Read it Again
3630 Peachtree Pkwy., Ste 314
Suwanee, GA 30024
770-232-9331
www.Read-it-Again.com

Waiting for the Girl Next Door

Book 4 in the Heart of Madison Series

sands press
Brockville, Ontario

Waiting for the Girl Next Door

Book 4 in the Heart of Madison Series

By Crystal Jackson

sands press

sands press

A Division of 3244601 Canada Inc.
300 Central Avenue West
Brockville, Ontario
K6V 5V2

Toll Free 1-800-563-0911 or 613-345-2687
http://www.sandspress.com

ISBN 978-1-988281-94-0
Copyright © Crystal Jackson 2021
All Rights Reserved

Publisher's Note
This book is a work of fiction. References to real people, events, establishments, organizations, or locales, are intended only to provide as a sense of authenticity, and are used fictitiously. All other characters, and all incidents and dialogue, are drawn from the authors' imaginations and are not to be construed as real.

No part of this book may be reproduced in whole or in part, stored in a retrieval system or transmitted in any form or by any means, without the prior written permission of the publisher.

For information on bulk purchases of this book or any book published by Sands Press, please call 1-800-563-0911.

1ST Printing

To book an author for your live event, please call: 1-800-563-0911

Sands Press is a literary publisher interested in new and established authors wishing to develop and market their product. For more information please visit our website at www.sandspress.com.

Acknowledgements

The Heart of Madison series started with a vision—not of a series of books but of a woman in a faded dress in an antique store quoting Mary Oliver and inspiring the owner of that store to think about the choices he was making with his life. Everything that happened from that scene until now has been a delightful surprise.

To my readers: Thank you for opening your hearts to this world I created in this town that I love. I hope you have loved the characters as much as I do.

It's impossible to thank every single person who uplifted and inspired me along the way—but you know who you are. Thank you to Shannon for loving my book and being its champion. To Perry and the team at Sands Press for getting this series into the hands of readers. To Laurie for your editing prowess.

Thank you to Jessica and Jenni—for being my first readers when this series was nothing but a dream. To the Madison Writers Group for supporting my vision and inspiring me to improve my craft. To the city of Madison for being a source of constant inspiration. To Michael, Anna, and Colby for the memes, inside jokes, and laughs that kept me going while releasing books in the middle of a pandemic. To Carmen and Parisa for your support. To Sully Archer McPuppy (yes, I'm thanking my dog) for your company through the editing process of this book (and for being a cozy foot warmer while I worked). To Lindsya, Carolyn, and Christy for always having my back. And to David—for making me believe again in romance off the page.

And last but never, ever least: to Luna and Linus, my biggest fans. I hope you know I'm your biggest fan, too.

To my Grandmama, Margie Peoples
Thank you for handing down your love of romance novels.

*"The world breaks everyone, and afterward,
some are strong at the broken places."*
~ Ernest Hemingway

Chapter 1

Layla Westerman kept one leg hanging over the side of the hammock, so she could occasionally make it swing. She glanced over at the baby on the floor who had her entire fist shoved in her mouth and grinned.

"I could get used to this," she said with a sigh, glancing over at Lindy who was lying on her stomach on the wide screened-in porch holding a toy out for Maya to grab. Maya kept ignoring her, pulling out her fist and looking at it before popping it back in.

"Why do I bother buying her toys?" Lindy asked with a sigh, sitting up. "Get used to the baby or the hammock?"

"Oh, I'm not ready for a baby yet," Layla said with a wry smile, although her heartstrings pulled every time she looked over at Maya with her bright eyes and chunky cheeks. "This, the hammock, the whole thing," she sighed happily.

She was relaxed and being relaxed was still rare enough that she appreciated it. She didn't like to talk about the panic attacks she'd been having. Or the nightmares. In fact, her sister Presley only knew about the nightmares because they had lived together. Layla had sworn she didn't remember them when she woke up. Of course, she was lying. She looked over at Lindy with her dark hair braided over one shoulder. She looked back at Maya. "She looks so much like you."

"Well, she's got Dean's smile," Lindy admitted with a grin.

"Dimples, too. She's perfect."

"Isn't she?" Lindy agreed. "You are perfect," she told Maya, leaning forward to kiss her nose. Maya started to giggle, her belly bouncing and her fist popping out of her mouth with a wet sound. Lindy looked up at Layla over Maya's head to ask, "Are you unpacked yet?"

"Yeah, it wasn't so bad. I didn't have that much really." They both paused, remembering why. When Lindy had been giving birth to Maya, Layla had been out in the waiting room breaking up with Noah. She'd finally admitted to her sister and their friends that he was abusive, and after she'd said the words, she couldn't imagine going back home with him. Her sister, father, and new friends had all stood with her when she faced him. Her new stepbrother had helped escort him out. But of course, he hadn't gone peacefully. He'd burned most of her possessions. She'd even lost a few precious photos of her mom and a couple of mementos that couldn't be replaced.

It could have been so much worse, she reminded herself. After the breakup, he'd hung around her classes and called her phone repeatedly. She'd changed numbers and jobs, and he hadn't been around in months. She wasn't sure why, but she was grateful it all seemed to be over. Not the panic attacks or the nightmares. But the rest of it seemed to have settled back down.

She looked over at Lindy who had a smile on her face that mirrored her child's. She counted back. Maya was seven months old now, making it seven months since she'd left Noah. She'd lived with Presley for six of those, and they'd actually gotten along better as adults than they had as teenagers, though she sometimes suspected it was because Presley was worried about her. Still, it was nice. She hadn't been close to her family since her mom got sick. It was good to spend time with them.

Lindy was family, too, now. She'd invited Layla to come hang out with her over on the porch. It was the end of January, but it was still in the 70s. Typical Georgia weather, Layla thought. She laughed as Maya toppled over and then righted herself.

"Did you know the house next door sold?" Lindy asked. She watched Layla's body tense. "I met one of the owners. Nice enough guy. They said there might be some work being done in the next couple of months."

"Nice to give you a heads up," Layla said carefully, closing her eyes. She tried to remember how to relax her body as Presley had taught her to do when she'd tried to get her into yoga. It wasn't working.

"I don't know if they're keeping it or flipping it," Lindy said conversationally, trying to lighten the mood. "But everyone mostly keeps to themselves around here," she reassured Layla. "If they're going to stay, I might invite them over and get to know them."

"Probably a good idea," Layla said absently. Lindy looked over at where Layla lay with her eyes shut and made a decision.

"Hey, can you take Maya for a minute? I need to run inside real quick." She picked Maya up and all but shoved her in Layla's arms.

"Okay, sure," Layla said in surprise, looking up at the baby sitting firmly on her belly with her legs splayed in front of her. Maya grinned and leaned forward to grab handfuls of her hair. Layla remembered suddenly why Lindy had started braiding her long hair back. She grinned back at Maya. "Look, monkey, you're going to have ease up on your grip," she told her, prying the chunky hands from her hair and making sure to remove the stray strands that came out in her hand.

Layla's hair was nearly black and mid length. It was curly where Presley's was straight, and she'd let it grow to just below her shoulders. Where Lindy's was more of a dark chestnut and midway down her back, Layla's was shorter, darker, and a riot of curls this morning in the humidity. She shoved it back over her shoulders and held Maya out of reach.

"Don't even think about it," she said, as Maya opened and closed her fists in the direction of her hair. She thought about sitting up but wasn't sure she could manage it without toppling them both to the floor of the porch. She grabbed each of Maya's hands and patty-caked them together, which made Maya giggle.

"I thought I heard my best girl," Dean said in the raspy voice of the newly awakened. Layla looked up and felt her mouth go dry. Dean stood there in low slung, faded jeans rolled up at the bottom and barefoot. He was wearing a plain black T-shirt and leaning on a crutch. Layla imagined she could just about make out a six pack under the shirt and averting her eyes to his well-muscled arms didn't help. He just grinned at her, used to the impression he made.

"Don't let Lindy hear you saying that," she warned him, turning back to Maya. Dean was pretty. God knows he knew it, she thought. But he was also Lindy's husband and Maya's father. Besides, Layla reminded herself, men were just trouble. Still, she liked to listen to his deep southern-fried drawl. It didn't have that twang of country found in some of the more rural areas of Georgia. It was definitely more Rhett Butler than Larry the Cable Guy. She grinned at the thought and decided to enjoy the view.

"Lindy knows the pecking order around here," Dean said with an easy smile, shifting around on the crutch. He only used it reluctantly and was switching to a boot soon enough. He was still recovering from an injury he'd sustained fighting a fire, and he was hoping to be back to work in the next month, if everything went well with rehabilitation. Still, it didn't affect his easy grace much. His blonde hair was carelessly mussed as if he hadn't done anything but run a hand through it when he woke up. He turned green eyes on Maya, and even Layla could see them light up.

"You want her?"

"'Course I do," he said, leaning over to scoop his daughter up with one hand. She giggled, and Layla swung her leg over and sat up.

"Where's Lindy?"

"You didn't see her inside?" Layla replied, her brow furrowing.

"I was getting more coffee," Lindy said, as she walked out, letting the door slam behind her. "It was an emergency," she added with a grin.

"Maya kept us up a little last night. Teething," Dean said.

"It was Dean's turn to sleep in, and I'm catching a nap with her later on," Lindy explained, sitting down on the floor beside Dean's chair and leaning her head against his knee. Maya turned and started reaching for Lindy's hair. She reflexively moved her braid out of the way and reached up to hold Maya's tiny hand.

"My turn," Dean reminded her with a grin.

Layla looked at the two of them and felt a stab of envy. She'd never even had a healthy relationship, much less the kind of love story that Lindy and Dean had. She'd thought Noah was the one. He seemed so unlike anyone she'd ever dated. He was smart. Like really smart, she thought, and he was in culinary school to be a chef. Attractive, smart, and could cook? She'd thought she was dreaming.

Only it was a nightmare. His dark red hair and freckles had been as disarming as his wide smile, and just as deceptive. He hadn't been her usual type, not the usual blue-collar bad boy she'd been known to see socially. He'd been sweet, maybe even a little nerdy. She closed her eyes briefly as she remembered how it had all been sleight of hand. She'd seen exactly what he'd wanted her to see. He was really someone wholly different than the man she had fallen in love with.

It wasn't until she'd found out he'd been hurting someone else, too, that she'd had the courage to break away from it all. She'd started to believe what he'd told her, that she'd never find anyone else who would want her. She didn't talk about it to anyone but Naomi. After all, it had happened to her, too, and at the same time. No one else could really understand just how it was to be with someone who could be so sweet and so toxic in the space of a few minutes. She envied Lindy and Dean their easy relationship. They both had assured everyone that it had been far from easy, but it looked easy from where Layla was sitting. She didn't realize she'd let out an audible sigh until she caught Dean and Lindy looking at her.

"Want some coffee?" Lindy asked sympathetically, guessing where her thoughts might have drifted.

"Sure," she agreed, not quite ready to go home yet.

"I'll get it," Dean said, placing a soft kiss on the top of Maya's head with its downy dark hair and handing her to Lindy. "How do you like it?"

"Sweet," she said with a grin. "Just pour the cream and sugar in."

"I thought you'd be coffee-black," Dean told her with a grin.

"Surprisingly, that's Presley. Although, she's more likely to grab a chai or a green tea these days."

"One coffee coming right up," he said, heading inside. Lindy and Layla watched him go.

"Um, no offense or anything, but your husband is one beautiful man," Layla said with a smile.

"I'm not offended. Just don't let him hear you say it. His ego is enormous enough as it is."

"I might have drooled a little when he walked up," Layla admitted with a laugh.

"Yeah, he has that effect. I was immune for years. Until I wasn't."

"Did you get glasses? Contacts?" Layla asked incredulously.

"I practically grew up with him. He was just Seth's bratty friend. Until he wasn't," she said with a shrug.

"That's pretty cute actually."

"Yeah," she sighed. "The guy before him was a real ass."

"He really was," Dean agreed, coming out with the coffee. "Are we talking about exes?" he asked with interest.

"Not yours," Lindy told him decidedly. "We don't have time."

"She was dating this pretentious art asshole," Dean began.

"Hey!" Lindy said. "I mean, yeah, but ..." She nodded toward Maya.

"She's not exactly talking yet," Dean argued. "Okay, fine," he relented, holding both hands up after Lindy sent another significant look at the baby. "He was a super not nice guy. A real prick," he said in an exaggerated baby voice and then looked at Lindy. "She doesn't know what that means."

"He's not wrong. About the guy. He was kind of a tool," Lindy said with a roll of her eyes. "I mean, not like …" She trailed off, a little embarrassed at their banter.

"Like Noah, I know. Continue." Layla waved off the embarrassment. She couldn't avoid the subject forever.

"He didn't think much of the fact that I went to art school only to open up my own canvas studio teaching painting to regular people," Lindy said with a shrug. "Though it seems like it ended for a bunch of reasons."

"And then she couldn't resist my charms," Dean filled in with a grin.

"Um, that is not how it happened," Lindy said with a roll of her eyes. "If I recall, you followed me around like a puppy until I had no choice but to give in."

"Something like that," he agreed, picking up her hand and kissing it, with a wink.

"Stop," she said, pulling her hand away and laughing. "He was a real pain in the …" She glanced at Maya. "Anyway," she shrugged. "Now here we are," she said, gesturing around them.

Lindy had once lived in the carriage house where Layla lived now. She'd moved into the big house when her mom had married Layla's dad, Theodore, and moved in with him. Dean had moved in with her. After all, by then they were already pregnant with Maya. She'd thought the relationship with Dean would run its course, and he'd go back to serial dating. But it hadn't. He hadn't. They'd gotten married on New Year's Eve. She sighed happily and then turned back to Layla.

"Are you dating anyone?" she asked, curiously, ignoring Dean's warning look.

"No. Not right now. I'm just getting used to the new job and everything." Layla had gone to school to be a CPA, and she'd taken a job at a local firm after her internship ended. The pay wasn't extravagant or anything, but she was doing okay, she thought. She enjoyed playing around with the numbers. Presley said tax law seemed boring, but Layla liked seeing how much she could help her clients get back. A lot of the families lived paycheck to paycheck, and it made her feel good to be able to help them get more than they expected. Plus, it was soothing just to focus on numbers for a while.

"How's that going?" Dean asked, changing the subject easily.

"I like it. It's different, but I think it's a good fit for me," Layla told them. Dean shifted Maya onto his shoulder, and she laid her head sleepily down, nuzzling against his neck.

"If she's ready for a nap, I'll take her up," Lindy volunteered eagerly.

"Give her a minute," Dean said, waving her away and snuggling in. He looked at Layla. "Just let us know if you need anything over there. We're thinking about putting security cameras up around the perimeter since we have Maya. It's a safe neighborhood, but it'll still be good to have. Make sure none of the kids TP our house come Halloween," he told her with a grin. "Not that they would want to mess with Lindy if they did," he amended, shooting his wife a look.

Layla looked down, covering a sudden surge of emotion that might have been relief and gratitude. "You can never be too careful," she said, quickly adding, "I think I'll go unpack those last couple of boxes. Thanks for coffee."

Lindy and Dean watched her cross the yard. "Dean Walton, that was really sweet," Lindy told him.

"I'm sweet sometimes," he said with a grin, while his wife looked at him with amusement.

"Give me my baby back," she said, but added a smile.

"If you remember, this is my baby, too," Dean reminded her.

"Yeah," she said, leaning up to kiss him soundly on the mouth before sliding Maya off his shoulder. "We're going to take a nap.

Don't forget to put our mugs in the dishwasher," she told him as she headed inside. Dean smiled and grabbed the mugs. He wasn't going to forget. He thought a nap sounded pretty good himself.

Chapter 2

Presley Westerman sipped coffee that had already grown lukewarm and made a face. She set the mug down on the desk and made a few notes on the chart after a quick glance at the clock. She was ready to go home. More than ready. It had been a tough night. A routine delivery had turned into an emergency C-section, and she'd had to step back and let Dr. Isaacs take over. Of the doctors on staff, her patient couldn't have ended up in better hands, but she'd still been surprised at the night's plot twist.

She rolled her shoulders and decided that she really needed to take the time to schedule a hot stone massage. Or at the very least a chair massage, she thought. She couldn't imagine finding the time, although Layla kept reminding her it was more about making the time. She thought that was fairly hypocritical of her sister to say when you considered that she had turned into a bit of a workaholic herself when she wasn't holed up in her new apartment.

Presley sighed and reminded herself that Layla had good reason. She'd just managed to get out of an abusive relationship, and she was entitled to deal with it however she needed to. Still, Presley thought, she hoped she'd start taking her own advice sometime soon.

"I'm out," she told Gemma, who was leaning against the front desk flipping through charts.

Gemma pirouetted in her direction with a grace that was surprising when Presley considered how infamously clumsy the nurse was. In fact, the charts started to spill out, but Erin at check-in reached up from her chair across the desk and steadied them automatically with one hand while answering the phone with the other. Gemma grinned at Erin and turned back to Presley who observed that today's scrubs were covered in ocean life. Gemma's hair was woven into intricate dark braids, and a bright smile stretched across her face as she raised an eyebrow. Presley wondered absently what skin product she used to keep that luminous tone, and then nearly shook her head at her own wandering thoughts.

"Just the one shift today?" she asked Presley, taking a sip from the coffee in her hand.

"Yes, thankfully," Presley said, rolling her shoulders again. She'd spent most of the winter covering for a colleague out on maternity leave. That had included a few double shifts she was grateful to leave behind.

"How did Mila do this morning?" Gemma asked, referring to their patient. Gemma was one of Presley's favorite nurses, although she liked most of them—with one obvious exception, she thought darkly.

"Baby was breech. Dr. Isaacs has her now," Presley explained.

"Is she totally freaking out?" Gemma asked with a sympathetic smile. Mila had been difficult in some ways, but she was endearing all the same. They had a number of teenage pregnancies, but Mila seemed like she'd actually put some thought into making a real go of motherhood. It was nice to see when you considered the ones who acted like their lives wouldn't change a bit, likely saddling their parents with their infants the moment they stepped out of the hospital.

"Pretty much," Presley agreed. She reached up and pulled her short dark hair out of its ponytail, feeling some of the pressure release. Her tired eyes were a pale blue and were framed by a thick fringe of bangs that she kept thinking she'd grow back out. One of these days. "She'll be okay. Text me if there are any problems?"

"You know it." Gemma paused, pursing her cherry red lips together as she thought about what she was going to say next. Presley had a moment to admire today's lipstick. Gemma wore a variety of all-day shades, and Presley had to admit that they seemed to last through even the longest shift. She was about to ask for the name of the brand again when she caught Gemma's look.

"What is it?" she asked with trepidation. "Something wrong? Did my sister call?" She didn't mean to automatically think of Layla, but the last year had been tough on them both. They'd spent a lot of months looking over their shoulders, waiting for the fallout of her having left the abusive ex. There hadn't been any, but Presley wondered sometimes.

"Maybe you should give it a few minutes," Gemma suggested helpfully. "Or take the stairs instead of the elevator. Hey, that would get you some extra steps in for the day," she said, nodding to Presley's step counter on her wrist.

"Okay, what's up?" she asked suspiciously.

"It's just that, um, Derrick and Amber were just pulling up when I came in," Gemma said, shifting nervously and almost knocking over her coffee. Erin moved it carefully over and continued typing.

"What's he doing here?" Presley asked surprised. Derrick was her ex, and as a sales rep, she knew it was possible to run into him in the hospital. She mostly managed to avoid it. Amber had once worked closely with her before she'd decided to make a play for Presley's then-boyfriend. It was still galling that almost all her colleagues had realized what was going on before she had. She felt her face flush in embarrassment and kept her gaze averted so she wouldn't have to see naked pity on Gemma's face. Of course, there wasn't any pity there when she finally ventured a glance over. Gemma's face was tight with anger.

"Who knows? Parking on this side just seems like rubbing it in," Gemma said in annoyance. "You know how she is." They exchanged an understanding look.

"It's been over a while now. Me and Derrick, I mean," Presley said, with a seemingly careless shrug of her own. She hadn't seen him since her father's heart attack when she'd been trying to get to the hospital.

"Did you really almost run him over?" Gemma asked, her face lightening at the thought.

"Where'd you hear that?" Presley asked, with a flash of amusement. Erin raised one hand as she continued to reassure the patient on the phone. She mouthed, "I saw the whole thing."

"I didn't run him over," Presley said with a laugh. "I wanted to though," she admitted. "It might have been close."

"Too bad. I always thought you were too good for him," Erin said, with her hand over the mouthpiece.

"Next time give me a heads up, okay?"

"None of us liked him. Next guy? You let us meet him and look him over first," Gemma suggested, patting her arm.

"Where do you get this done?" Presley asked, tapping Gemma's carefully made up nails with the designs. Gemma's nails weren't long, but they were carefully manicured to match her outfit. Presley considered herself pretty low maintenance, but lately she was tempted to give herself a makeover.

"I'll get you a card when I'm at the salon next time. You'll love it," she said, eyeing Presley's nails. "Quit biting them," she ordered.

"I don't. Mostly," Presley amended. "I'm working on it." She'd chewed just the one edge ragged with stress over the last few months. She hadn't even realized she was doing it again. It had been years—since back when her mom was first diagnosed—since she'd bitten her nails. She sighed. "Alright, I'm not here."

"Take the stairs," Gemma ordered.

"Yeah, sure." She wasn't really in the mood to deal with either Derrick or Amber today.

Presley headed down the stairs quickly, her bag slung over her shoulder. She thought she'd head home and take a book with her into the bath. That's all she wanted: a good read, a long bath, and maybe she'd book the massage in the morning when she woke up. She opened the door at the bottom of the stairs, and there they were, clearly trying to use the back way, too. She held the door open wide and let Derrick reach out to grab it. She spared him the briefest glance and didn't bother to look at Amber at all, as she brushed by them and headed toward the exit. She sensed them hesitating behind her, but she didn't slow down.

As she walked across the parking lot, she let a stream of expletives run through her head. It didn't help that Derrick still looked good or that she still felt a little bit of a spark as she brushed by him. He hadn't exactly stepped entirely out of the way, and she thought darkly that he'd probably done it on purpose just to wind her up. Well, mission accomplished, she thought grimly.

The drive home didn't take long, but it was later than she'd realized. She parked near her apartment, and noticed that her neighbor's pickup truck was once again parked sideways. Newer neighbors hated that, but Presely had come to accept it as a part of the deal. She usually parked about three spots down to give him a wide enough berth. She slid out of the Ford Focus she'd bought last month. The gas mileage was good, and she'd liked driving Layla's when she had that flat tire after Christmas. Her model was a little newer, but she'd still bought it used. It was white, like Layla's, but she reminded herself that beggars couldn't be choosers. She'd much rather have had it in black or maybe even a silver. She could have afforded a new car, but who wanted a payment anyway?

She jogged up the stairs to her apartment and turned when she thought she heard a sound behind her. She glanced back but didn't see anything. Probably the stray cat that the college kid downstairs kept feeding. They'd all told her to stop, but she never listened. Presley shook her head and unlocked the door to her apartment. It had been a long day. Running into Derrick had been … jarring, she decided. She thought about that long bath with a book but decided that a quick shower and collapsing into bed might be the better option.

Chapter 3

Presley took off her sunglasses as she and Layla stepped into the store. It was bright outside, but a chill had set in. That was January in Georgia for you. Warm one minute, cold the next. She wondered if they might even get snow this year. She loosened her scarf a little in the over-warm store. She'd paired a brown leather jacket with jeans and a simple blue sweater. She'd wrapped the infinity scarf with its swirl of blues around her neck and slipped into her favorite boots.

Of course, Layla, walking next to her, looked like she'd stepped out of a fashion magazine. Right after her breakup with Noah, she'd hidden in over-sized shirts and leggings or yoga pants, but lately she'd started dressing up again. Layla wore a fitted sweater dress in red with knee boots that had a heel that had her towering over her sister. She had a black thigh-length coat that would have made Presley look silly but looked perfect on her sister.

Presley wanted to ask Layla if she was wearing eyelash extensions, but she felt foolish even asking. Still, her sister's eyelashes were thick and curled more than normal, and she had this smoky thing that Presley had tried and failed to replicate, opting instead to go with a light neutral eye color that she could manage without feeling like a failure. She did have on a bright, pretty plum lipstick. She'd bought some from Gemma who sold the brand. It had made her smile when Layla had immediately demanded to know where she could get it.

"What are we looking for again?" Layla asked with a sigh.

"Just something for Dad's birthday," Presley reminded her, knowing she hadn't forgotten. "Something that suits him. He loves these antique stores."

"How many is this? Four?" Layla asked, looking around. Antiques weren't exactly her thing, though she had to admit that shopping with Presley was sort of fun.

"Five, I think," Presley returned with a grin. "Fifth time's the charm?" She wondered, walking through the crowded aisles. They had tried on hats in the last one, and Layla had snagged one in a fancy hat box that she swore would be perfect for a derby party in the spring. At the store before that, Presley had come across a pair of earrings she liked. They were clip on, but they had a lot of style. Presley sometimes suspected she didn't have much style anymore. She was just too busy.

"Let's do lunch after this one," Layla suggested. "Brews?" she asked, referring to Brews and Blues, the local coffee shop that doubled as a popular lunch spot.

"Either that, or we could hit up the Mexican place that just opened," Presley said absently, focusing in on an old-fashioned shoe shine kit that was almost right but not quite.

"That's boring," Layla told her, sitting it down. "Wait—how do you feel about day drinking?" she asked her sister in a mock-serious tone.

"What's not to like? Margaritas?"

"Depends. Strawberry with sugar or salt on the rim?" Layla demanded, as if the answer was of great importance.

"I prefer salt," Presley admitted, wondering if that was the right answer.

"Damn right you do," Layla agreed. "Okay, let's do that."

"Want to call and invite Naomi?" Presley offered.

"No, she's working. I ran into Beth this morning." Beth was Seth and Lindy's cousin and Naomi's boss at the bookstore. "We could ask Libby," Layla suggested, referring to Seth's wife.

"She's out of town on an assignment, Dad said, this morning." Presley shrugged. They were quiet for a minute, separately wondering why they always felt the need to add others to the mix, as if they couldn't have lunch with just the two of them. Both of them thought that a buffer might make things easier, but no buffer was available.

"Lindy's out having lunch with Dean. We could ask Keely," she suggested hesitantly. The whole stepmom thing was just too weird.

"No, she and Dad are having a day to themselves on the farm," Presley answered, picking up and putting down a tie pin. Dad didn't need any more of those.

"So … margaritas?" Layla confirmed.

"Sounds good to me," Presley said. "Oh, look at this."

They both gravitated over to a bee-themed display. Layla looked at it wide-eyed. "I think we're going to need a bigger boat," she quoted.

"I think you're right." Presley picked up a queen bee curtain tie back in bronze. Their dad kept bees, but he had also written a novel that centered around bees. It had become a surprise bestseller, and he was currently fine-tuning a sequel to it now. She kept the bee ties in her hand and reached over to stroke an antique bee smoker, exchanging a look with Layla.

"Okay, let's just grab a few things," Layla said with wide eyes. "Oh my God, he's going to love this stuff," she said, finally getting into the spirit of their shopping venture. "We can celebrate with those margaritas."

"I like the way you think," Presley said, scooping up a tie tack and deciding that the little bee made an appropriate addition to their haul.

When they sank down into the booth at the restaurant, their wallets were lighter, but so were their moods. Layla immediately ordered the largest pitcher of strawberry margaritas after making sure Presley wasn't on call. Presley ordered a taco salad, and Layla sprung for nachos while she waited for her fajitas. She looked around with a grin.

"I'm really beginning to love this place," Layla said with a smile.

"Wait until we've at least tried the drinks," Presley cautioned her with a quirk of her brow.

"No," Layla laughed. "Madison. I thought it was sort of a backwater at first, but it's actually pretty cool."

"Yeah, I like it. It's easy to see why the others love it here," she said, referring to their new extended family.

"The house beside me sold," Layla said carefully, inserting it awkwardly into the conversation.

"To anyone we know?" Presley asked lightly, gauging the mood.

"We don't really know anyone," Layla said with a shrug. "Lindy met one of the owners. Said he seemed decent enough."

"That's good," Presley said, knowing instinctively why a new neighbor might make Layla nervous.

"Dean said he was going to install a security camera out back. You know, because of Maya. The neighborhood is safe enough," Layla said casually.

"That's good." Presley felt a wave of relief. She wondered when they'd both stop feeling on edge. She was grateful when the server deposited the large pitcher on the table with a flourish.

"Come to mama," Layla said with a grin, eyeing her well-salted and filled-to-the-brim glass and drawing it closer to her with a gleam in her eyes.

"We're going to need an Uber," Presley commented seriously.

"We could walk to my place from here if we need to and come back and get your car later," Layla noted, grabbing a chip and dragging it through the queso.

"How is the new place? I mean, other than new neighbors and all that. Is it weird living so close to Dean and Lindy?" Presley asked curiously, depositing a pile of chips on her plate and inching the salsa closer.

"Not at all. We mostly stay out of each other's way, but it's friendly. And I have to admit that Dean is eye candy," Layla said with a twinkle.

"You said it," Presley agreed fervently, taking a sip of her drink. "Does he have a brother?" she asked cheekily.

Layla shrugged. "Wouldn't that be great?" she agreed. "Are you still doing the online dating?"

"No, I'm going to pass on that for a while," Presley said and then paused with a chip hovering near her mouth. Her brows drew tightly together for a minute, drawing a line between them.

"What's up?" Layla asked.

"I saw Derrick yesterday," she admitted. "And Amber."

"At the hospital?" Layla asked, her own brows drawing together sharply. "I hope he looked like hell. I hope they both did."

"Thanks for that, but they looked pretty much the same," Presley said with a shrug. It had been long enough that she should really be over it. More than a year now, she remembered.

"Did you at least manage to run him over this time?" Layla asked, her face brightening hopefully. Presley let out a dramatic groan.

"I will never live that down," she said, leaning back in the booth. "It was only a little awkward. I just wish I didn't have to run into exes at all. Especially that one." She paused, then added, "Besides, I wasn't even in my car."

"There's always next time," Layla said comfortingly, letting out a happy sigh as the plates of food were set down in front of them. She looked up at the server and thanked them enthusiastically. Presley just rolled her eyes, unused to her sister being so cheerful.

"So, what's with you?" Presley asked curiously. "Did you get laid or something?"

"What? No," Layla said, darting an embarrassed glance around her. "I mean, I wish. But no. It's just been a good week. I like the new job, and everyone's been great. I honestly couldn't have afforded my new place in a million years if Lindy hadn't cut me a deal. It's great!"

"Nice to have family connections," Presley agreed. "Weird to think that she's family now though. Have you talked to Dad lately?"

"I talked to him last night. He stopped by with Keely to play with the baby."

"Well, I can't wait for him to see all the stuff we found. Did you order the cake?"

"Of course. Though I guess I could have baked one," Layla admitted. She'd learned to bake and even cook with Noah. He'd enjoyed teaching her what he'd learned in his culinary classes. She'd thought it was sweet until she realized that he was really just grooming her to be the kind of person he wanted. A frown started to form as she thought about it.

"Time for a refill," Presley insisted, filling Layla's glass. "We really don't have time to bake one," she reminded her sister, suspecting where her thoughts had gone. She knew Layla better than her sister thought. "We're both working up until his birthday dinner. I've got clinic, and you're doing that training thing."

"I guess that's true," Layla said, her face clearing. "Want to walk over to my place when we're done and check it out? I finally finished unpacking."

"Sure," Presley still wasn't used to how much their relationship had changed, but she was glad that they were starting to be friends again. It hadn't been easy. There was a lot of water under that bridge, but they were both trying to do better.

***

At Layla's apartment, Presley marveled at how much had been done. She wasn't much for decorating herself. She liked what she liked, but she had never had Layla's natural style. It wasn't just with fashion and makeup. She just knew how things were supposed to look and assembled them accordingly. She had an instinct for it. Presley was surprised when she went into accounting instead of design or something more creative, but Layla had shrugged and said she just liked numbers.

"It looks good," Presley said, wishing she was more comfortable with openly praising her sister's talents. She was still a little reserved around her, so afraid that things would go back to being contentious between them. "When do the new neighbors move in?"

"I don't know. Soon, I guess. Lindy said they're going to be fixing up the place," Layla said with a shrug, glancing out the kitchen window where she could see the house next door. She wondered if she should get curtains, maybe thick ones. She sighed and turned around. "They may just fix it up and flip it and not really stay there." She was reminding herself more than Presley. "I guess we'll just have to wait and see."

Presley flopped on to the couch and stretched out, still buzzing a little from the half-pitcher of strawberry margaritas she'd consumed. "I could get used to this."

"There's something we usually don't see. Presley at rest," Layla joked, sitting down and curling up in the chaise lounge.

"I could be one of those live art exhibits and just lay around while people walked by, maybe nap a little." She closed her eyes and smiled.

"You'd last five minutes," Layla told her.

"I could do thirty," Presley said with a rueful grin, peeking open an eye. "Maybe an hour."

"Are you on call this weekend?"

"Yeah. But then I'll have a couple weekends off after that." Presley reached to the top of the sofa and pulled a soft chenille blanket down on top of herself.

"Did you even sleep after you got home from work?"

"A little. Kept having ... weird dreams."

"You can nap for a while if you want," Layla commented—but Presley was already fast asleep. Layla rolled her eyes. She'd always envied Presley's ability to sleep anywhere, even if she never stayed down for long.

She reached over to the coffee table and picked up the book she'd been reading. Naomi had turned her on to it after the last book club. It was a thriller, but Naomi assured her that it didn't have any triggers. Naomi had been seeing a counselor for some of her anxiety, and she said *triggers* like it was something Layla should be aware of. Layla was enjoying the book. It had kept her firmly on the edge of her seat every time she'd had a chance to sit down over the past couple of days.

But she wasn't so much enjoying Naomi's insistence that she see a counselor, too. Naomi was the only person in her life who could really understand what had happened with Noah, and Layla didn't want to go tell a stranger about things they could only understand in theory. This wasn't a theory. This was her life. She was managing the stress the best she could, and she didn't think going to talk to a stranger was going to make anything better. If it worked for Naomi, great. But it wasn't for her, Layla told herself as she opened her book to where the bookmark was wedged a third of the way through.

Chapter 4

Layla stood in front of the carriage house and watched Presley drive off. Her sister had woken up with bedhead and a dazed look, but she'd taken the time to share a snack before heading toward home. Layla stood barefoot for a minute in the grass and stretched her arms high above her head. The sun felt warm on her skin even with the cool breeze, and she was feeling relaxed from the margaritas. She checked her phone for the time and decided to swing by the bookstore to see Naomi.

She went inside and pulled on her boots. The advantage of a small town, she thought to herself, is that you could just walk over and say hello to a friend without having to drive. She slipped into her jacket and remembered to grab her keys. She locked the door behind her and then checked it again before walking to the back door and doing the same. Satisfied that everything was secure, she headed toward the bookshop in town.

It was strange to see so many flowers in bloom in January. Maybe there had been flowers in bloom in Athens a year ago when she was still living with Noah, but she didn't recall them. She couldn't decide if it was because she had been under a great deal of stress or if there hadn't been any. Still, it seemed that Madison maintained a perpetual spring, except for the bare trees. She walked with a light step toward the bookshop, waving at an occasional passing car or saying hello to shopkeepers she knew as she walked along. She put her hands in her pockets and thought about how this town was starting to feel like home. She felt the panic that lived perpetually in her chest ease a little.

Stepping in to the bookshop, she immediately shrugged out of the coat and waved to Beth at the counter. It was warm in here, and

Beth had recently used a hygge vibe in the whole store. The last time Layla had stopped in, Beth had regaled her at length about the whole Danish concept of coziness and how she'd incorporated it into the store. Layla had to admit that it was nice.

"Hey, you," Beth said with a smile, brushing her red hair back from her face and adjusting the horn-rimmed glasses she preferred. "Naomi just took a break, but she'll be back in a few minutes if you want to take a load off." She gestured toward the plush sofa and chairs that were nestled in a corner.

"Don't mind if I do," Layla said with a smile, selecting a chair that she could sink down into and smiling up at Beth who was heading her way.

"Mind if I join you?" Beth asked and then sat down without waiting for an answer. Layla grinned at her. She didn't know Beth well; she was her stepbrother's cousin, her new stepmom's niece. Layla nearly rolled her eyes at how Southern that sounded, the mixed up and complicated family tree. "How's the carriage house working out?"

"I love it," Layla said with a sigh. "I've unpacked everything, and I've been in full decorating mode. You should come by and see it."

"I might do that. I'll call first though," Beth said with a smile. "I heard the house next door finally sold." Beth's own home was a couple streets over, and she took an active interest in the community.

"Yeah," Layla agreed, her good mood fading as the pressure in her chest increased.

"I'm sure Dean will go over and chat them up if Lindy doesn't. Get the lay of the land," Beth said reassuringly, knowing that Layla had good reason for her anxiety. "They may just flip it. I guess we'll find out."

"I guess so," Layla agreed, looking around the room. "I could live here," she admitted. "I have to admit the whole cozy thing really works. I kind of want to curl up with a blanket and read."

"That's the point. You'll read enough that you just have to buy it to finish at home," Beth said with a grin, leaning her head back on the sofa with a sigh. Layla started to relax, but she jumped a little when the door opened, which let her know she wasn't quite successful.

"Hey! When did you get here?" Naomi asked, coming in and shutting the door firmly behind her.

"Just now," Layla told her, watching as Naomi unwound the seashell pink scarf from around her neck and hung it up.

Naomi took off her lined jacket and hung it up beside the vintage fur coat that Beth told everyone was only faux fur. She turned toward Beth and Layla in her tight jeans and sunset pink sweater that suited her girl-next-door look. Her face was lightly made up but didn't quite cover the smattering of freckles. Her brown eyes matched the exact tint of her hair, and she had it straightened and then pulled carelessly back into low pigtails that Layla suspected would have made her look ten if it wasn't for her impressively robust figure.

"I still have a couple of hours before we close," Naomi told her, sitting down beside Beth. "Was it busy while I was gone?"

"Nope. One customer came in on her way to the tearoom." Beth nodded toward the next room. "But that's about it," she sighed deeply. "You two talk, and I'm going to go pretend to be busy over there in case a customer comes in," she said, gesturing over to the antique register at the front of the store.

"Were you on lunch?" Layla asked. "It's kind of late for that."

"No, I went to see my therapist," Naomi said, without any embarrassment.

"Did you change your day?" Layla asked, confused.

"No, I just needed an extra session. I went on a date with that guy I showed you on the dating site, and it didn't exactly go well," Naomi admitted with a grimace.

"Mansplainer?" Layla asked.

"No," Naomi grinned.

"Fuckboy?" At Naomi's laugh, she continued. "Married? Was it a cat-fishing situation?"

"None of that. He was nice actually," Naomi said. "It was going pretty well, but then he walked me to my car. It kind of fell apart from there." Her eyebrows drew together as she looked away. "I thought he was going to kiss me, and I got that panicky feeling here." She touched her chest lightly, right over her heart. "I kind of freaked out and pushed him away and drove home. I'm not actually sure how I even made it back."

"Damn," Layla said quietly, wondering how long the fear was going to stay with them both. She knew exactly how Naomi felt because her own boyfriend was the one who'd assaulted her. Ex-boyfriend, she corrected herself. Layla hadn't known about it until later, but when she'd found out, she left him. It had been scary all around, and she couldn't even imagine dating right now.

"Yeah," Naomi agreed. "He was actually sweet about it though. He sent me a text to make sure I got home okay. I'm so embarrassed, though, I don't really know what to say to him. It's a little soon to tell him about all of that, and I don't think he'll want to repeat the experience anyway." She shrugged and let out a long sigh. "Anyway …"

"Are you sure you're ready to be dating?" Layla asked in concern.

"I'm sure I *want* to be ready, which is practically the same thing. Anyway, I talked to my therapist, and I feel better about it." Naomi looked squarely at Layla. "I know what you're going to say, but I really wish you'd go talk to him. It's not weird at all, and it really is helping."

"Is it?" Layla asked skeptically.

"Well, panic attack aside," Naomi said with a small smile. "But I'm not having them as often, so that's something. I do feel better. I'm finally realizing it wasn't my fault." She gave Layla an even look.

"Or yours either."

"I never said any of it was my fault," Layla said uncomfortably, casually eyeing the exit.

"No, but then you don't have to either," Naomi countered. "I just think you'd feel better. Maybe start sleeping better."

"I'm okay," Layla insisted. "I really don't need my head examined," she said. "I'm glad if it's helping you, but I really just want to forget about it."

"It's kind of hard to forget without help," Naomi pointed out. "Well, not forget so much as work through."

"That's why I have you," Layla said with a grin. "I'll just take a little second-hand therapy."

"Whatever," Naomi said. "He's actually pretty easy on the eyes if you want to make an appointment. The eye candy value alone might make it worth it."

"Tempting, but I can go next door if I need eye candy," Layla said, referring to Dean.

Naomi grinned. She'd dated Dean, after all, before the whole incident with Noah. She'd been angry when he'd ended it suddenly, dismissing her like every other woman he'd dated until Lindy. But she'd moved on. "That's a good point. He *is* pretty."

"Speaking of pretty …" Layla nodded toward the door where a well-muscled man in his twenties came in carrying a large box of books. He was bald, tattooed, and had bold, even features that made both women sigh as he headed toward the counter where Beth was doing a spontaneous happy dance before launching herself into his arms.

"Why didn't you date him?" Naomi asked, curiously. She knew that Layla had been in some of the same classes as Jamie last year.

"Not really my type, I guess," she admitted with a little twinge of regret. "Clearly, my type needs work," she said wryly.

"Well, Noah was an anomaly," Naomi said.

"Everyone I dated before him was blue collar and a little rough around the edges. I actually thought I was doing a little better. He was charming and romantic, and I just ..." She left it hanging, and Naomi nodded.

"Yeah, I know. Who would have thought he could be such a monster?" Naomi said with a shudder. "He was smooth, I'll give him that. I never saw it coming."

"Me either. He was great until we moved in together," Layla admitted. "Then it just started unraveling. Or he did. I don't know."

"Well, at least he's left us alone since then," Naomi reminded her, seeing that tight look of anxiety on her friend's face. It was a little bit of a pinch around the eyes and a loss of color in Layla's cheeks. She'd witnessed one of the panic attacks and knew it could hit quickly. "Anyway," she continued, "I'm going to give the dating app another shot after I apologize to Will for being so sketchy." She rolled her eyes. "You should try it."

"I'm not ready yet," Layla said firmly. "But when I am, I'll let you know. I guess I'm going to head back home. Presley was over earlier, and we found Dad the best present. I think I'll go ahead and wrap it."

"Is Presley doing okay?" Naomi asked. She didn't know Layla's sister well, but she knew they had a somewhat fractious history.

"Yeah, we actually had fun. There might have been day drinking involved." She grinned over at Naomi with a twinkle in her eyes.

"Yeah, well, careful with all that," Naomi smiled, but she had a little worry behind it. After all, she strongly suspected Layla wasn't dealing with the anxiety as well as she maintained.

"It's not a usual thing for us. It was nice today though. I think I'll wrap the gift and then just relax the rest of the day," Layla said, standing up and stretching again. "God, that chair is comfortable."

"I know. We've sold a lot of books from that chair," Naomi said with a grin. "Look, call me later, and maybe I can bring over a movie if you want to hang out."

"You just want to come over and steal a peek at my eye candy."

"Honey, if I want eye candy, I can just go see my therapist," she said with a mischievous grin. "In fact, I feel a little panic attack coming on right now."

"Too bad you're a client and can't actually date him," Layla pointed out.

"Yeah, Doc Dreamy will just have to remain a fantasy," Naomi agreed. She hugged Layla tightly. "Call me later, okay?"

"You know I will," Layla agreed, waving at Beth and Jamie who were deep in a conversation at the counter.

"Text me when you get home," Naomi commanded.

"Okay, Mom," Layla joked as she sauntered out, swinging into her coat.

"Whatever. Just do it," Naomi called out as Layla opened the door.

Layla waved and kept moving. She'd text Naomi because she appreciated that someone would check in on her like that. Right after everything had gone down with Noah, she hadn't wanted to be anywhere alone. She certainly wouldn't have wanted to walk around town on her own with all the tourists and strange cars driving by. She made it home and took her boots off on the doorstep. She'd been careful to keep her home clean and had to remind herself that it was because she liked things tidy and not because Noah had made her do so until it became second nature. Still, she eased them off with that tight feeling in her chest, and then her gaze caught something off-kilter.

She straightened and eyed the truck parked next door. It was black and big with a scuffed, clearly well-used toolbox on the back. Layla realized that either the neighbors had moved in or workmen were starting on the house. She grabbed her boots with one hand and fumbled with the keys with the other. She opened the door with shaking hands and firmly shut and locked it behind her before carefully placing her boots on an organizer in the front closet. Then she dashed to the back door to check the locks there. She let out the breath she'd been holding when she realized that everything was locked up tight, and nothing was out of place.

Layla stood at the kitchen window and tried to see if she could see anything else, but the house next door didn't seem occupied. She put a kettle on and reached for the chamomile tea that Naomi swore helped with her stress. She really didn't think it would work, but she didn't have anything stronger in the house. She tried to slow her breathing, yoga-style like Presley had encouraged, and reminded herself that Dean had installed cameras. She wasn't alone, she thought to herself. Lindy and Dean were just across the way. They would hear her if she screamed.

She leaned against the counter and sank to the ground. *They would hear her if she screamed.* The thought hit her hard. Noah had covered her mouth when she tried to scream, and when she'd tried, things were so much worse for her in the days afterward that she'd just stopped and learned to swallow it down when the terror rose inside her. She wondered if she would even scream now if she were truly afraid, or if she'd just be locked inside that silent terror. She closed her eyes and put her head between her knees and thought she heard herself screaming until she realized that it was only the tea kettle. She stood shakily, bracing a hand against the counter and slowly rose to standing, reaching to remove the kettle from the stove.

She pulled the mug toward her, automatically reaching for the chamomile tea and placing a bag in the mug with still-trembling hands. She poured the water over the tea and set the timer. Then she turned back toward the kitchen window and looked out at the house next door, wondering how she was supposed to sleep now.

Chapter 5

"Now I told you; don't push. I'm a nurse, not a doctor, and I didn't sign on for delivering babies," Presley heard the words, as she paused outside the room for a quick glance at the patient's chart. The words were said severely, but she knew that Clarissa was among the best and most tender of nurses. "Now didn't I tell you the midwife would be right in?" Clarissa asked the laboring mother who returned her smile with a look of relief.

"Hi, Vashti. Are you ready to have this baby?" Presley asked, as she came into the room with a smile.

"Just about," Vashti smiled wanly. "Loving the epidural, but I'm getting a little tired, Presley."

"The contractions are coming along nicely," Clarissa said, updating Presley on her patient's progress.

"You've been in the best hands on this floor," Presley told Vashti, nodding at Clarissa.

"I know it. I don't think I could have done this without her," Vashti agreed.

"Where's your partner?" Presley asked. "You're not doing this alone, are you?" She checked her notes in concern. Few of her patients gave birth alone, and she didn't recommend it.

"No, Donovan's just running late. As always," Vashti said, rolling her dark, heavily lashed eyes with their smear of smudged mascara and blowing back her long dark hair where it was coming down from the messy bun she'd thrown it into. "I took an Uber the second the first contraction hit," she said with a laugh.

"Well, you're just about ready to push," Presley said, checking Vashti's cervix to make sure, and trying to withhold judgment on the father who couldn't even give the mother of his child a ride to the hospital. "I hope you decided on a name."

"I was thinking Natalia Jasmine," Vashti said with a wide smile.

"That's pretty," Presley commented, relieved that it was, so she wouldn't have to fake enthusiasm over a ridiculous name.

"Awfully fancy," Clarissa commented, shifting her weight into the seat. Her iron gray hair was cut in a no-nonsense style she'd kept for the last twenty years. She kept saying she'd retire, but most of the staff figured she'd outlast them all. She seemed to fit perfectly into the chair where she sat, a short, round woman with a wide smile, that she gave out only when she felt it was warranted, and soft, wrinkled hands that were tougher than they looked. She'd held many a woman's hands during contractions, with or without the epidural.

"She'll grow into it," Presley said, coming over to pat Vashti's hand in encouragement. "It's almost time."

"I'm here, I'm here! Don't start without me," a deep, panicked male voice said from the door.

Vashti and Presley looked up at the same time, and Donovan smiled, bemused. He noted that they both had the same dark hair, more black than brown, but Vashti's was long and tied up in a messy bun where the nurse seemed to have hers in a short ponytail with a straight fringe of bangs across a face that was much more pale that Vashti's warm Persian coloring. She also had light eyes that were striking in her face while Vashti had those big, dark ones. They made an interesting picture.

"I hope I made it before the doctor," Donovan Clairmont said with a grin as he walked over to kiss the top of Vashti's head. "How are you doing, sweetheart?"

"Better when I push this baby out. And this is Presley, my midwife, you Neanderthal," Vashti said with a rasping laugh that just made Donovan grin.

"Sorry about that. I'm Donovan," he told Presley, flashing a charming smile.

"You're late," she replied, and then made an effort to soften her tone. "But not too late. Vashti is just about ready to push, aren't you?"

"Let's get this over with," Vashti said, gritting her teeth through the effort of another contraction. "Then I want a nap," she paused, thinking and trying to take a deep breath. "And a big ass cheeseburger with everything on it." She paused for another breath. "And fries. And a Coke."

"I feel like I should be writing this down," Donovan said with a grin, patting his pockets for a pen.

"You can have all that and more once we get your daughter out," Presley said. "Now I want you to breathe through this and push as hard as you can. You'll feel the pressure."

"Oh, I feel it alright," Vashti said breathlessly.

"You've got this," Donovan told her, patting her hand.

"You're going to need to do better than that, Coach," Presley told him. "Try to help prop her up to push. And breathe with her," she told him, getting ready.

Thirty-five minutes later, Vashti was still marveling at Natalia's little fingers and toes. Donovan was sitting with her on the bed making the appropriate admiring noises but had yet to ask to hold the baby. Presley finished delivering the placenta and cleaned up, surreptitiously checking Donovan out. The guy shows up late and doesn't even try to hold the baby, Presley thought to herself, wondering what kind of dad he'd be with so little effort. He leaned his head of full light brown hair close to Vashti's dark hair to look at the newborn.

"Well, I think she definitely looks more like you," he said with a grin, admiring the baby's dusky skin and dark head of hair. "She's definitely got your hair," he said, yanking a strand of Vashti's with a grin. He turned and looked over at Presley with a smile, and she saw his eyes were brown, too, and crinkled at the corners. "How'd she do, doc?" Donovan asked.

"I'm a midwife, not a doctor," Presley corrected automatically. "They both did great. Perfectly healthy, beautiful baby. And mother, too," Presley said, softening her smile as she aimed it at Vashti. "You'll need to get some rest, but the nurses will be in to check on you. If you need anything, you're familiar with the call button." They exchanged a grin, as they both recalled just how many times she'd pressed it before the epidural arrived. "A lactation specialist will be in to make sure everything is going well on that front, but I'd recommend getting some sleep while you can. Tomorrow, we'll get you up and around, but for tonight, call a nurse if you need to use the restroom. Just try to rest while you can."

"After the cheeseburger," Vashti agreed, turning a pointed look at Donovan who looked surprised.

"You want to eat after all that?" he asked incredulously.

"Damn right. All the toppings," she reminded him. "Now would be good," she told him with a grin.

"And fries. And a Coke. Yeah, I remember." He stroked a hand over her head. "I'll see you in a while then."

"I could use a cookie, too," she called after him, as he headed out the door just after Presley.

Presley walked toward the nurse's station, planning to do her notes as quickly as possible and end her shift. After all, she'd pulled a double, subbing in for a doctor who had a family emergency. She sighed, wishing for a cheeseburger herself, or a nap, in equal measure. She didn't even realize that Donovan was on her heels until he nearly ran into her when she stopped abruptly to look down at the notes in her hand.

"Hey, sorry," Donovan held out his hands in a gesture of peace. Presley noted that he was quite a bit taller than her, but then decided that he wasn't quite six feet. Presley, at 5'5", considered herself pretty average in height. She moved to let him pass.

"There are a couple of fast food places down the street, but the restaurant on the corner has a really good burger that's about a dozen steps up from that. You can call in an order, and they'll let you pick up curb-side," Presley told him absently, looking down at her notes. "There are some menus in the waiting room if you want to grab one."

"Are you working all night?" Donovan asked curiously.

"No, just wrapping up my shift now," Presley said, still distracted.

"Want to share a burger with me?" Donovan asked. "I can drop one off with Vashti and maybe meet you a little later?" he asked with what he probably thought was a charming smile that Presley found suddenly repulsive. She was aghast. Was he hitting on her, mere minutes after Vashti had given birth? She looked up at him incredulously.

"I don't think so," she said flatly, turning and walking away.

"Alright. Well, it couldn't hurt to ask. No harm, no foul," he said, wondering what he'd done to get under her skin. He shrugged, as she turned to level a look of loathing over her shoulder. He shook his head and moved to the elevator. He'd try the restaurant she suggested, maybe bring her back a burger. It must have pissed her off when he came in late, he thought, as he headed to the door. She sure was awfully worked up for such a casual request.

***

Presley came in the next night to do her rounds and stopped in Vashti's room last, hoping to avoid another run-in with Donovan. She'd called Layla on the ride home to bitch about the dad who'd hit on her before he'd managed to grab a burger for the new mother. She had worked up quite a head of steam about it and still hadn't quite simmered down. When she walked in to Vashti's room and saw her crying, she immediately went into Mama Bear mode.

"What happened? Are you in pain?" she demanded, coming into the room and sitting down to take her hand.

"No, it's not that," Vashti cried. "Natalia's dad is a prick! Always has been, always will be," she said angrily. "He doesn't even care to come see his own child, said he had to work! Work, my ass. There's probably someone else," she said, swiping tears out of her eyes.

"Well, I wasn't all that impressed with him to be honest," Presley said with a shrug. "You're probably better off without him."

"Wait—was he here?" Vashti asked hopefully, her face clearing.

"Wasn't he here yesterday?" Presley asked, confused.

"He didn't come see me. He wouldn't even take my calls until this morning," Vashti said, confused herself. "Are you sure it was him?"

"Wait—who was the guy here with you when you had the baby?" Presley asked.

"Oh, that's my brother, Donovan," Vashti said. "Sorry, I keep forgetting you've never met Eric. Of course, you thought Donovan was ..." She started to laugh. It started as a giggle, but then she was braying with laughter, tears running down her cheeks in amusement. "Not impressed, huh?"

"Sorry," Presley said with an embarrassed smile, trying and failing to stop the blush that stained her cheeks. "It's just ... you two don't really look alike."

"Well, we wouldn't. My mom, his dad. We're steps. Anyway, at least that took my mind off Eric for a minute," Vashti said with a side smile. "He's the asshole who won't show up. Donovan has been the only support I've had with our parents out in Arizona."

"I think I owe your brother an apology," Presley said with a cringe of embarrassment and a long sigh.

"What'd he do?" Vashti asked with interest.

"He hit on me, and I ... well, I wasn't very nice," Presley admitted, embarrassed.

"Oh my God, you thought we were together and he ..." she took a deep breath and tried to stop giggling. "Easy mistake though. I'm sure he'll understand."

"Understand what?" Donovan asked from the door with a quizzical look on his face.

"She thought you were the baby daddy," Vashti said, rolling her eyes.

"I just got my wires crossed," Presley explained, wondering if this could get any more humiliating. "She just told me you're her brother. I, um, thought … Anyway, sorry about that. Really."

"Oh," Donovan looked over at Presley, assessing her reaction carefully. He thought the blush was pretty, even if she clearly wanted to be anywhere else in the world at the moment. "And you thought … huh. Well, that makes more sense. I wasn't sure how I'd offended you, but now it all makes sense." He started to grin. "Well, you can always make it up to me. Maybe buy me a cheeseburger sometime," he said with a wide smile.

"Yeah, I may have to do that. Again, I'm very sorry," Presley said, trying not to get her back up at his obvious enjoyment of her discomfort. After all, she'd been rude and firmly in the wrong. Still, did the man have to look positively gleeful about it? "I just wanted to check on you before I head out," she said, turning to Vashti and focusing on her instead of her annoying brother. "Looks like everything is good here."

"It's fine. Thanks for stopping by. Best laugh I've had all week."

"Glad I could help," she returned wryly. "On that note, I'm going to go before I embarrass myself any further," Presley said. "I'll check on you again tomorrow if they haven't already released you. You follow up with me in a week."

"Yes, ma'am," Vashti agreed, with a little salute.

Presley waited until she'd slid into her car before she dialed Layla's number. Normally, her sister would be the last person she'd call with something like this, but they'd started to become friends again, however slowly. Presley was hoping to catch her before work, if she could. Then she remembered that it was Saturday, and her sister wasn't working at all. She almost hung up the phone, but her sister picked up. Presley began without preamble, "Okay, so you won't believe what stupid thing I did ..."

Chapter 6

Presley decided she had the best seats in the house. She was kicked back in the hammock watching Dean and Lindy argue over the grill. She pulled her blanket up firmly to her chin. It was a little chilly, but she couldn't resist the pull of the hammock. The wide farm table was set up with a brightly patterned tablecloth in the center of the garden. Libby was sitting on a porch swing with Keely while Layla leaned on the railing beside them cooing at Maya who was playing on a blanket on the porch. Seth was somewhere inside cooking, and her Dad came through the screen door mid-argument.

Her family had definitely expanded, Presley thought. Her dad's birthdays used to be tense dinners with just her and Layla trying not to argue and leaving as soon as they could reasonably get away. Her dad had eloped with Keely the year before, a whirlwind romance that had taken them all by surprise. And Keely was a package deal. Now Presley had a stepbrother and stepsister, which still felt surreal. But nice-surreal, she thought with a grin as she settled in for the live entertainment.

"You're going to burn them," Lindy said sharply over at the grill.

"I know what I'm doing," Dean insisted, bumping her with his hip to shift her away. "This is not my first time at the grill."

"Hard to tell," Lindy returned with a roll of her eyes and a firm step back toward the grill.

"I told you that I'm grilling today," Theodore insisted affably, waving them aside.

"And we told you it's your birthday, so we should do it," Dean countered easily.

"It's my birthday, so I get to say what I do with it," he returned with a deceptively friendly smile.

Presley grinned, suspecting already who would win this argument. Her dad looked dapper and easy going, but he had a stubborn streak. She and Layla had inherited it honestly enough. Her dad was in the tweed jacket with patches at the elbows that he loved and that she and her sister often teased him about. He might have been turning sixty, but he looked a good decade younger. He had a full head of silver hair with a short beard, and he kept in shape. Presley could admit that he was an attractive man, and he and Keely together were a handsome couple. She watched as Keely got up to wade into the fray.

She smiled privately to herself when Dean and Lindy retreated and allowed her dad to stand at the helm, so to speak, of the grill on his own, a look of deep satisfaction on his face. Keely stood beside him, leaning in as they exchanged a private word. She felt a pang then of what could only be envy. Even with Derrick, she'd never had that easy rapport. She'd always felt like she had to dance around his insecurities and fear of conflict. He'd always brushed lightly over her tough days at the hospital, preferring not to talk about them. She wondered absently if he did the same with Amber.

She'd missed him for a long time. The breakup had been sudden and humiliating, but what was infinitely worse was missing someone who had chosen someone else. She watched her dad and Keely smiling warmly at each other and wished wistfully for that.

Of course, she thought, she'd actually have to date if she ever wanted to find that. Her thoughts automatically went to Donovan, and she nearly groaned out loud. When would her humiliation end? It was bad enough that Derrick and Amber had made the rounds of hospital gossip before Presley had found out about their affair, but now the nurses on the floor were circulating the story of how Presley thought the brother was the husband and coldly rebuffed him. It would be hilarious, if it had happened to someone else. As it was, Presley shifted uncomfortably in the hammock and tried not to think about the clear amusement in his eyes. Or the attraction that had been undeniable.

"Are you joining us or just going to lay over there all day?" Seth called from the table. He was setting covered dishes out.

"You all seem to have this under control," Presley called back with a grin. She was glad she had a couple of days off before her next clinic. She was hoping the gossip would have blown over by the time she got back. She swung her legs over the side of the hammock and pushed the blanket to the side. She got up and walked over slowly. "Everything smells so good," she told him with a sigh.

"I think we've got a little bit of everything today," Seth agreed.

"My family used to throw on burgers and dogs and call it a BBQ," Dean said with a mournful shake of his head, chiming in to the conversation as he took a seat at the table. "The first time I went to a BBQ at Seth's, I didn't know what to think. Pulled pork, brisket, chicken. The whole she-bang."

"What can I say? We like food," Lindy said, sliding in beside him.

"A fact for which I'll always be grateful," Dean told her fervently as she grinned at him.

"After that, we couldn't get rid of him," Lindy explained to Presley.

"She spent years pretending to hate me," Dean told Presley, nodding his head toward Lindy.

"I wasn't pretending," Lindy said with a laugh.

"They fought all the time. Could have knocked me over with a feather when I found out they were dating," Seth told Presley. She'd heard the story before but grinned with amusement at the banter. "Especially since I'm pretty sure I told you she was off-limits," Seth said with a significant look at Dean who held up his hands in a gesture of peace.

"You're not the boss of me, Seth Carver," Lindy pointed out wryly.

"Hey, man, can I help if I'm irresistible?" Dean asked, as Lindy gave him the side eye.

"It's that pretty face of yours," Presley nodded in mock seriousness.

"It's a curse," he told her, a smile pulling up the corners of his mouth.

"How about you and Libby?" Presley asked Seth. "How'd you two meet?"

"We were kind of set up by my mom," Seth admitted with a laugh. He waved Libby over from the porch. "We're about ready."

"Not just yet," Theodore called over from the grill where he was listening to their conversation. "Give it a few more minutes."

"Keely set you up?" Presley asked curiously. "Um, you were actually set up by your mom?"

"Well, she introduced us anyway," Seth explained with a grin. "She threatened to introduce her to Dean, and I wanted to save her from that heartbreak."

"My hero," Libby said with a wide smile, as she walked up and wrapped her arms around his neck from behind.

"He was just afraid you'd meet me and then fall helplessly into my arms," Dean explained with a sly look as Libby gazed over at him fondly.

"Absolutely," Seth agreed exchanging a grin with his best friend since childhood. "Anyway, Mom introduced us, and I wasn't looking for anything, but then Libby was just … perfect."

"Hardly," Libby said wryly as she walked around and slid onto the bench beside him, squeezing his hand. "I had issues."

"But charming issues," Seth countered. "And no more than me."

"That's true enough," Libby agreed. "Anyway, fast forward through some rough patches, and here we are. Are you dating anyone?" she asked Presley with interest.

"Me? God, no. I don't have time to meet anyone," she told them with a shrug.

"Well, I hear that's not entirely true," Keely said with a warm smile, coming over to pass Maya to Lindy. "She's hungry, if you want to feed her before we eat."

"Do you know something I don't?" Presley asked with a laugh.

"I heard you met someone at the hospital," Keely said.

"Stop telling my business!" Presley told Layla as she walked up with a guilty grin and a pitcher of tea. She slapped a hand to her face, "And the humiliation continues."

"Okay, I've got to hear this," Lindy told her, as she adjusted Maya at her breast.

"No, you really don't," Presley muttered into her hands. "I'm not telling you anything private ever again," she said peeking out her fingers toward Layla. "You're the worst."

"Oh, don't act like you wouldn't do the same," Layla said with an easy laugh, grateful that she and Presley could play-argue rather than the real arguments they used to have.

"It was just a stupid thing. Seriously not worth telling," Presley said dismissively, straightening and reaching for one of the covered dishes.

"We'll be the judge of that," Seth said.

Theodore walked over from the grill with the meat piled high and gestured for everyone to sit. "You talk while we eat," he said, pointing to Presley.

"I guess everyone else in the free world has heard about it so why not? Okay," she began, drawing a breath. "So, there I was in the middle of delivering just the cutest baby girl when this total dipshit of a dad finally shows up. Then, right after the baby is out, the guy follows me into the hall and hits on me. I was so pissed. Anyway, I pretty much let him have it and then vented about it later when my patient was crying about her asshole baby daddy." Presley burned with embarrassment as she thought about how unprofessional she'd been. "Anyway, she started laughing and said the baby daddy hadn't even shown up for the birth. Her brother had. So, there I was with foot-in-mouth syndrome. It was just the worst."

"Good thing you're a doctor," Keely said with a smile.

"Midwife," Presley said automatically.

"How'd you dig yourself out of that hole?" Theodore asked, grinning at his daughter.

"Oh, his sister thinks it's hilarious. She told him, and I apologized. But, oh my God, the entire floor has been talking about it. I barely got through my shift. Then Big Mouth over here tells Keely so …" She shrugged helplessly. "Now everyone knows."

"Sorry," Layla said, mouthing "Sorry not sorry" at her food.

"I saw that," her sister said, sticking out her tongue.

"They never really grew up," their dad said with a grin, looking proudly over at the two of them getting along so well.

"Anyway, that's it. No love story. Just me making a total ass of myself," Presley finished, turning to the heaping plate of food she'd been filling up as she told her story. She leaned close to breathe in the aromas and then tucked into the meal with a gleam in her eyes. "Come to mama."

"First, you're being uncomfortably intimate with your food," Lindy said with a grin. "Second, you left out the most important part."

"I did?" Presley asked when she finally stopped chewing.

"You did," Keely confirmed.

"What? Is my humiliation not complete?" she asked, quirking her eyebrows.

"On a scale from one to Holy Wow, how hot was this guy?" Libby demanded.

"What makes you think he's attractive?" Presley asked with a carefully blank expression.

"Yeah, he's definitely hot," Lindy said with a nod.

"I'm guessing Holy Wow," Layla piped up. "It wouldn't be nearly as embarrassing if he'd just been, you know, *meh.*"

"That's not even a real word. You guys are the worst," Presley groaned. "He was alright," she conceded before turning pointedly back to her food.

"Sure, he was," Dean said with a grin. "See? That's the kind of denial you used to have," he told his wife with a sly smile.

"Not everyone was taken in by your charms, Dean Walton," Lindy said, waving a fork in his direction while Maya slept in the sling.

"Well, you did marry me," he pointed out as the others laughed.

"Fair point," she conceded. "The real surprise was Seth and Libby though. First, they were on. Then off. Then back on. It kept us on our toes."

Presley cast Lindy a grateful look as the subject flowed to the relationship roller coasters of the last few years. She and Layla exchanged a grin. It was weird to have such a busy birthday dinner after all the quiet years of just the three of them. It was big and messy, but it was fun, too. They even teased each other like they'd always been family. She had to admit, it was pretty nice. But she was grateful that her own embarrassment was forgotten as the conversation flowed. By the time the cake was brought out, it seemed to be forgotten. She only hoped it was being as easily forgotten at work.

Chapter 7

Layla woke up the morning after the family dinner and sighed as she looked around her bedroom. It was really starting to feel like home. She'd hung up a few paintings she'd found around town and set out the candles that she loved but had stopped bothering with when things with Noah had gotten particularly grim. She was reclaiming her space and her life. It wasn't happening quickly, but she was slowly letting go of that tight fist of anxiety she'd carried after she'd moved in with him.

She'd been surprised that she enjoyed her dad's birthday so much. Everyone had been welcoming, and her dad had been so pleased to have both daughters there that he couldn't stop hugging them and patting their shoulders as they passed. It had been endearing but a little heartbreaking, too. There were so many years when she had only seen her family when she had to, so sure that she wouldn't have a good time. She had thought they always expected the worst from her, and she usually lived up to that expectation, no matter how hard she wanted to prove them wrong. After everything fell out with Noah, her dad and Presley just stepped up as if she hadn't spent the last few years being a total brat every time she came around. She rolled her eyes at how easily she could self-sabotage her own life. She was glad they all seemed to be getting over their earlier distance.

It wasn't always easy. Her knee-jerk reaction was still to assume the worse. It had been like that for years, since they'd found out their mother wasn't ever going to get better. She'd just withdrawn from all of them, turning to boyfriends and friends and partying to try to get through it. She regretted that now, but at least she was getting another chance. Layla rolled out of bed and headed downstairs to make coffee. She grabbed a cup from the shelf and smiled. The mug was in the shape of a slipper and said, "One shoe can change your life. ~ Cinderella" She thought that was true enough and glanced ruefully at her own bare feet and remembered how she'd once had a closet full of shoes—before she'd moved out and Noah and torched her remaining possessions. Of course, she could always buy more. She was just glad she had a life she could change.

She looked out the kitchen window with a frown. She'd finally given up on sleeping with all the banging at the house next door. She'd been warned there were renovations coming, but this was ridiculous. After all, what sane person woke up this early on Saturday if they didn't have to? She glanced over at the clock on the oven and grimaced. It was earlier than she'd realized.

Of course, she hated to complain. After all, she'd kind of fallen into a sweet deal with the rental anyway. Layla looked around the house and wondered if she'd ever get used to it. She'd only been living there about a month, having moved out of Presley's apartment to relocate for her new job to Madison. Her step-sister had offered her the carriage house in her own backyard when she heard she needed a place to stay. She had a beautiful home and was surrounded by people she knew and liked. It was the perfect situation.

Bang. Bang. Bang.

Surrounded by people she knew, she thought, and the world's most annoying neighbor. She went over to the window to look out. She could see one man outside, hammering away at something. She couldn't make out much of his features, but she did zero in on the man bun holding back his long hair. She rolled her eyes. It was just one more irritation.

She looked down at her pajamas to make sure she was at least decent. She had on a college sweatshirt that used to belong to an old boyfriend, not—thankfully—the most recent one who had turned out to be a nightmare, but some guy before that. She wore black leggings underneath it, and she slipped her small feet into a pair of boots by the door and headed out with her coffee.

"Hey!" she called, walking over to the black wrought iron fence that separated the properties. She had to call out a couple of times to get his attention.

"Well, hey," he said with a slow smile, checking her out. Layla squared her shoulders and tried to stop the trembling that always seemed to start up now when she was around men she didn't know. She took a moment to check him out and assess her surroundings. She was on her side of the fence so she should be safe enough, but she took a cautious step back toward the house. He had dark blonde hair. Highlighted, she thought in disgust. He had a full, groomed beard and easy enough features. She might even have found him attractive if he wasn't currently disturbing her REM cycle every morning. His eyes were light, but he was squinting so it was hard to tell.

"Something I can do for you?" he asked her

"You could stop hammering away over there before eight in the morning," Layla suggested severely, grateful that her voice, at least, didn't shake.

The man walked over to the fence, causing Layla to take an instinctive step back and spill a little of her coffee over the side of the mug. He stopped, cocking his head and looking at her. He stood with one hand on his hip, and she could see that he had that lean, sort of rangy body that came with the type. You know, the kind of guy who works on houses. Your usual blue-collar fantasy, she thought, remembering all the other guys just like him she'd dated when she was going through her string of bad relationships. She could see the muscles even with the long sleeve T-shirt, and she had to admit he looked good. Just not good for her, she reminded herself.

"Sorry about that. I forgot that not everyone is a morning person. I'm Jude Anderson," he said, staying where he was and just looking at her. He waited a beat. "Do you have a name?"

"I'm Layla." She just looked at him, unsure. "Westerman," she added.

"Who lives in the big house?" Jude asked, curious.

"My stepsister and her husband. He's a firefighter," she added. "And their baby who probably likes to sleep in the morning," Layla told him, looking at him intently until he seemed to get the message.

"Right. Well, I'll stop by later and see what a good time would be to work. For the baby's schedule and all that," Jude said with a shrug.

"You set your own hours?" Layla asked skeptically.

"Something like that. My boss is a bit of a slave driver, but I'm sure we can work something out," he said. "Besides, he doesn't care when I do it, as long as I get it done on time."

"Jude. That's not a name you hear every day," Layla commented, struggling to find something to say while he just stared at her with a patient gaze.

"My mom is a Beatles fan. Your parents dig Clapton?" he asked her with a grin.

"My mom," Layla said shortly. "But she just loved music. I have a sister named Presley," she said with a small smile.

"Your mom has good taste," Jude told her with a wide smile.

"She did," Layla commented shortly.

"Sorry," Jude said, sounding sincere.

"It was a long time ago. Just … maybe start a little later, okay?" Layla asked. When he only tilted his head, she continued. "With the work. Some of us like to sleep in on weekends," she pointed out, taking a sip of the coffee in her hand.

"So noted. Sorry again," he said, putting the ear bud that was hanging down around his neck back in his ear. He took it out and beckoned her over. "You'll never believe this," he said, holding the ear bud over the fence toward her to hear.

"What is it?" Layla asked, unmoving.

"It's Clapton." Jude said with a grin. "I like him, too."

"I'll just take your word for it," Layla said. "Is it *Layla?*" she asked curiously as she started back to her house.

He shook his head. "*Wonderful Tonight,*" he answered with a grin, watching her nod before she quickened her steps.

"Nice to meet you, Layla," Jude said, a little louder now that his ear buds were back in. She gave a little wave and stepped back into the house. She looked out the little window at where he'd gone back to working. Weird guy, she thought.

***

Outside, Jude put down the hammer and decided to go make some breakfast before continuing the work on the house. It wouldn't do anyone any good to annoy the neighbors right off. Besides, he needed to check with the stepsister and see when the baby was sleeping, make sure he hadn't been an annoyance already. He looked over toward the small carriage house from the kitchen window. He hadn't realized anyone lived there. He'd sort of assumed it was a garage, or storage.

"You didn't tell me you had a cute neighbor," Jude told John-Paul as he walked into the room.

"The firefighter?" JP asked with a grin. "Yeah, I couldn't agree more."

"No, I mean the woman in the carriage house," Jude said with a laugh.

"You mean Layla? Her sister told me about her. I've seen her out a couple times, but she's more of the indoor type, I think. She's cute enough. A little overly made up for my taste," he said with a shrug.

"Really? I just met her. Didn't look like she was wearing any makeup at all," Jude said with a shrug.

"Well, most people are asleep this early on a Saturday unless they have work or kids," JP pointed out. "How's the work coming?"

"Faster if you would help," Jude suggested.

"Well, what's the use of having a brother who's handy if you can't get a little help with renovations?" JP asked, settling himself onto a stool at the breakfast bar.

Jude's brother was similar in coloring. They both tanned easily, and Jude's highlights were from the sun while JP had chosen to have a few extras strategically added at the salon in his somewhat shorter hair. Jude kept his tied back while he worked, especially now that it had grown so long. JP kept his face clean-shaven, but otherwise the brothers had strong features, strong enough that strangers used to mistake them for twins when they were little, although there was a two-year age difference between them.

"Are you heading into work?" Jude asked JP with a sigh, giving up on ever getting help from that quarter.

"For a while," JP said. "I need to check in on my clients, make sure everything is in order."

"It's insurance, JP. I think the office will be fine without you for a weekend," Jude told him, warming up the skillet for French toast.

"I've got to make some calls," JP said with a shrug.

"On a Saturday?" Jude asked skeptically.

"Well, if you must know, I have a breakfast date."

"Yeah, I thought so," Jude said. "Someone new?"

"His name is Jake, and I met him at the gym," JP said, reaching to pour himself a cup of coffee and adding in the cream and sugar he liked. "Not my usual type, but he seems nice."

"Well, your usual type has been shit lately. Probably a good idea to try something new," Jude told him.

"I know you're right," he said with a sigh. "Why aren't you dating anyone?"

"No reason. Just haven't met anyone lately," Jude said, his eyes inadvertently drifting to the kitchen window.

"Ah," JP said.

"No 'ah'. No anything," Jude told him. "She was rude actually." Although he wondered if it was something else. "And, I don't know, kind of skinny."

"Women call that petite. Not skinny. No one likes 'skinny'," JP pointed out.

"Fine, petite," Jude said, rolling his eyes.

"But you said cute, if you'll recall." JP took a sip his coffee.

"Yeah, I guess I did," Jude agreed.

"So why aren't you asking her out?"

"I just met her."

"Is there a rule about how long you have to wait that I don't know about?" his brother asked him with a grin. "Should I write this down?"

"I like to get to know a person first," he answered with a laugh. "Besides, she seemed a little nervy."

"Well, you do it your way, and I'll do it my way, but it wouldn't hurt to be neighborly and stop by to invite her for a drink sometime," JP said, as Jude turned back to the stove to slide on the first piece of toast. "And you're good with nervy."

"That may be," Jude agreed. "Still, that doesn't mean I want to date someone like that." But he let his eyes wander back to the window and he wondered what she was doing.

***

Inside the house, Layla took a shower and changed into jeans and a sweater. She dried her hair and curled it, and then she started the makeup routine she had once enjoyed before Noah. Now, it took her several tries to do any of it without shaking or dropping anything. She sighed. The relationship had ended months before, and he'd finally left her alone. But she could still remember what it was like to live inside that relationship, how he'd constantly poked holes into her self-esteem until she didn't have any. But she'd always enjoyed makeup, and she was determined to recapture that feeling.

She applied it carefully, making decisions based on what she liked and not what she remembered Noah liked. She took a deep breath and finished by selecting the bright red lipstick Noah had told her made her look like a slut. After all, she liked red, and it had always looked good with her pale coloring and dark brown hair. When she was done, she looked into the mirror with a small smile. She thought she looked pretty good.

She headed downstairs and glanced out the window. At least it was quiet at the neighbor's house now. The hammering would probably start back up soon, and she planned to be out of the way well before that happened. She walked outside, putting on a jacket as she did.

"Hey. What happened to all the noise?" Lindy asked, standing in the backyard in leggings and a T-shirt, looking cold.

"I asked him to quiet down so early in the morning," Layla said with a shrug.

"Well, go back and tell him to get back to work," Lindy said irritated, her dark hair twisted carelessly on top of her head and listing to the side. Her blue eyes narrowed, "Maya likes rock music and hammering, apparently. Since she started teething, she screams unless there's noise. I'm tempted to have Dean drive her around in the fire truck with the sirens on just so we can get some sleep."

"Um, that's weird, isn't it?" Layla asked, puzzled.

"Yeah, but that's how it is. So maybe tell Man Bun to get back to work?" Lindy suggested, shooing her toward his house. "I'm begging you."

"Fine. But you're going to make me look weird," Layla told her. She turned back around. "You call him Man Bun?" she asked with a giggle.

"Well, I didn't know his name, and Dean might be offended if I called him Hot Dude," she said with a grin. "But he is." When Layla hesitated at the gate, Lindy softened. "I've met the brother. Nice guy. Hunky. They're good people," she told her. "But maybe get a move on," she said, spinning on her heel and hurrying back inside from the cold.

When Lindy opened the door, Layla could hear the baby wailing. She took a deep breath and walked through the gate. She knocked on the back door, and the hunky brother opened it. "You must be Layla," he said with a grin.

"I must be," she said uncertainly, trying out a small smile. "Do you have a minute?"

"Come on in," JP said, holding open the door.

"Um, okay," Layla said, stepping just inside. She could tell JP was making faces behind her, but she didn't know what to make of it. She looked over at Jude and then back at JP. "I guess you're the brother?" she asked. "Lindy said she met you."

"Lindy's a peach," he said, leading Layla further into the roomy kitchen. Her eyes went to the large fireplace where a fire was already warming the room. Her eyes widened a bit, and her shoulders relaxed a little. "I'm John Paul, but everyone calls me JP," he said with a smile, extending his hand to shake hers. His grip was firm, but his eyes were kind. Layla began to relax a little.

"John Paul. And Jude," she smiled slowly.

"Yep," Jude said from the stove, following her train of thought. "Her sister is Presley," he explained to his brother with a grin.

"So, our parents were all nuts. Or leftover hippies. You be the judge," JP said with a laugh. "What brings you over?"

"Well, um, Lindy happened to mention that Maya, that's the baby, likes the sound of the hammering. She's teething," Layla explained with a shrug.

"Are you saying it's okay if I get back to work?" Jude asked, sending a slow smile her way that made Layla catch her breath.

"Um, preferably as soon as possible," she said, shifting her weight on the balls of her feet.

Jude took a last bite of his French toast and stood up. "Here's what I'll do. I'll get back to work, and you can finish this French toast." He sent a look over at his brother. "JP, fix her a plate for me, will you?"

"Oh no, I didn't come over here for that!" Layla exclaimed uncomfortably. She hadn't meant to come inside. She was just going to deliver the message and leave. She shifted where she stood, and Jude pulled out a chair and beckoned her over.

"Sit, eat, and I'll tell you all about the date I'm going on in the next hour. That should give Jude time enough to get the baby to sleep," JP began, glancing at his brother who was pulling on a jacket and zipping it up. He turned to Layla and picked up on the story as if he'd already been telling it. She sat down hesitantly and instinctively picked up the fork and leaned toward him as she tried the French toast.

"So there I was, running on the treadmill, trying to go just a little faster than the elderly man on the one next to me when the most beautiful man I've ever seen starts checking out the stair climbers in front of me." Layla grinned and found herself taking a bite of the cinnamon raisin French toast. It was good. Really good. She glanced down at it and then back up at JP, deciding she might as well enjoy herself.

When the hammering began, she jolted, but JP continued on smoothly. "So, you know I had to check him out, but I was trying not to be obvious. Turns out I'm not very good at that," he said with a grin, snagging a piece of bacon from the corner of her plate and then launching into a description that made Layla's smile widen and her body finally relax.

By the end of the story, Layla had forgotten about the hammering outside and had begun to enjoy JP's company when Jude walked in.

"I just met Dean. He came out to tell me I could take a break. They're taking the baby over to her mom's for a while." He looked over at Layla, who was standing awkwardly and starting to look uncomfortable again. He wondered if uptight was just her usual setting and then reminded himself not to be so judgmental. Not everyone was as comfortable with strangers as he was. "How was the French toast?"

"Great. Actually, really great. Thank you," she said, standing up and pushing back the chair. "I should go. Good luck on the date," she told JP and picked up her plate, looking hesitantly around for the sink.

"I don't need luck," he said with a wink, taking the plate out of her hands. "Come back and visit me again. I'll tell you all about it."

"Okay. Thanks again," Layla said uncertainly, waving to them both and slipping out the back door.

"There's a story there," Jude said quietly, watching her go and wondering.

"I know. But she might not be ready to tell it," JP reminded him. "She's sweet."

"Yeah?" Jude asked.

"Once she warms up a bit. She liked me," JP said confidently. "She's not so sure about you."

"Well, I did wake her up hammering," Jude said wryly. "I guess I can't blame her for getting her back up about it."

"Not everyone is a morning person like you," JP countered, pouring coffee in a mug to go. "Don't wait up," he said cheekily, as he grabbed his keys and strode out.

Jude shook his head and went to look at his notes. He had a few things that needed to be fixed today while JP was out, but then he was planning to head to the lake, maybe take out the kayak. He glanced toward the neighbor's house and shook his head. Sweet, maybe. Closed off? Definitely. He turned away from the window and didn't know that Layla was on the other side of hers, too, wondering about them both.

Chapter 8

Presley was almost done with her clinic rounds when she looked down at her schedule. She'd dreaded this one, and it was her own fault. Vashti's appointment was her last of the day, and then she could go home. She took a deep breath and hoped that dealing with an infant would have her sleep-deprived and distracted enough not to bring up "the situation," as Presley was starting to think of it. She put on her professional smile and headed briskly toward the patient's room.

"Hello," she said, entering after a quick knock on the door. "How are my favorite patients?" she asked with a smile, noting that Vashti seemed surprisingly well-rested.

"Oh my God, she's just the best," Vashti gushed, placing a kiss on Natalia's forehead. "I don't know why everyone says this is so hard. She sleeps all the time."

"Let me take a look. She's so pretty," Presley commented with a smile. "Just like her mama. How are you doing? Other than getting so much sleep, I mean."

"I'm good, actually," the new mother replied with a tone of surprise. "I mean, all this squish was a little surprising, and I'm ready to drop the weight. But she's great."

"Has her father been in contact at all?"

"A couple of times. He hasn't seen her though. Actually, I decided I'm going to do this without him," Vashti said firmly. "I mean, I'm going to take his sorry butt to court to help pay for her, but I'm not going to try to make him a parent when he clearly doesn't want to be. Besides, Donovan moved into the guest room for a while to help out," she explained. "You remember Donovan," she said with a twinkle in her eyes.

"It would be hard to forget since I made a complete ass of myself," Presley agreed with a tight smile. "I'm just glad you were both such good sports about it."

"Hey, it was an easy mistake," Vashti said, reaching out to stroke a hand down Presley's arm. "Don't look so embarrassed."

"It's just not my first humiliation around here," Presley said with a roll of her eyes.

"That sounds like a story," Vashti commented, as Presley began the exam.

"Oh, it is, but I'd much rather hear about you and Natalia. We'll save my story for another day," Presley said, hoping that day would never come. "Now, let's get through this discharge paperwork and get you both home."

***

After Presley finished her notes, she grabbed the tote she carried and made her way toward the front of the office. She stopped a couple of times to say hello to patients who were in the waiting room seeing other doctors on staff. She pulled out her phone, turning off the Do Not Disturb setting, as she made her way over to the elevator. She pressed the down button absently and leaned against the wall as she began to respond to a text from her sister.

"Fancy meeting you here," a deep voice said beside her. Presley nearly jumped out of her skin. "Sorry. I didn't mean to scare you," Donovan said, holding up his hands in a gesture of surrender.

"I was just distracted," Presley explained, putting her phone back in her pocket without finishing the message.

"I can see that," he commented.

Presley looked at him and realized that he was just as attractive as she remembered and wished she hadn't made such a complete ass of herself. She could feel her cheeks flushing and cursed her pale skin.

"I heard you moved in to help with the baby," Presley said, making conversation and wondering why the elevator was taking so long. Maybe she should take the stairs, she thought absently.

"Well, I knew Eric wouldn't be around," Donovan said. "I hate that guy."

"I do, too, and I've never met him," Presley agreed, shifting away from the wall and turning to face the elevator. It never took this long, she thought with impatience.

"I never liked him," he told her. "He was never good enough for her."

"Do brothers ever think anyone is good enough for their sister?"

"This guy had a record, and he was just a punk," Donovan explained and then stopped when Presley let out a giggle. It was not a sound he expected from her.

"A punk?" she asked. "Really? I didn't know anyone said that anymore." She grinned over at him, finally meeting his eyes. He almost forgot what they were talking about with all that blue.

"Well, that's the nicest adjective I could think of," Donovan admitted. "Vashti's too smart for him. I don't know what she saw in him in the first place."

The elevator doors opened, and there was Derrick waiting at the door scrolling through his phone. He looked up absently and then jolted when he saw Presley. He backed into the corner, as Presley and Donovan stepped inside.

"Yeah, there's no accounting for taste," she told him with a grin, keeping eye contact with Donovan and ignoring Derrick completely. She could see him looking at the two of them speculatively.

"So, about that burger …" Donovan began, leaning against the wall, as the elevator descended. His body was angled toward Presley's, eclipsing Derrick.

"I didn't forget," Presley told him, blushing. "When is good for you?"

"Now? Is now too eager?" Donovan asked with a grin.

"I could eat," Presley admitted with a smile, glad for once that Derrick was around to see this.

"Good. How about I just drop Vashti at home, and then we meet up after?" he asked. "She's just down the road. Or, hey, why don't you ride with us?"

"Maybe she wants to grab a burger," Presley pointed out. "She does love them."

"I am *not* taking my sister with me on a date. Besides," he continued, "I happen to know we're approaching a regularly scheduled nap time. I'll promise to bring her a burger back, and she'll be good."

"Regularly scheduled nap time? She just had the baby," Presley said with a laugh.

"Okay, so most of the day is nap time."

Derrick shifted in the corner, trying and failing to ignore their conversation. Presley observed him out of the corner of her eye and was glad he was the one on the wrong foot for once. Donovan gestured for her to exit the elevator first when it finally came to a stop, and she could feel both Derrick and Donovan's eyes on her, as she walked out.

"Would you mind if I threw this in my car on the way?" she asked, gesturing to the large tote bag she carried for work.

"No problem," Donovan said, as Derrick walked slowly off in the other direction, glancing behind him a couple of times as he left.

"So, where's Vashti anyway?" Presley asked curiously.

"The cafeteria," he said. "I dropped her there after discharge. She's always hungry, but she suggested I hang back and say hello to you." He grinned at her. "My sister is a bit of a matchmaker, I'm afraid."

"Hmm," Presley wasn't sure what to say.

"So, who was the asshole in the elevator that you were ignoring so completely?"

"Oh," Presley let out a short laugh. "That's a long and humiliating story actually." She eyed him as they walked to the cafeteria. "I think I've embarrassed myself enough where you're concerned."

"You really shouldn't feel embarrassed about that," Donovan told her, as they walked. She looked up at him, noticing that he kept his stride shorter to accommodate her own. "It was sweet that you were so protective of her. Besides, I really should have been here with her when she first went into labor, but she called Uber before she called me and didn't bother to text me until she had the epidural."

"It's nice that you showed up for her. No one should have to go through that alone."

"Well, she's my sister," he answered with a shrug, as if that explained everything. "There she is," he pointed across the cafeteria where she was chatting up one of the doctors on break. "You know that guy?"

"I know *of* him," Presley replied honestly.

"Huh. Well, that says a lot. Let's go interrupt that before she gives him her number," Donovan suggested with a grin.

"I think she can handle herself," Presley muttered behind him.

"She'd say the same thing, and look: too late," Donovan said as he watched the doctor putting her number in his phone. "At least he has a job," he said in exasperation.

Before they made it across the room, Vashti had stood up with Natalia in the sling and hoisted the diaper bag over her shoulder. "I can carry that, V," Donovan told her.

"I'm not disabled," she said with a grin, surrendering the bag. "But I'll let you this once. Good to see you again, Presley. This one talk you into dinner?"

"Well, it helped that I asked her when we got into the elevator with some jerk she knows," Donovan asserted with a smile.

"I didn't say I'd go because of him," Presley told them, and then paused. "Okay, so not entirely because of him. But did you see his face?" she asked with a smile of her own.

"Yeah, that was almost the best part," he agreed.

"What could be better?" she asked.

"The part where you said yes," Donovan told her, meeting her eyes as they walked toward the parking lot. "No take backs," he warned.

"I do believe I said I owe you one," Presley countered.

"He's not going to let you pay though," Vashti warned her.

"Let me?" Presley asked with a tone of steel under the sweetness.

"Not like that," Vashti said waving her hands. "It's not chauvinism in this particular case. Donovan here is pure chivalry."

"Shut it," he warned her with a grin.

"Seriously, he's the real deal," Vashti continued, ignoring him.

"So … tell us about Elevator Guy," Donovan suggested.

"But I'm enjoying hearing more about you," Presley told him, as she slid into the front seat of the minivan after Vashti insisted on sitting in the back with Natalia who was still fast asleep.

"Yeah, I'm getting that. That's why I'm changing the subject. It's a short ride. Just enough time for the abridged version of your long story."

"No one wants to hear about that," Presley told them, putting on her seatbelt.

"Let's take a vote," Donovan said, and his and Vashti's hands shot up into the air as one. "We win. Let's hear it."

"That," Presley began with a sigh, "was Derrick. I'd been dating him for just shy of a year when one of my nurses tipped me off that something was up. Anyway, I found him hooking up with one of my nurses in the building where I work while I was on shift," she concluded to a near deafening silence in the van. "Nice ride, by the way," she told him, trying to break up the tension.

"It's mine," Vashti piped up. "I always wanted to be a minivan mom."

"You're the first mom I've ever heard say that," Presley observed.

"Well, I don't like to be predictable," she said. But she wasn't falling for the diversion. "So, this guy cheated on you with a coworker?"

"That's not even the worst part," Presley told them.

"There's a worse part than that?" Donovan asked.

"Everyone knew before I did. Everyone. Like the custodial staff and some of my patients. All the doctors and nurses I worked with and some I didn't. Everyone," she fumed. "It might have gone on longer if I hadn't been tipped off."

"Oh my God! That's the worst," Vashti exclaimed.

"Well, now they're busy talking about what an ass I made of myself with your brother here, so the gossip has kind of faded," she admitted ruefully.

"So that's why you were so embarrassed," Vashti said quietly. "I didn't realize."

"How could you?" Presley said with a shrug. "Anyway, it'll blow over. Gossip always does," she told them, although she had to admit that the gossip about her had lasted a lot longer than she'd thought it would.

"I'm really glad that I asked you out in front of him then," Donovan finally said. "Although I'd much rather have hit him, now that I have all the facts."

"Oh, that was a lot better than hitting him," Presley said. "Did you see his face?"

"Yeah, I did," Donovan agreed with a grin, glancing over at her as he pulled into a driveway.

"This ex of yours, Elevator Guy," Vashti asked as Donovan got out to go unlock the door, "is he hot?"

Presley glanced over at Donovan as she answered. "Not nearly as hot as your brother."

"That's what I thought," Vashti said, with a note of satisfaction in her voice as she reached in to release the baby carrier from the car seat. "That was my favorite part of the story."

"It was pretty satisfying," Presley admitted.

"Enjoy your dinner," Vashti told her, as she started to climb out.

"I've got it," Donovan said, taking the carrier. "Let me get them inside, and we'll head out," he told Presley.

"Take your time," she said. "I'm fine here."

"You're welcome to come in if you'd like," Vashti added. "Although it's a wreck right now."

"I'll just wait, but thank you." Presley settled back against the seat and closed her eyes while Donovan carried the baby inside. She kept thinking about the look on Derrick's face in the elevator, and a smile stretched across her face. When Donovan finally climbed in the van, she cracked an eye open at him. "I think I owe you one. Again."

"Please, you don't owe me anything," he told her. "Look, we could take my car, but I only have my work car in the garage. My other car is parked at home. I hope you don't mind the van."

"It doesn't bother me," she told him honestly. "It's comfortable."

"Hell, yeah, it is. I gave her a hard time about getting one, but I have to admit it's a pretty sweet ride. Though I'll call you a liar if you repeat that," he joked.

"So ... burgers?" she asked.

"Unless you want something else."

"I'm good with a burger." She turned in her seat to look over at him. "I don't want you to think that I was just using you to get at him," she said carefully.

"To be fair, I asked you right then because I sensed something was up," he admitted. "I think we're even as far as that goes. But I would have asked you anyway."

"I would have said yes anyway," she responded, blushing a little when he turned to look at her speculatively. "I would have," she insisted.

"Well, then pissing off Elevator Guy was just a bonus," Donovan said, pleased.

"Are you going to keep calling him Elevator Guy?" Presley asked curiously.

"I think that's the nicest thing I can call him, to be honest," he answered. "Besides, I'm hoping I won't have to call him much of anything. I appreciate you telling me the story, but I'd much rather hear about you, not the hospital gossip version of you."

"Oh, well, there's not much to tell," she told him. "You know what I do. Why don't you tell me about you?"

"What do you want to know?" he asked easily.

"What do you do for work?" She hadn't been able to peg his profession by just looking at him. He had a sort of military stance, but there wasn't a base nearby. She'd been too busy being embarrassed about how they'd met to give it any thought beyond that.

"I'm a cop," he told her, glancing over to see her reaction. "I don't usually lead with that since a lot of people have different ideas about cops."

"I don't have a problem with it," Presley said with a shrug. She paused, and Donovan glanced over at her.

"What?" he asked curiously. "Okay, spit out whatever cliché you're holding back over there. Yeah, I like a donut as much as the next guy. No, the coffee at the station isn't as bad as on TV." He rolled his eyes.

"I wasn't going to ask about the food. Or the coffee," she added with a grin. "So … you have a uniform? And handcuffs?" she asked him playfully.

"Yes to both, and I'm going to try not to think too hard right now about why you'd ask me that," he returned with a wolfish grin. "I'm going to think about that later though."

"It's just a cop thing. Like firefighters," she pointed out. "The uniform, the hose, the pole. It's hard to hear someone does that and not come out with a cliché."

"Firefighters," he scoffed. "Most of the ones I've worked with are lazy asses."

"Don't let my brother-in-law hear you say that," she said with a laugh. "He's far from lazy. He's actually pretty toned," she admitted with a grin.

"Must be out of a different house," Donovan replied. "But cops and firefighters don't always get on."

"Why is that?"

"No idea. It doesn't help we play ball against them," he said with a smile. "So, you have a sister then?"

"I have one sister, and last year I ended up with a stepsister and stepbrother. The firefighter is married to my stepsister. It's all kind of weird, actually," Presley admitted.

"Yeah, when my dad married Vashi's mom it was like that for a bit," he agreed. "But then we decided it was kind of nice having siblings. We have another sister now, and that was weird, too. But it grew on us," he explained. "Her mom was forty-two, and Vashti was just starting college. So, it was a surprise."

"I can imagine."

"You like your stepmom?" he asked, as they pulled up at the restaurant.

"She's really sweet actually. And beautiful. I mean, absolutely gorgeous. You know Helen Mirren?"

"Of course."

"She's beautiful like that," she explained. "She makes my dad really happy. They're kind of adorable about it."

"You sound close to your dad."

"Very."

"Daddy's girl?" he asked with a grin.

"I was all about my mom. But then she died. My dad was just the best single dad, and we got really close."

"What's your sister like? Are you two close?"

"We weren't at first, after my mom died. Actually, we've been a lot closer lately," she told him. "It was strange at first, but I really missed her."

"Nice that you're both getting another chance then," Donovan said with a smile. "Just wait here a sec," he told her, hopping out of the car. Presley watched him curiously, as he parked and walked around to her side of the van and opened the door.

"Thank you," she told him, sliding out and looking up. "I can't remember anyone ever doing that before. Other than my dad a million years ago."

"Well, that's because you've been dating people like Elevator Guy."

"That's true enough. I'm done with Elevator Guy, though."

"No lingering feelings?"

"It was nice to wind him up today after everything he put me through, but I think I'm over the rest of it," she said with a shrug, feeling for the first time like it was the truth.

"Good to know," Donovan said easily, opening the restaurant door for her.

"I'm really liking this chivalry thing."

"You sound surprised."

"Well, the only chivalry I've ever experienced is the kind that covers misogyny," she commented with a shrug.

"Yeah, I know the type," Donovan agreed. "If I promise I'm not the type, will you let me pay for dinner and maybe take you out again this weekend? If you're not working, I mean."

"First of all, I think I owe you the burger, if you remember correctly. And don't you want to see how this date goes before you schedule another?" she asked him, as they followed the server to a table by the window.

"First, I just said that to get you to go out with me," he returned with a grin. "And second, I like how this date is going. I'm pretty confident I'm going to want another, and I don't want to forget to ask you later because I'm distracted by your eyes."

"My eyes?"

"You probably hear all the time you've got great eyes," he said easily. "I might get distracted and forget, and then you might make other plans that don't involve me."

"I'm glad you think I have such a busy social life," she said with a laugh. "What'd you have in mind?"

"Depends. How do you feel about sports?"

"I'm a fan," she said cautiously, tilting her head. "Can you be more specific?"

"How do you feel about target practice?" he asked, after they'd placed their orders.

"I feel pretty strongly about not going shooting with someone I just met," she pointed out.

"Okay, fair point. But what if we weren't talking about guns?"

"Why don't you tell me what we are talking about, and then I'll tell you what I think about it," she said rolling her eyes.

"How about axe throwing?"

"Axe throwing. As in …"

"There's a place in town. We can get drinks and throw hatchets at targets. It's fun."

"Drinking and throwing weaponry." Presley thought about it. "I'm in," she said, taking a sip of the Coke she'd ordered.

"Do you want to go this weekend?"

"I'm good with that."

"Maybe we could grab dinner after. Or dinner before?"

"Eager, aren't you?"

"I'd like to get to know you," he admitted. "Are you on call this weekend?"

"Not this one. Next."

"Yeah, me, too. That works then," he said. "Must be fate."

"Must be," she said skeptically, sighing happily when the burgers and fries were served. "Thanks for this," she told him. "In case I get distracted by your pretty face and forget to thank you later," she continued with a grin. He laughed and leaned in to snatch a fry off her plate. "Hey, you've got your own!"

"Yeah, but I'm betting you're going to steal a couple later."

"Well, I am now," she told him with a short laugh, slapping his hand away when it came close to her plate again.

"Fair enough," he told her, picking up the large burger. "I'm glad we did this."

"Yeah, me, too," she said with a smile. "Now shut up and eat."

Chapter 9

Layla stood back and surveyed her work with satisfaction. She had literally rolled up her sleeves for this project and twisted her thick black curls into a messy bun at the top of her head. She was wearing an old shirt of her dad's, a button-up in a pale blue that matched her eyes, over a pair of jean leggings. The shirt was flecked with paint now, and she stood back and crossed her arms, rubbing them a little to warm herself. She smiled to herself and did a little happy dance of pleasure at the effect of the honey-colored door against the gray carriage house. When she heard clapping behind her, she spun around and nearly fell into the still-wet door.

"It looks good," JP said from where he was leaning against the fence with an over-sized mug of coffee. "I liked the dance best though," he admitted with a warm smile.

"Why are you lurking?" Layla asked with a smile of her own, feeling her nerves start to calm. She wasn't sure why JP didn't make her nervous when Jude so clearly did. She didn't think it was because he was gay. Physically, he was as strong and intimidating as his brother. She thought it was probably because he was just so friendly and laid back in a way that didn't feel threatening. Although she had to admit that the fact that he wasn't interested in her as a woman probably did have a little something to do with it.

"This is my yard. It's hardly lurking," he said with a smile. "Mind if I come over and take a closer look?"

"Um, okay," she said hesitantly as she observed that he was already making his way to the front gate to come to her side. She decided that maybe she wasn't so relaxed after all.

JP walked over and nodded at the door before sinking down on the porch swing with a happy sigh. "I'm a little surprised at your music selection. I figured you'd be out here painting to Clapton," he said, nodding to the small set of speakers she had plugged into her phone. She'd been singing along to Taylor Swift while working and wondered self-consciously if he had heard her as well as seen her. She didn't like the feeling of having been observed while she was unaware. "No leave it. I like it," he told her when she moved to cut it off.

"I like Clapton. I like classic rock in general, but I listen to other things, too," she said with a shrug, remembering how Noah had criticized her taste in music. Of course, there was little he hadn't criticized in the end.

"God, you must be freezing," JP told her, standing up and setting his coffee mug on the porch railing. "Let me help with that."

Layla didn't realize she'd been shaking. Somehow the thought of Noah could still rattle her, sending her from a place of pride at the work she'd done to the quivering mess she'd been with him. She let JP gingerly take the brushes from her and put them in the buckets of water she'd set out. "I guess I am cold," she agreed with a shrug, glad she had an easy excuse for her reaction. She couldn't talk about why she was shaking, not even with Naomi. Everyone would just tell her to see a therapist, and that she wouldn't do.

"Why don't you come over and have a cup of coffee? Just while these dry," he suggested, breaking into her thoughts.

"Thanks. I could use a cup," she told him gratefully and then wondered if she was foolish to trust someone she'd just met. "Is Jude home?" she asked, wondering which answer she was hoping to hear.

"He is, but he's probably still sleeping," he told her. "He had a late night last night."

"Oh?" she asked, wondering what a late night for Jude entailed.

"No rest for the weary," JP said with a grin, leaving her with her curiosity. "Ah, he lives!" he said dramatically, as they walked into the kitchen where Jude was pouring a cup of coffee.

Layla immediately took in all of Jude—and there was a lot to take in. He was standing in the middle of the kitchen, barefoot and in pajama pants. He hadn't bothered with a shirt, but then he probably wasn't expecting neighbors to just drop in. He looked like a man who was used to manual labor, and she remembered that falling for his type was the reason she'd had garbage relationships. She pointedly looked away from him and tried to focus on anything else.

"Sorry. Wasn't expecting company," he said evenly, observing the thoughts that had played on her face from the moment she'd stepped into the room. He guessed that she was terrible at poker. "I'll just grab a shirt."

"Show off!" JP called out, as he walked away. "I'm personally working on my dad bod right now," he told Layla conspiratorially, patting his stomach. "It's the in thing."

"Is it?" she asked with a grin. She didn't take anything he said seriously, not with that tone.

"How do you like your coffee?" he asked her, moving over to the pot.

"Light and sweet if you don't mind," she told him, leaning on the breakfast bar.

"You know, you don't seem the sunny door type, if you don't mind me saying so," JP said, passing her the cup.

"Oh? What type do I seem?" she asked, trying to keep defensiveness from creeping into her tone.

"I figured you for brooding colors," JP told her easily, smiling to soften his words.

"I'm not sure what type I am," she said, rubbing her arms again and sliding off the stool to walk over to the fireplace. She thought it was nice that they already had a fire going so early in the morning. She'd started painting early after a nightmare had kept her from getting any sleep, and she was starting to feel the effects of being up for so long.

"Nothing wrong with experimenting some," Jude said, as he walked into the room, dressed in jeans and a sweater. "Sorry about my earlier state of undress. I wasn't expecting company," he explained, shooting a look over at JP. "Late night."

"I heard," Layla said shortly. "JP invited me over for coffee," she said, holding up her mug in explanation. "Which I appreciate."

"Any time," JP returned with a smile, refilling his own mug. "Layla's been out doing a little painting this morning."

"Dressed like that?" Jude asked sharply.

"What's wrong with how I'm dressed?" she retorted, feeling angry and embarrassed at the same time. She'd woken up from the nightmare flustered enough that she'd simply pulled on the first shirt she'd found and gone outside to paint, not even noticing that she was cold until she'd finished.

Jude looked her up and down, taking in the men's shirt she was wearing so casually with the leggings and boots. At least, he thought, her shoes were sensible enough. "Do you have any idea how cold it is outside?" he asked her and then broke off and stormed out of the room.

"What is his problem?" she asked his brother.

"Oh, well, that's Jude for you," JP said with a shrug.

"Here," Jude said, thrusting a sweater at her as he came back into the room. "You're going to freeze to death."

"Um, thanks?" she asked, raising her eyebrows. "I can't wear this. I'm still covered in paint," she explained holding out her arms to show off the paint-flecked shirt.

"I don't care if it gets a little paint on it," Jude told her evenly. "I care that you don't freeze to death because you didn't have the sense to dress for the weather."

"Excuse me?" she asked, her voice tightening dangerously. She was getting pretty tired of having men tell her that she wasn't smart enough. She could feel the anger starting to move her, heating her more effectively than the fire burning behind her.

"I don't think he meant it that way," JP began uneasily, sensing the tension. "He's just a worrier, our Jude."

"Thanks for the coffee, JP. I think I'll head home now," Layla said stiffly, ignoring Jude completely and setting the sweater down on a chair.

"Oh, don't be stubborn. There's no way the door has dried yet, and you're clearly freezing," Jude said sharply and then took a deep breath. "Look, I'm sorry for being an ass. Rough night," he said, rubbing his tired eyes.

Layla reached for the sweater and pulled it on, deciding she could still be pissed off wearing the damn thing. She had to admit that she was freezing, even if she didn't admit it to him. "Just don't take your hangover or whatever out on me," she told him, as she sat down at the breakfast bar. Then she inhaled sharply. "How did you know I painted a door?" she asked him tightly.

"I saw it from the window when I went to get dressed," he answered easily. "It's not like doors just change colors on their own," he reminded her, although he was watching her carefully.

"Oh. Okay," she said, satisfied with the explanation. She didn't like being watched, and she sipped her coffee and wondered how long it would take for the door to dry. She needed to grab a shower, and then she was planning to curl up with her book club read before the meeting tonight. "You're not working today?" she asked Jude.

"I'm taking the day off," he told her shortly. "So why the yellow?"

"For the door? I don't know. I just wanted the change," she explained briefly, not able to put into words how much effort simply choosing a color had been for her. She'd come to a point of second-guessing every decision she made, trying to beat back the inner dialogue that kept telling her that nothing was good enough. She knew that voice was Noah's and not her own, but it was still present with her. She'd gotten rid of him and yet hadn't, really. She'd felt such a sense of satisfaction when it was finished, knowing that Noah would have hated it, but she loved it.

"Well, I like it," JP told her. "Now if you two will excuse me, I need to make a call," he said, nodding at his phone where he'd been texting on and off since they'd come in.

"The new guy he's dating?" Layla asked with interest.

"No, that didn't work out. I'll leave him to fill you in on the story there. Apparently, it wasn't the worst date of the century, but it made the top five."

"Well, that's too bad. He doesn't exactly seem heartbroken though."

"No, he met someone else," Jude said with a roll of his eyes. "So ... why didn't your boyfriend help with the door?"

"What boyfriend?" Layla replied, wishing JP had stayed a little longer.

"Figured you were wearing his shirt, after all," Jude pointed out.

"Oh, this," Layla said, her smile transforming her whole face. Jude raised an eyebrow. "Um, this is my dad's shirt."

"Huh." Jude wasn't sure what to say. He'd just assumed it was a lover's shirt, past or present. Now that they'd clarified her relationship status, he had to admit that he was interested. She was probably trouble and definitely high maintenance, he reminded himself. "So, no boyfriend in the picture?"

"No," Layla said, her smile slipping away. She remembered the last one and swallowed, hard. When she looked up and caught the spark of interest in Jude's eyes, she knew she had better make things clear. "I'm not dating right now," she told him firmly.

"Why not?"

"Is that really any of your business?"

"No. But you seem pretty definite about it. I figured there was a reason."

"My reasons," Layla returned evenly. "Besides, I don't think this would be a good idea," she said, indicating the two of them.

"Did I ask you out?" Jude asked blandly.

"Well, no," Layla said, feeling embarrassed. "But I just wanted to be clear. About the no dating thing," she explained, feeling wrong-footed and defensive. She hadn't felt this way in a while, and it was starting to annoy her.

"About the no dating me thing, specifically."

"It's just, I've dated men like you before. I don't think it's a good idea for me," Layla explained shortly. "No offense."

"I really don't think you have," Jude said evenly. "And anyway, you're not my type," he told her breezily, standing up to open the fridge. He pulled out bagels and cream cheese, tossing them on the counter. He took the bagels over to the toaster and turned to look at Layla where she stood, her eyebrows drawn sharply together in a look he'd have found cute if he wasn't annoyed by how badly he'd botched the entire conversation.

"Excuse me?" she asked him, sharply, not expecting that reply.

"You're a little high strung. And definitely high maintenance," he said with a shrug, knowing he was making things worse but too tired to care. After all, he thought, it rankled that she'd judged him without knowing anything about him at all. "No offense," he added flatly.

"I think my door is probably dry now," she told him, standing.

"Oh, don't be like that. Take a bagel," he said, handing one to her and inadvertently stepping into her personal space.

"Don't tell me what to do," she said, sharply, slapping it away. It rolled around the floor, and they both watched, shocked. "Sorry," she said quietly. "I, um, need to …" Layla didn't finish the sentence, darting instead for the back door.

"Shit," Jude muttered, as she practically ran across the yard. He headed out to follow her and only caught up as she was climbing the porch steps. "Hey," he called out, she whirled around, and he noticed how pale her face was. She also seemed to be struggling to breathe. He knew a panic attack when he saw one. "Just wait. Breathe. Layla, breathe."

Layla sank down on the back porch steps and couldn't even think beyond the next breath to feel embarrassed that she hadn't quite made it home to hide the attack. She put her head between her knees and felt Jude join her. He put a hand on her back, lightly, and reminded her to breathe. She sat like that for a few minutes and then finally noticed that his feet were bare. She sat up, a rush of color returning to her face. "You're freezing," she told him, looking into his eyes.

"I'm okay," he told her, waving off her concern even though he had wondered how long it took to get frostbite. "Are you okay?" he asked quietly.

"Yes," she said, feeling the rush of embarrassment.

"Hello?" Layla and Jude both looked up, as Presley came striding around the corner. "Do you have any idea how long I've been knocking?" she demanded, and then noticed her sister's face. "Is this guy bothering you, Layla?" She narrowed her eyes at his bare feet and the fact that her sister was wearing a man's sweater. "Oh my God, am I interrupting?" She wasn't sure which possibility worried her more.

"Oh, no, it's nothing like that," Layla said, exchanging a look with Jude who stood up quickly and took a couple of steps toward Presley.

"I'm the neighbor," Jude said, nodding toward the house next door. "Jude Anderson."

"Presley Westerman." Presley looked down at his feet. "Leave in a hurry?" she asked suspiciously.

"Layla was having coffee with me and my brother, and I was a bit of an ass. Long night, long story. Anyway, I was rude, and I came over to apologize," Jude explained, leaving out the panic attack.

"That's pretty much it," Layla agreed, standing up and edging toward the house. "Anyway, apology accepted, and I was just about to head inside."

"Alright," Presley said, feeling like she was missing something. "Nice to meet you, Jude. Are you coming in?"

"No, I better get back and have some breakfast. Nice meeting you, Presley," he said, with a wave.

"Holy cow, is that Man Bun?" Presley asked, as they went inside. "You didn't mention he's hot. And when did you paint the door?"

"This morning, and he's alright, I guess. For that type," Layla said with a shrug.

"It's barely 9:00 a.m. How long have you been up?" Presley asked with concern.

"A little while. Anyway, if you think he's so hot, why not ask him out?" she countered, wondering why she felt so uncomfortable at that thought.

"Who says I'm not already dating someone?" Presley asked with a smug smile.

"Who?" Layla demanded and then looked closely at her sister's face. "Oh my God, you're not dating the patient's brother, are you? Can you do that?"

"Well, he's not my patient," Presley said, rolling her eyes.

"Okay, how did this happen? I thought you were hoping never to see him again?" Layla asked, settling into the sofa and pulling a blanket around her legs. Her arms were warm now, but her legs were freezing. She took a deep breath and noticed how much Jude's sweater smelled like him and then wondered uncomfortably if she should have given it back.

"Well, I was already deeply embarrassed, but I ran into him right as I got into an elevator with Derrick," she began, and then told her sister all about Jude asking her out in front of him.

"I would have paid good money to see that," Layla said with a grin.

"Yeah, it was pretty great," Presley admitted. "We've been out on one actual date, but we've got another later tonight so … it's kind of nice."

"Okay, I need to see this guy," Layla said curiously. "Do you have a picture?"

"Of course. I've already cyber-stalked him," Presley joked, holding up his social media profile. "This is Donovan."

"He's hot. What's he do?"

"He's a cop," Presley said with a grin. "Uniform and everything."

"Nice."

"So, what's Jude do?"

"Contractor maybe? I don't know. He's working on their house," Layla said with a shrug.

"He could just be handy," Presley said, raising her eyebrows. "Are you sure that's what he does for a living?"

"I don't know. It hasn't really come up," Layla said with a shrug, realizing she'd just assumed and hadn't really asked him.

"You two looked cozy enough."

"I'm not ready to date, Presley. Anyway, he's just a neighbor. It's not a thing."

"I'm just saying he looked interested."

"Well, he's not. I'm not his type either."

"Well, then he's an ass, and it's his loss," Presley said staunchly. "You can do better."

"Fine, but I'm not trying to date right now," Layla pointed out. "Tell me everything about Donovan and then tell me again about the look on Derrick's face in the elevator. That was my favorite part."

***

Next door, Jude poured another cup of coffee and looked out the window at the yellow door. Well, he'd pretty severely botched the entire morning, he decided with a sigh. He'd have to apologize again when she wasn't trying so clearly to hide a panic attack from her sister.

"Where's Layla?" JP asked.

"Well, I pissed her off, and then she slapped a bagel out of my hand before running out the door," Jude recapped.

"What has been happening here? I step out for two minutes, and you manage to screw it up with the pretty neighbor," JP noted in exasperation. "What did you say?"

"She told me flat out I'm not her type, and it pissed me off. So I told her she's not mine either," Jude said with a sigh. "I'm just not having the best morning."

"What happened last night? A suicide?" JP asked, his face showing his concern.

"Attempted. I called it in early enough, but then I had to spend the night and the better part of this morning getting him admitted into a treatment facility. It was—rough. And the parents were angry about the medical costs, like that matters," Jude said, rubbing a hand over his face.

"It was a kid?" JP asked, shocked.

"You know I can't talk about it. Anyway, it made for a long night."

"And then you were tired and a total ass to the pretty girl," JP sighed. "Did you at least apologize?"

"Yeah, I went over to apologize right after she left," he paused and decided that Layla's panic attack was her own business. "I met her sister as I was leaving."

"What's she like?"

"It's hard to say. Protective of her sister, for sure," Jude said. "She couldn't decide if we were lovers or if I was bothering her. You know, because Layla was wearing my sweater."

"Well, there's definitely something going on with Layla. She about jumped out of her skin when I went over to talk to her this morning."

"Yeah, I've noticed that."

"You sure you want to get involved?"

"I don't know if I do. I guess I wouldn't mind getting to know her better, but I really don't think she's interested. She said as much."

"Well, you did insult her. And she thinks you work in construction," JP pointed out.

"She's already assumed a lot about me," Jude said. "I don't want to be dated for my resume."

"But you want to get to know her?" JP asked. "Attraction or professional curiosity?"

"I don't know," he shrugged. "Maybe both."

"Well, careful there."

"I thought you liked her," Jude said, cocking his head and shooting a glance at his brother.

"I do. I think she's sweet. But she might be trouble, too."

"Did you even have a phone call to make?" Jude demanded, cocking a hip against the counter.

"No, I just went into the other room to listen," JP said with a smile. "You definitely screwed it up, by the way. Maybe you should get her flowers." When Jude merely lifted up a finger in reply, JP chuckled. "Well, it's your funeral."

***

Layla walked Presley out to her car, looking forward to a shower and a book before lunchtime. She glanced over at her sister who was tucking her hair behind her ears and kind of half smiling, as if she was thinking of something sweet. Layla was pretty sure who had put that smile there.

"So, when are you going to bring Donovan around?"

"Can we get through a second date, at least?" Presley asked. "This may not even go anywhere."

"But you hope it does?"

"I don't even know him very well. I guess I'm just enjoying seeing where it does go. Look, can you not tell everyone? At least until there's something to tell? I think I've had enough embarrassment for one lifetime."

"I can keep my mouth shut," Layla said. She stretched and then stopped suddenly, as the sunlight caught the driveway. "Hey, Pres, wait a sec. There's glass all over." She bent down at the back of the driveway, wondering what could have broken. She looked up and down the street for a second. "You're lucky it didn't pop your tire when you drove in."

"I wonder what could have broken," Presley said, looking around. "You don't think—"

"No, I don't," Layla said flatly, knowing exactly what her sister was alluding to. "We have no reason to think it's anything but an accident. Let me clean it up first. Just be careful in case you already drove over a piece." Layla went inside to grab a broom, and Presley stood outside looking speculatively from her sister's place to the street around it and back over to the neighbor's house, wondering.

Chapter 10

Layla put the last of the glass in the recycling bin as Presley pulled away, looking carefully to see if she could tell where it had come from. She knew where her sister's thoughts had gone. Her own sometimes wandered in Noah's direction. It didn't seem like he'd give up so easily. Still, he might have found a new relationship. The idea of that made her suddenly reach up to rub warmth back into her arms. She hated the idea of him doing to someone else what he'd done to her.

"Do you ever dress warmly enough?" Jude asked from the other side of the fence. He was holding the gate, but he didn't approach. When Layla merely looked at him, he continued, "Can I come over for just a minute?"

"Only for a minute. I've got book club in a little while," she told him, straightening from where she'd bent down by the recycling bin for a closer look.

"Break something?" Jude asked casually, nodding at the broom and dust pan in her hands.

"There was glass on the driveway," she said by way of explanation.

"You're lucky you didn't get a flat. Where'd it come from?"

"No idea," she said with a shrug. "Is there a reason you're here?"

"You're clearly freezing. Can we step inside for just a minute?" he asked her. She looked at him, and he could read the flash of emotions skim over her face. Then she nodded.

"Sure," she turned and headed in, holding the door open for him.

"Nice place," he commented, as he followed her into the bright kitchen. When she finally looked at him, he held up the bag she hadn't noticed in his hands. "Here."

"What's this?" she asked, gingerly taking it from him.

"What does it look like?" he asked, an edge coming into his voice. Her nervousness irritated him, and he tried to shake off the resentment.

"I mean, it's clearly a wine bag. I meant why."

"I was an ass," he said shortly. "There's chocolate in there, too," he added. At that, she opened the bag and dug in, and he chuckled. "Well, I know your weakness now."

She looked up at him sharply. "Were you looking for one?"

"Are you always this prickly?"

She rubbed a hand across her eyes. "I wasn't always," she answered, looking tired at the thought.

"So, what happened?" he asked her, wanting to know what had made her react the way she did. He knew he was being nosy, but he didn't care. After all, nosiness was his stock and trade.

"My mom got sick," she said shortly. "Want a glass of wine?"

"I wouldn't mind," he said, surprised that she'd answered at all with anything other than a retort to mind his own business. She opened the bottle easily and poured two glasses and then walked into the living room where she sank onto a chaise lounge. He sat down carefully on the couch, sipping the wine.

"Anyway, it was the kind of sick where there was no getting better," she continued. "I was a bratty teenager, and when we found out she wasn't going to be okay, I got worse." She shrugged.

"Because you felt guilty," Jude said, not asking.

She looked up, surprised. "Yeah. I'd been such a bitch to her. Not all the time, but enough."

"You were a teenager," he replied evenly.

"Yeah," she said, grateful that he understood. "Anyway, the sicker she got, the worse I got. I just resented everyone. I stayed like that for a really long time."

"But you got better?"

"For a while. I met someone," she explained, looking down at her glass of wine. "He made me want to be better, at first."

Jude waited, sipping his wine and wondering why he cared so much to hear her story. Her eyes were on her glass, but he could see the rapid play of emotions. He caught fear and grief and a little flash of anger. "But later?" he asked, finally. She looked up slowly and met his eyes.

"Then he changed," she said simply and then shook her head. "No, he was always that way. I just didn't see it. Then, I did, and I was too ashamed to leave."

"Ashamed or afraid?"

"Both. Equally," she answered honestly, feeling the tightness ease in her chest a little at admitting it.

"He groomed you."

"Yes," Layla said with a sigh. "I was just an easy mark."

"But you got out," Jude pointed out, leaning back in the seat with an appraising look. "Seems like that took a lot of courage."

"Oh, I didn't do that alone. I found out he was doing the same thing to someone else, and word got back to my family." She shook her head in wonder. "I don't know if I'd have had the courage to do it if they hadn't been there when I found out."

"Don't sell yourself short. You're a smart woman. I'm guessing you'd have gotten away eventually."

"Maybe," she replied doubtfully. "I don't like to think of what that might have cost me." She looked up at him suddenly. "You're a surprisingly good listener."

"Thanks," Jude said with a grin. "It's a specialized skill."

"Use it a lot at work, do you?" she asked, her eyebrows raising in humor.

"Well, yeah," he answered honestly, knowing that he should probably explain. He'd started to when she spoke up.

"I really do have to get ready to go to my book club," she told him. "But thanks—for the wine and the listening."

"Sorry about what I said earlier," Jude said, standing up and following her to the kitchen with his glass.

"Yeah, me, too," Layla told him with a small smile. "I don't mean to be that way," she shrugged. "I can't seem to help myself."

"Well, I was being an ass," he answered with a grin. "I can't really blame you."

"Truce?" Layla asked stretching out her hand.

"Yeah, why not," he said, taking her hand in his own to shake. Her hands were icy, as he'd expected. She always seemed cold. But he was startled by the warmth that shot through him when he touched her. It was cold but soft, and he thought she was a little softer than he'd expected. He met her eyes speculatively and could see a similar reaction surfacing there. "Maybe we could grab dinner one night," he suggested before he could stop himself.

"Jude." She said just his name, and his breath caught.

"You don't think it's a good idea?" he asked her, letting go of her hand reluctantly.

"I can't keep repeating the same patterns," she told him softly. "You seem really nice, but I have to be more careful."

"Do I remind you of him?" he asked her, surprised and a little hurt.

"No, not at all. He was … I don't know how to explain it," she said. "He was different from anyone that I had dated. He seemed more together. Everyone before him was a little rough around the edges and just not … good for me," she finished. "He was different. Turned out to be a different kind of bad for me."

"Ah. I remind you of the others," he said, understanding and wondering if it was too late to correct her on the assumptions she'd made.

"Sorry," she said, sounding regretful.

"You have to do what makes you happy," Jude answered easily.

He didn't have to like it, but he got it.

"Yes," she replied gratefully, relieved he'd understood, but somehow feeling wrong-footed again. She was doing the right thing, she thought to herself, so why didn't it feel right?

"I'll go and let you get ready. I'm glad we had a chance to talk. I hope we can at least be friends."

"I'd like that," she told him, feeling a little better. "Thanks for the wine and everything."

"I'll see you when I see you."

"See you later," she said softly as he left.

Layla turned to head upstairs and wondered if Naomi was right. Maybe she should be talking more about what had happened. But when she thought about talking to a professional, she cringed. She didn't mind so much with Jude. He was just a neighbor, maybe a friend, and when she'd started telling him, she did it because she didn't think he'd care anyway. But then he'd listened so well she'd almost forgotten her resolution not to date that type anymore. She went into her room to change into something for the book club and glanced out the window toward his house, lost for a minute in thought.

***

"I'm not late," Layla said, as she came through the door.

Naomi was standing beside the refreshment table near the front of the room and grinned at her. "Cutting it close there, Westerman."

"It's hard to know who you're talking to when you do that," Beth said with a grin, nodding to Keely, the tearoom and bookstore's owner and Layla's new stepmother.

"It's nice to see you, Layla," Keely said warmly, bringing in another pot of tea and sitting it on the warmer at one of the tables. She came over and enveloped Layla in a hug, which always took her a little by surprise.

Layla returned her smile and was glad that the tension between them had eased. She had resented Keely, and it was only after she moved out of Noah's place and into Presley's that she'd been able to really find an appreciation for her. Keely hadn't been judgmental, and she didn't even ask questions. She just showed up with some things that Layla might need and remained supportive throughout the ordeal. It reminded Layla so much of her own mother that she finally stopped hating Keely for not being her.

Keely turned to greet another guest, and Layla marveled at how put together she seemed. She was nearing sixty, and yet her face was nearly unlined. She had the same bold blue eyes as Seth and was nearly as tall as Lindy with hair that was silver and swept up elegantly. She looked more like an aging Hollywood movie star than a business owner in a small town. It was easy to see why her dad was attracted, but she could also see why he fell in love with her. She was sweet, but she was also strong, having raised two kids on her own when her husband left. Her dad and Keely had the single parenting in common, even if they'd come at it from different circumstances.

"Can I help with anything?" Layla asked Beth.

"Nope. Grab a drink. We're still waiting on a few stragglers," she said, heading back toward the kitchen.

"Like you," Naomi said with a grin. "Finish the book?"

"Of course, I did," Layla said. "Okay, I finished it this morning, but I still read it in time."

"I figured you'd be here early," Naomi said, thinking about how Layla didn't like walking on her own when it started to get dark.

"My neighbor stopped by for a minute," Layla said by way of explanation, unwinding the scarf and slipping off her jacket. She looked around at the tearoom where they were holding tonight's book club meeting. The tables had greenery as centerpieces, and they had lit candles around the room. They'd finished a book on hygge the month before, and they had decided to incorporate some of the

Danish ideas on a cozy atmosphere into their winter meetings.

"Man Bun?" Naomi asked, her eyebrows shooting up. "I thought you didn't like him."

"He's nicer than I thought," Layla said with a shrug. "Not like that," she added sharply.

"He's hot though, right? That's what Beth said," Naomi pressed. "She saw him the other day when she was at Lindy's."

"If you like that type."

"Hot?" Rebecca chimed in behind her. "Hot is everybody's type." Rebecca was the local librarian, but she was nothing like the librarians of Layla's youth. She was mouthy, profane, and dressed like someone's idea of a sexy librarian with buttoned up shirts, pencil skirts, and usually just one more button opened than she should have, with lace peeking through. She even had her curly blonde hair twisted into a bun, but of the messy variety, and she had glasses she wore only for reading, which added to her whole vibe. Layla rolled her eyes but smiled widely. She liked Rebecca.

"I'm not saying I don't like hot," Layla explained. "He's just too much like my exes. You know, rough around the edges, good with their hands—"

"I'm not seeing the problem here," Jill interrupted. She was sitting beside Rebecca. They were roommates and book club regulars. Jill's boy-short silver hair had purple tips these days, and she had switched out the nose stud for a ring and added one to her eyebrows, too. On anyone else, it would have looked tough, but she looked like a sassy pixie next to her voluptuous roommate. "Good with his hands? A little rough around the edges? *Mmm*," she commented, licking her lips.

"Right?" Naomi returned. "What's the problem?"

"I've just dated that type. They're great in bed but usually trouble. You know, they don't really commit. They're rarely stable," Layla explained. "I mean, the guy is in his thirties and living with his brother."

"Maybe his brother is living with him," Naomi pointed out.

"Sorry, you lost me at *great in bed*," Rebecca returned with a grin.

"Ignore her," Jill said with a smile, bumping Rebecca's shoulder with her own. "Not everyone has your appetites."

"Sad for them."

"I just need to be more selective this time. I'm just going to be friends with Jude," Layla told them.

"Maybe I should meet him," Jill suggested.

"Get in line," Naomi put in. "He sounds pretty yummy."

"Isn't it time to get started?" Layla said.

"Alright, you're off the hook for now," Naomi said with a grin. "But we're not done with this conversation."

"Whatever," Layla said, but added a smile.

She hadn't had girlfriends like this in a long time. In high school, she'd prided herself on having more male friends than female ones. Looking back, she could see that all those "friends" she'd been so proud of had just been trying to sleep with her. She'd thought she was a guy's kind of girl, but then she realized that they thought about her differently than she saw herself. When they got girlfriends, they'd drop her, usually at the girlfriend's request.

After that, she'd been more of a loner than she liked to admit. She and Naomi had bonded after Noah, but she'd gotten to know Jill, Rebecca, and Beth a little through the book club. It was nice having a group of women to talk to, particularly the kind that didn't judge her.

She looked at Naomi who was heading over to Beth to get things started with the club. She'd have to tell her about the panic attack later. They'd promised to be honest about that sort of thing. But for now, she just wanted to enjoy a little time out with friends. Plus, she had a lot of opinions about the book, and it was nice to be able to talk them out. She poured herself a cup of tea and waited for the meeting to begin.

Chapter 11

Presley paused outside the donut shop and glanced at her fitness tracker with a grin. She'd made good time, but now that she'd finally stopped, she realized that it was really cold outside. She opened the door to the shop and walked in with a happy sigh. She liked a good workout, but she also liked a good donut, she told herself. She ordered and then took the hot glazed donuts and coffee over to a table as far from the door as possible. She didn't want the draft since she was in a racer back tank and yoga pants. She was glad she'd opted for the pants and not the shorts, but she was wishing pretty desperately for a jacket. Those five miles hadn't taken long, but she'd have to run back rather than walk if she wanted to keep warm. She bit into the donut and thought it was probably a good thing for her to do ten miles anyway.

She felt her phone vibrate and took it out of a pocket in her leggings. A text had come in from Donovan. She grinned, as she looked at it.

"Still on for tonight?"

"Yep," she answered shortly.

"Talk?"

"After my run," she told him. "30 minutes?"

"How far you running???"

"5 more miles," she typed out with one hand, eating her donut with the other.

"5 MORE??? You taking a break?"

"Having a donut."

"You are weird", he replied and then followed it with the laughing emoji faces.

"Now you know," she told him, sending a picture of a face with a tongue sticking out.

She tucked the phone away. She had to admit that she liked Donovan. It didn't hurt that dating him had changed her work humiliation into the cutest meet-cute story in the history of the world. Everyone had gone from laughing at her to sighing wistfully that she was now dating the hot guy she'd mistaken for her patient's husband. Word had even gotten back to Amber who had just shot Presley dirty looks when their shifts overlapped. Of course, Presley reminded herself, that wasn't exactly unusual. Dirty looks and smug looks were the usual ones she got from her.

Still, it was nice to be the object of envy rather than pity and speculation. Not that it was the point, of course. Donovan was interesting. The first date had been nice, even if he hadn't kissed her at the end. She wasn't used to that. He'd driven her back to her car and hugged her before she got in to drive home. He'd even waited to make sure she got out of the parking garage safely. It was nice, but she wondered what his deal was. He was clearly interested, she thought. But he hadn't made a move. She had strongly mixed feelings about that.

She finished the donut and lingered over her coffee, remembering how cold it was outside. She knew after the first mile, she'd heat back up, but she made a mental note to do more to prepare for the weather than grab yoga pants and a stretchy headband to cover her ears and keep her hair out of her face. She took a last drink and then put the mug on the counter, waving to the kid behind as she left.

She was about to start running when her phone started vibrating with an incoming call. She set off at a brisk walk and answered it in annoyance. She didn't like her running time interrupted.

"Hello," she answered briskly. When there was no answer, she glanced at the screen. It was an unknown number, and she had good reception. "Hello?" she asked. There was the sound of moving in the background. "I think we have a bad connection," she said uncertainly.

When she heard the click, she rolled her eyes. She was getting a lot of wrong numbers and sales calls lately. She reminded herself to put her phone number back on that Do Not Call list to keep solicitors from calling her private cell number. She took off at a run after silencing her calls and tucking the phone back into the pocket in her leggings.

She kept her pace brisk and only slowed down at intersections where she had to wait at crosswalks. She ran in place while she waited, to keep her heart rate up. After all, she had indulged in two donuts today. She was a little curvier right now than she preferred. She blamed it on the short torso that came with her small stature. She'd been slim as a reed growing up, like Layla still was now, but she'd put on a little weight during nursing school and then a little more when she was finishing up school to be a midwife. When she finally graduated, she'd started back to running, hoping to keep her weight in check. She wasn't heavy, but she felt like she was a few donuts away from going there if she didn't stay active. Still, she liked running, so it wasn't all about weight.

Her phone vibrated again, but it didn't ring. She made a mental note to check it when she got home and picked up her pace. She had an errant thought that it could be her dad. The year before, he'd had a cardiac incident, as he liked to call it. She'd spent a few days at the hospital between shifts, as he recovered. It had been terrifying, and now a ringing phone automatically took her back to that memory. Presley knew it was worse for Layla. When the phone rang more than once, she had the knee-jerk reaction that something had happened to her dad or that Noah was bothering her again. Of course, that fear had let up after she changed her number.

By the time she got home, she'd forgotten about the calls and jumped in the shower. She wasn't on call, and she didn't have to be tied to her phone after all. She sang along to Norah Jones as she showered, and then she snagged her phone to send a text to

Donovan about their date. She saw that she had one text from him, a smiley face response to her last message. She shot a winky face back. Texting made her feel like a teenager. She replied to a text from her sister about the next book club pick, and then she shot a text to Donovan to figure out what time they were meeting at this axe throwing place.

"Pick you up?"

"Going to drive over from my dad's. I'll meet you there," she explained.

He replied with the time, and she put the phone down, still on silent, and began drying her hair. It was short and mostly straight, but it was too cold to let it air dry. She figured she'd swing by her dad's and say hello for a while before her date. At least they were doing an activity, so she could dress casually enough.

She experimented a little with her makeup, swiping on a turquoise eye shadow that looked so cute on one of her colleagues. She took a quick picture and sent it to her sister in a text.

"Does this make me look like a hooker?" she asked. Layla was her go-to person for all style and makeup questions. Her sister could have made tutorials she was so good, if she'd been interested in that sort of thing.

"Yes. But a cute one," she replied. Presley rolled her eyes.

Message received. She typed, "Taking it off."

"Neutrals are better for you anyway," Layla replied. "Hot date?"

"Yep," Presley replied. "Axe throwing."

"Seriously???"

"Yep."

"Less is more then."

Presley picked up the phone and called her. "What the hell does that mean?" she asked without preamble.

"Go for a more natural look. Light on the eyeshadow, something neutral. A more natural tone for the lipstick. Go peach for the blush.

That pink doesn't suit you," she said, sounding distracted.

"You busy?"

"Just woke up."

"Oops. Sorry."

"What are you doing up this early?" Layla asked, covering a yawn.

"Went for a run and grabbed donuts. I'm going out to Dad's for a little while since I'm not working." She put the phone on speaker and wiped off the turquoise eye shadow she had known better than to buy. "Then I have the date after."

"Let me know when you get home," Layla told her. "After, I mean."

"Since when do I call you after a date?" Presley asked, amused.

"Since you started throwing weapons with guys you don't know," her sister replied. "It's like the start of an episode of *Unsolved Mysteries*."

"You're too young to remember *Unsolved Mysteries*," Presley pointed out with a short laugh, remembering how she used to be fascinated with it when she was little.

"So are you," Layla countered. "Fine, *Forensic Files*," she amended. Presley knew that Layla only knew about *Unsolved Mysteries* because it was syndicated, but she'd never watched it like Presley had. Of course, Presley only watched it because *Rescue 9-1-1* came on around the same timeframe, and she liked everything medical. Layla, Presley remembered, had been playing with Barbies around that time.

"Ha! I told Donovan the same thing when he asked me," Presley said, amused that they'd had the same reaction.

"And yet you're still going," Layla pointed out. "Just because he says he's not a serial killer doesn't mean he's not one."

"We're not throwing axes in the secluded woods. There's a gym where people do it. It's a whole thing. I looked it up," Presley explained, amused. "It's legit. We'll have some drinks, throw some axes. It'd be kind of hard to murder me and hide the body with so many witnesses."

"Okay, that sounds better. Still, call me after please," Layla asked.

Presley relented, "Fine. But you worry too much." She smiled. She liked it better when Layla worried about her. They hadn't gotten along for years. It was nice to be friends again and not just sisters. "Okay, I'm texting you a picture. Tell me what you think."

"That's much better," Layla told her after a minute. "It'll be cold, so you can wear your hair down."

"Any other tips?"

"Don't talk about Derrick," Layla suggested.

"I don't talk about him all the time," Presley objected, affronted.

"I guess that's true. You used to, though."

"Besides," Presley pointed out, "He already knows about Derrick."

"That's true. Good that's out of the way," Layla said. "Just have fun."

"That's the plan. Are you coming over to Dad's for lunch?"

"Yeah, but then I'm meeting Naomi afterwards for a movie, so I might leave before you do."

"That's fine. See you in a little while. Love you," she added, still feeling the strangeness of saying what they used to never say. After Noah had scared them all, it seemed important to say it.

"Love you back, weirdo," Layla said, and Presley could hear the smile in her voice before the call disconnected.

"You're the weirdo," Presley told the phone before turning her attention and grinning at her reflection. What are my bangs doing, she asked herself, looking closely in the mirror. She sighed and took out her straightener to fix the part of the fringe that was sticking out a little. There. All done. As natural as she could get while actually wearing makeup, she thought to herself.

***

Presley found a parking spot in a self-pay lot as close to the axe throwing place as she could get. It was in a building downtown—

one she hadn't noticed before and close enough to all the action in Athens that she didn't really have a reason to be afraid. It was already getting dark outside, and she looked around, wondering if Donovan had driven Vashti's van or brought his own car. She wasn't sure what he drove, other than a police cruiser, which she was pretty sure he wouldn't be driving tonight. She got out and immediately heard his voice.

"Why would you park beside an unmarked, windowless van?" Donovan asked her, exasperation in his voice.

"It's the closest parking spot, short of parking in the handicapped lanes," she said. "Hello to you, too."

"It's important to be aware of your surroundings," Donovan pointed out.

"Thank you, Mr. Safety Officer—says the man who's taking me out to throw weapons on our date."

"A perfectly safe activity with plenty of witnesses," he reminded her, smiling suddenly. She liked the way it crinkled around his eyes, and she smiled back. "We'll even have someone teach us how it's done."

"True," Presley said. "And I promise to grip my keys in my hand when I come out afterwards."

"Good thinking, but I'm walking you back to your car," he said, eyeing the unmarked van.

"You look like you're thinking about giving them a ticket," she said with a grin.

"Yeah, well …" He shrugged.

"Are you always so suspicious?"

"I like to think of it as safe."

"Occupational hazard?"

"Pretty much. You look beautiful, by the way," he said. "I'd have said that first, but I got distracted."

"By the lecture, yeah. I noticed," she grinned. "Thanks. You look good, too," she told him, thinking that was the understatement of the century. He looked, she thought, delicious. She wondered absently what he looked like in his uniform and thought he probably looked pretty damn good if he looked this hot in regular clothes.

"Thanks," he grinned at her, reaching for her hand and leading her away from the van. "Am I going to be able to talk you into a late dinner or a drink afterwards?"

"What is it with you and securing the next date before we've had the one we're on?"

"Confidence?" he asked with a laugh. "Isn't the motto, be prepared?"

"Were you even a Boy Scout?" she asked him, as they approached the studio. Inside the windows, she could see targets separated by cages. It reminded her of batting cages, except people were hurling tiny axes at targets. When they walked in the noise was louder than she'd expected. The sound of axes finding their targets was as common as the clink of them hitting the ground when they missed, and there was a general buzz of conversation from the watching crowd.

"I was a Boy Scout for a couple years," he answered, stopping suddenly and turning to face her.

"Shouldn't we go in?" she asked, raising an eyebrow and nodding toward the door.

"In a minute. Just thought I'd get this out of the way," he said, moving in and closing the distance between them. Presley didn't hesitate and met him there, sighing as she felt his hand reach up. His thumb stroked down her cheek while his other hand reached up to cup the back of her head gently. The kiss spun out, and Presley felt like she was spinning with it. When he stopped, she nearly swayed, and then laughed.

When he looked at her quizzically, a grin on his face, she explained, "I didn't think swooning was a thing. You've got good moves."

"So do you," he said, reaching for her hand again and heading toward the building. "I just wanted to get that out of the way. It was distracting me."

"I had wondered," Presley said.

"Curiosity satisfied?"

"Not yet," she told him saucily, feeling his eyes on her as she walked ahead of him into the building.

"Now I'm distracted again," he murmured into her ear as they joined the group waiting to sign in.

She looked up at him and smiled, her lips just a breath away from his as he'd been leaning down to whisper in her ear. She looked at his full lips and then back at his eyes. She could see the heat in them, and she felt her own body hum in response. "Later," she told him, turning back to the group and feeling him pull her back against him as the guide gave them a rundown of how things worked.

"That a promise?"

"*Shh* ..." she told him, smiling to herself.

They played Giant Jenga in the spacious lobby while they waited for a lane to come open. The guide had already apologized for the delay and gave them free drinks on the house while they waited. Presley managed to beat Donovan in the first round, laughing when the blocks crashed down, but after that, she was clearly outgunned—although, she thought, she was never going to admit it. She eyed the tilting tower and walked slowly around it.

"Can't find a good one?" Donovan asked with an innocent smile.

"Shut it," Presley warned him, bending down to inspect the tower and then sighing when it swayed again.

"Donovan?" a guide called out.

"Right here," he replied, holding up a hand.

"You're up."

Presley picked up her drink and started walking away from the tower.

"Where are you going?" Donovan asked in amusement.

"Time's up," Presley said, gesturing toward their lane.

"I was winning," Donovan pointed out.

"Were you?" she asked, as she walked toward the lane. He followed with a grin and watched as she picked up an axe and tested the weight. She put it back and tried another while he lifted one that caught his eye.

"I didn't know you were so competitive," Donovan commented, as the guide went off to get scoring cards for their round.

"You don't really know me that well, do you?"

"I'm learning," Donovan said, stepping up to put into practice what he'd learned about the axes. When the first bounced off, he turned around to meet Presley's eyes. She smiled at him but waited for him to retrieve it before she went in for her throw. Instead of the one-handed style Donovan had favored, she took the axe in both hands and got a running start, stopping on the line and hurling it at the target. It missed the bullseye, but landed just above it.

The guide whistled as he set down the pad of paper and looked at Donovan. "I really wouldn't piss her off," he said with a grin. Presley laughed and took a drink.

"So," she asked. "How many points is that?"

***

When they walked to the parking lot after their time was up, Presley smiled and pointed to her car. "See? The windowless van isn't even there anymore."

Donovan rolled his eyes. "But look how your car is so isolated right there," he pointed out. "If you'd parked nearer those other cars, it would be safer."

"But I thought this was the closest parking spot."

"There's another on the other side. Better lighting," he told her. "When I didn't see you over there, I came here." He walked her to the car, and when she turned to answer him, he pulled her to him and then backed her against the car. His mouth was on hers before she could do anything but take a breath. When he finally pulled back, he rested his forehead against hers. "We still on for that drink?"

"Sure. Your place or mine?" she asked him, meeting his eyes.

"Don't tempt me," he told her. "I thought we'd take this slow."

"Why?"

"I can't think of why right now," he admitted, kissing her forehead. She closed her eyes. She wasn't used to tenderness accompanying heat.

"Fine, have it your way. A drink then."

"Now I think I'm disappointed."

"I can do slow."

"Hmm … I'm not going to think about that right now," he told her with a grin. "Okay, how about this? Let's drive back to your place," he paused to roll his eyes when she grinned. "Just to drop off your car, and then we can take mine to get that drink."

"I don't know. Sounds like that would be too tempting," she told him with a smile, craning her head back to fully meet his eyes.

"I'm not going to get out of my car when we get to your place," he promised. "Just park and then get in mine."

"I don't even know what you drive," she told him. "I could get in with a stranger."

"I've got a black Expedition. I'll follow you if you'll give me a couple minutes."

"Sure," she told him and gave him a quick kiss before unlocking the door.

"You have a manual lock?"

"It's an old car."

"Get in, and then I'll go get my car."

"Bossy," she mouthed, as she slid in.

"Just looking out for you," he told her, bending to kiss her again.

"You're sweet. Weird, but sweet."

"See you in a few," he told her. "Wait for me."

She sat in the car for a few minutes, a smile on her face. When she saw the lights behind her a couple minutes later, she pulled out and drove home, reminding herself to tell him that he was following too closely. When she turned into the apartment complex, she parked and waited a second for him to pull up.

"Following a little close back there."

"That wasn't me," he said with a laugh. "You let that other car pull out between us," he said. "But it turned in the other direction, and I was able to catch up. Couldn't you see my car?"

"It's dark outside. All SUVs look the same to me in the dark," she said as she slid in beside him. He leaned over to kiss her. "Keep that up, and we'll just stay here."

"Stop tempting me," he joked. "I have a place in mind I like, if that's okay with you."

"Lead the way," she told him, putting on her seat belt. "If I forget to tell you later, thanks for this."

"Any time," he said, leaning over for a last quick kiss before putting the car in reverse.

Chapter 12

Layla groaned aloud when she heard the quick tap at the back door leading to the garden. She didn't want to move. She'd been staring at webinars most of the day at work, and she was pretty sure her eyes were bleeding. She peeked one open, hoping whoever it was would go away. Tap, tap. No chance. She got up slowly and called out, "Just a second."

Lindy was standing there, one hip cocked, and Maya perched there with her wide owl eyes peeking out from a hat shaped like a puppy. Lindy raised an eyebrow as Maya greeted her with a gummy grin. "Did I wake you up?"

"If only," Layla said with a sigh, reaching up to tickle Maya under her chin. "God, she's pretty."

"We're grilling out," Lindy told her without preamble. "Want to come over?"

"It's January," Layla said.

"February now, actually," Lindy shot back. "You sure you weren't asleep?"

"Sorry, long day," Layla said running a hand through her disheveled hair. She'd stretched out on the couch when she'd gotten home and hadn't moved in the last hour. She'd thought about dinner a time or two, but she'd only had the energy to kick off her shoes. "You're grilling out? It's cold out here."

"Well, we're not going to eat outside," Lindy said, shifting Maya.

"You want to come in and sit down?" Layla asked, feeling awkward inviting Lindy in to what used to be her house.

"Nope. Dean told me to fetch you for dinner. I'm fetching," Lindy said, but a smile stretched wide to soften her words.

"Let me just grab my shoes. Want me to bring anything?"

"Do you actually have anything?"

"Okay, point taken. Just getting my shoes," she said, turning to grab them from where they'd fallen on the floor by the couch. "What are we …" Her voice trailed off, as she realized that Lindy had left already. With anyone else, she'd have thought they were being rude, but Lindy was just like that. She was probably cold and wanting to get the baby back inside.

"Hey, Dean," she called out, as she walked through the garden. Dean Walton really was eye candy, Layla thought. He was tall with a slimmer build than Seth. She had reason to know that slim body was in very good shape, as she had glimpsed him without his shirt on a couple of times over the summer. He turned to her, the winter sun glinting off the dark blonde hair that was getting long again. He squinted his green eyes at her and grinned.

"Guess Lindy talked you into it."

"She didn't exactly present it as an option," she admitted, smiling. "What are we eating?"

"What aren't we eating? Little bit of everything."

"Is it just us?" She'd noticed that Lindy's family tended to get together often, just to hang out. While she and Presley were spending more time together and with their dad, regular family gatherings hadn't been a part of their lives in a long time.

"Lindy invited a couple people," Dean told her, eyeing the grill and then Layla. "You've got to be freezing. Go on in. They won't bite."

"That little one might," Layla referred to Maya with a laugh.

"I'd be more worried about Lindy, to be honest," he joked, as Layla headed up the porch steps into the screened-in porch. She took a deep breath and then pulled open the door that led into the kitchen at the back of the house.

"Hey," she said in surprise, as JP nearly bowled her over coming out.

"Hey, yourself," he said with a grin. "Sorry about that. You okay?"

"I'll live," she told him, returning his smile. "Did Lindy make you come?"

"Well, she didn't exactly twist my arm," he replied. "She said food, and I may or may not have started walking over before she could ask. I'm shameless."

"Where are you going?" she asked, stepping out of the way of the door and trying to decide if they were going out or back in.

"I'm assisting Dean at the grill. Jude's inside with a beer and the baby." He paused. "The beer's not for the baby, of course."

"I could stay out and help," she offered, feeling suddenly nervous at the thought of seeing Jude again after everything she'd told him.

"Nope. You're not getting away that easy," he told her, shooing her inside.

"What do you mean?" she asked, feeling defensive. She wondered if Jude had told JP what she'd said. After all, she hadn't explicitly said she was telling him in confidence, but she'd assumed he would understand that. Her arms crossed at her chest.

"I just know the two of you got off on the wrong foot. I heard you threw a bagel at him," he said, lightening the mood easily.

"That is *not* what happened," she told him, uncrossing her arms.

"Well, at least call a truce around the baby," he suggested and then turned to head outside.

Layla walked into the kitchen but didn't see anyone. She wandered into the dining room and noticed the table was set for a group. She counted the places and wondered who else was coming. With this crew, it could be anyone. Seth and Libby were regular visitors, as were her dad and Keely. Beth and Jamie stopped by fairly often, since Beth was Lindy's cousin and Jamie and Seth were friends and coworkers. It really was a small world, Layla thought with a sigh. She walked into the living room and stopped dead.

Jude was holding Maya up above his head. Their faces were nearly touching, and Maya was giggling. Her chunky hands had reached out to grab two full handfuls of Jude's hair, which he'd made the mistake of leaving down. He was trying to talk her into letting go, and she was shaking with laughter. Layla felt the smile stretching across her face.

"What's going on here?" she asked with a laugh in her voice. Jude was stretched out in khakis and a button up shirt, looking a little more dressed up than she'd seen him so far. He was sprawled on the living room floor and darted a look at her from where Maya had him by those warm blond highlights in his dark hair.

"Good! Reinforcements," he said. "We were playing airplane, and then she got distracted. I'm a little stuck."

"Have you been like this long?" Layla asked, sitting down in the floor beside them.

"A few more minutes than strictly comfortable," Jude admitted.

"Why didn't you put her down?" Layla asked with a grin.

"Well, I tried that, and she may have started pulling," Jude said with a laugh. "It seemed better just to wait for Lindy to come back. She ran upstairs to change."

"Come here, baby," Layla said softly, and Jude's eyes widened. He'd never heard her voice with that gentle tone. She reached out her arms, and Maya bounced in Jude's hands and stretched her hands toward Layla, releasing his hair. He passed her over with a sigh.

"She's heavier than she looks," Jude said with a grin, pulling his hair back out of his face.

"Here," Layla said, sliding a rubber band off her wrist and passing it to him.

"Thanks," he told her gratefully. He pulled his hair back, twisting it easily in the back, and Layla was surprised when she felt heat warm her face. That shouldn't be sexy, Layla thought, turning her eyes to Maya.

"You might want to do something about yours before she gets you next," he suggested with a grin.

"Oh, can you hold her for a second?" she asked, seeing Maya eye her hair with speculation. It was a little wild today, the dark curls brushing her cheeks and running riot down her back. She'd pulled it back for work but had released it the moment she'd gotten into her car to come home.

"I can do one better. Do you have another band?" Jude asked. Layla held up her wrist where she had two more.

Jude reached for her hand and slowly removed one band, and Layla prayed that he didn't notice the goosebumps rising on her arms as he held her wrist gently. He motioned for her to turn her back to him, and she shifted, making faces at Maya to keep her entertained. Layla held herself completely still as Jude gathered her hair in his hands. She tried to focus on Maya and not the warmth shooting through her body. She could feel him lift her hair and start pulling it through the band, gently. When he let go, she looked over her shoulder and met his eyes, which immediately caught and held them.

"I didn't know we were doing hair. Am I next?" Lindy asked wryly from the doorway. Layla jolted and turned awkwardly to face her.

"We had a bit of a hair crisis," Jude admitted. "When you left me here with this tiny terror, she grabbed on to mine when we were playing airplane and held me captive until Layla saved me. My hero," he said, grinning at Layla and patting his heart.

"We decided having hair down might be a mistake," Layla admitted, wondering how long Lindy had been standing there.

"Well, if we're done playing beauty parlor, the food's almost done," she said with a grin, walking into the room and scooping up Maya. "That's my girl," she cooed at the baby. "We do like a man with pretty hair," she said, nuzzling Maya's cheeks and then grinning at Jude. "I like the man bun," she told him with a laugh.

"Yeah, Dean told me that's what you call me."

"Well, to be fair, I didn't know your name."

Layla sat quietly, trying to settle herself. She couldn't quite forget his hand on her wrist or pulling her hair back and up. She was sure her face was flushed still, and she gave herself a minute to gather herself as the conversation flowed around her. When Jude stood to his feet, she looked up and noticed how tall he was compared to her, especially since she was still sitting cross legged in the floor.

"Need a hand?" he asked, extending his own. She took it and pulled herself up, feeling the calluses on his hand and reminding herself that she'd been down this road before.

"Thanks," she said casually, trying to dispel the tension that had risen between them. She could still feel that pull toward him and wondered how she was going to avoid temptation with it living right next door.

"Least I could do for my hero," he said with a grin, patting his chest again. Layla rolled her eyes in response and then followed Lindy to the kitchen where she was pulling glasses down from the cabinet. Maya was on the floor playing on a rug filled with toys.

"Can I help?" Layla asked.

"You both can help," Lindy told her, nodding to include Jude as the doorbell rang. "If you could just get the door, Layla, I'll have Jude help me get the drinks ready."

Layla walked toward the door, wishing she could have helped with the drinks instead. She really wasn't comfortable with new people. She opened the door slowly and then grinned. "What are you doing here?" she asked Presley.

"Eating," Presley said shortly. "I'm starved." Presley came in and shrugged out of the leather bomber jacket she was wearing. Layla noticed it was the one their grandfather had given her ages ago and was a little worse for the wear. Still, it suited Presley. She'd paired it with a long rust-tone sweater over leggings the color of sand. Her boots were short and heeled, and she'd pulled her hair to the side in a style that made her look years younger.

"I thought you were working today," Layla commented.

"I'm back on days," Presley answered with a shrug. The doorbell rang again, and Layla turned back to open it.

"Hey, that was quick," Seth said with a grin, his gloved hand in Libby's.

"Presley got here just before you did," Layla answered, grateful that she knew everyone who'd been invited. She mentally counted the place settings and knew no one else was coming.

"We're freezing. We walked over and regretted it about halfway here," Libby admitted, stepping inside the warmth with a sigh. Layla looked with envy at Libby's Hepburn style dress in a pale pink with the flared skirt and leggings. She'd added black ballet flats with a small pink bow to the ensemble. Layla loved the look, but she could never quite pull it off herself.

"Nice flowers," Presley commented, nodding toward Libby's other hand. Layla noticed Presley was carrying a bag of wine, and she wished that she had thought of that. She always had wine on hand, she thought, feeling awkward about coming empty-handed.

"I'll go put them in water," Layla offered, taking the bouquet from Libby. She looked at the roses mixed with carnations and leaned forward to smell them. Libby fell into step beside her with Presley and Seth behind.

"I don't usually like carnations," Libby said. "But I couldn't resist these roses."

"They're pretty," Layla told her truthfully. "I wish I'd thought to bring something."

"I'm sure Lindy ambushed you," Libby said with a laugh. "Honestly," she leaned in to tell Layla confidentially, "I bought these for home, but then I grabbed them when I heard we were coming over for dinner." They exchanged a smile, and Layla felt herself relaxing.

"Who else is here?" Presley asked, eyeing the table.

"Lindy invited the neighbors," Layla explained, as they walked into the kitchen.

"Hey, Jude," Presley sang out, as they walked through the door.

"Yeah, I've never heard that before. Nice seeing you again, Presley," Jude said from where he was filling the last glass.

"I didn't realize you'd met," Lindy said curiously.

"He was at Layla's the other day," Presley said with a shrug, and all the eyes in the room turned to look at Jude and Layla with clear speculation.

"I'll head outside and check on Dean, make sure he hasn't burned the food," Seth said, heading for the back porch and effectively breaking up the tension.

"What were you doing at Layla's?" Lindy asked, while Libby made faces at her from behind Layla's back. Layla could feel the looks being shot back and forth behind her and tried to think of a reasonable explanation that didn't go into the whole bagel-throwing incident again.

"Just stopped by to lend a paint brush," Jude lied easily, catching Layla's eyes. "She was doing some painting, and I thought she could use a couple more brushes if she was going to do a few more projects around the house."

"I just painted the door," Layla said casually, shooting him a grateful look and picking up with the story.

"I noticed that when I was out running the other day," Libby commented, going up to the counter and picking up a tall glass of tea. "It looks great."

"I like your dress," Layla told her honestly, grateful to move the subject away from her and Jude.

"Thanks," Libby said, as they turned toward the sound of the porch door banging open.

"It's freezing out there," JP said as he came in. "I'm leaving them to it."

"John Paul, this is Presley and Libby," Lindy introduced them.

"Well, you're clearly Layla's sister," JP told Presley. "You can call me JP."

"Layla mentioned we all share crazy parents," Presley said with a grin.

"I just met your husband outside," JP told Libby.

"Yeah, that's Seth," she told him with a soft smile. "It's so nice to meet you. Are you going to stay in the house or flip it? I heard you were doing some renovations."

Layla shot her a grateful look. She'd wondered herself but wasn't sure how to ask without doing so abruptly. She looked at JP with interest.

"We thought about flipping it," he admitted. "But we're just going to play it by ear."

"So, you two live together," Presley commented. "How's that working out for you?"

"Well, we get along most of the time," JP said with a shrug.

"It works for now," Jude said easily, exchanging a look with JP. "We didn't exactly plan it, but it's working for us."

"Sounds like a long story," Layla commented curiously, thinking of the circumstances under which she'd moved in with her own sister for a few months.

"The food should be out in a minute, but we've got time," Lindy said easily.

"We don't want to pry," Layla told them, knowing that she'd hate airing her own story so publicly.

"Speak for yourself," Lindy said with a grin, and Libby laughed.

"She's naturally curious," Libby explained.

"Nosy is what you mean," Lindy replied with a roll of her eyes. Dean and Seth came in from outside carrying the food from the grill, and Lindy eyed the brothers. "We're not done," she warned them, grabbing glasses and heading toward the dining room.

They all sat down at the large dining room table, and Dean scooped Maya out of the swing Lindy had put her in when she'd grown tired of the toys on the rug. She'd fallen asleep in the swing, and he moved her into a pack-n-play in the living room while they were eating. When the baby was settled, he came into the dining room and sat down at the head of the table with a sigh.

"I remember when your grandfather used to sit here," Dean told Seth with a smile.

"Yeah, good times," Seth agreed. "This was my grandfather's house once. My mom moved in after our dad left." He exchanged a look with Lindy and then continued. "We grew up here," he explained to the newcomers.

"And you lived nearby?" JP asked Dean.

"Seth and I have been friends since we were kids."

"We couldn't get him to leave," Lindy put in.

"I'm here to stay," Dean pointed out, exchanging a smile with her. "Anyway," he returned to the group, "I grew up in Madison but met Seth in school. Then I pretty much stayed here until they made me go home."

"So, your mom married their dad?" Jude asked, indicating Seth and Lindy and then Layla and Presley. "How old were you?" he asked.

"Last year old," Presley said with a grin. "It's all new for us."

"Nice though," Layla said, speaking up and surprising herself.

"Nice for us, too," Libby told her with a smile.

"So, how did you two end up living together?" Lindy abruptly returned to the previous conversation.

"Ignore her. She's nosy. It's like a weird form of Tourette's. She can't even stop herself," Seth said, rolling his eyes.

"You don't ask, you don't know," she pointed out evenly.

"I had a little legal issue a couple years ago that made my finances less than stellar," JP admitted wryly. "And then," he looked at Jude for confirmation before continuing, "Jude got divorced."

Layla looked over at Jude quickly, surprised by this information. He'd never said he'd been married. Not that she'd asked, she reminded herself. She wasn't sure why the fact of a wife, ex-wife she reminded herself, made her so uneasy.

"We decided to pool our resources and buy the house while things are being sorted," JP finished. "It gives us both time to figure some things out." He looked over at Jude with an inscrutable expression.

"The divorce is done, but there's been," he paused, his brow furrowing, "custody issues."

"You have a kid?" Layla asked, surprising herself again by speaking up. He turned to her, a nervous expression crossing his face.

"Two," he admitted.

"I haven't seen any kids—" she began.

"Well, you wouldn't," Jude said shortly. Then, sighed. "That's the problem. The ex is a bit vindictive. She's made visits difficult."

"That's awful," Libby said sympathetically.

"Do you have a good lawyer?" Dean asked, frowning at the thought of someone being kept from their kids.

"Yeah. It's just taking time," Jude admitted. "I may have to sue for full custody. She'll fight it, of course."

"How old are they?" Presley asked with interest.

"Kelsey is six. Connor is two."

"Pictures," Lindy demanded. Jude got out his phone and showed them his screensaver.

"Gimme," Lindy said, holding out her hand. She took the phone and looked back at him. "Cute kids. Your son is your mini-me," she told him. "Daughter's got your hair," she added with a grin.

Lindy passed the phone around, and Layla found herself looking at two kids and then up at Jude where he was watching her carefully. She wanted to know why he wasn't seeing them and why she even cared. She looked back down and had to admit that Connor did look like Jude. Kelsey had his hair and smile. She passed the phone back to him. He looked at it and then put it face-down beside his plate.

"So, we hear the two of you just got married," JP spoke up, changing the subject, and turning to Dean and Lindy. "Do tell."

Layla watched Jude's shoulders start to relax as the conversation moved away from him. She studied him casually and then turned back to her dinner. She had to shift her idea of him around the idea of a marriage and divorce and two kids. She hadn't pegged him as a dad, but what did she really know about him? She let her thoughts wander over what they'd spoken about since they'd met, and she realized she'd made a lot of assumptions without asking a lot of questions. Her eyebrows drew together as she puzzled it out, and then she looked up to tune back into the conversation around her.

Chapter 13

As she was walking home, Jude fell into step beside her. "See you at home," JP told him, passing the two of them and heading to the fence. "See you later, Layla." Layla waved and then glanced at Jude.

"Why didn't you say anything?"

"I don't like to talk about it," he admitted.

"But I told you about my situation. I don't like talking about that either," she told him evenly.

"I know. It just seemed like you had enough on your plate without my situation," he explained, although he admitted to himself that wasn't entirely true.

"Are you really going to try to get full custody?"

"I think I need to," Jude said, frowning. "I know they need their mom, but they need me, too. Of the two of us, I'm more stable," he said, shrugging. Layla wondered about that. After all, he was living with his brother, and she didn't know anything about his job. She wondered what his ex was like.

"Why did you get divorced?"

"Is it ever just one thing?" he asked. "That might be a story for another day. But I do owe you a story."

"You don't owe me anything," she said quietly, arriving at her little house. She looked back at Lindy's, how it was lit up, and she could see Seth and Lindy loading the dishwasher in the kitchen. Maya's laugh floated out to her, and she looked at Jude. No wonder he'd been so good with Maya. She had a feeling he had probably been a good dad, but then again, she was still making assumptions, she thought to herself. "Want to come in for a drink?"

"Another time," he promised.

***

When he headed home, Layla walked inside and immediately sensed that something was out of place. Slowly, she backed out of the room and ran up the path to the back door. She opened it quickly and called out softly. "Hey, Dean, can you come here a minute?" She motioned him outside, and Seth followed behind.

"Look, I know this is going to sound crazy, but I think someone's been in the house."

Dean and Seth exchanged a glance and immediately headed down the path. "You want to wait inside?" Seth asked her.

"No, I'd like to come with you, if you don't mind," she said nervously. "I mean, I could be wrong."

"Did you lock the door when you came over?" Dean asked.

"I … no, I don't think so," she admitted. "I just came straight over."

"I've got the security cameras up. I'll check the footage later. Though I don't know if they cover the front entrance," he said, thinking it through. "I'll make sure they do from now on."

They stepped into the house. "Just hang back a little," Seth told her, as they walked through the rooms, Layla a step behind them.

"Anything missing? Or out of place?" Dean asked, looking around.

"Just little things. I know this sounds weird, but I know how I left everything," she said, feeling foolish.

"No, I get it. Libby's the same way," Seth offered. "I could move something an inch over, and she'd know."

"I know I had a bottle of wine on the counter that I set there when I came home," she pointed out. She remembered that she hadn't removed it from the bag, but she'd put it there on the counter. The bag was gone, and the wine was moved over a little more to the center. "I think there are some pictures gone, too," she told them quietly. "They were on the fridge."

"Couple of things," Dean said quietly, assessing. "First, Seth can go up with you while you throw a few things together," Dean began, holding up a hand to silence whatever objection she was about to come up with. "You can stay at our house until we get the locks changed and I set up the security cameras outside. We'll put one in here, too," he told her. "Second, you're not drinking this wine. I'll get you another bottle," he told her, and she felt a chill at the thought. "I'll look around while you pack. Take whatever you need for a couple of nights. If you need anything else, one of us will come over with you to get it."

As they walked up the stairs, Layla felt the panic rising in her throat. "Have you heard from Noah lately?" Seth asked quietly, as she stood looking around her room and feeling sick that anyone could have been in her space.

"No, not in months," she admitted shakily.

"Do you think this was him?"

"Who else could it be?" she answered, her eyes meeting his. "Nothing of value was taken. My laptop is still here. My jewelry," she indicated the overflowing jewelry box. "Not that I have much, but nothing that is worth anything is gone."

"It might be time to file a restraining order."

"We don't know that it was him," she said. "I mean, we don't have proof."

"I think, after everything, we need to go with your gut feeling on this."

"It's just a piece of paper," she told him helplessly.

"Yeah, but it's a record, too," he told her, reaching over to rub her arm where she had them crossed tightly around her. "Throw some things together, and we'll head back. You shouldn't be alone right now."

"I don't want to be," she told him honestly, moving to grab an overnight bag out of her closet. She started throwing things in, thinking of what she might need for the next couple of days for work. She straightened, "Can you not tell Presley?" she asked. "She worries about me."

"I'm not going to tell her," Seth said evenly. "You are. She needs to know."

"Yeah, I guess you're right. I just ... don't want to dredge it all back up," she said with a shrug, feeling the anxiety float from her throat to her stomach and back again. "Seth ... I think I'm going to be sick." She ran into the bathroom and threw up, sinking back on the floor after. He'd been in her house, she thought. Or someone had. She looked around and wondered when and for how long.

"You okay?" Dean asked from the doorway, Seth beside him.

"I need to get out of here," she told them. She stood up, and Seth held her bag out.

"Do you think you've got everything you need?" he asked. "We can come back tomorrow if you forgot anything."

Layla reached over and grabbed the over-sized makeup bag from the counter and held it up. Seth opened the bag, and she put it inside. "That's enough for now. I need to grab my purse and my book downstairs. That's all," she said, feeling exhausted in a way that she couldn't even articulate. This had been going on too long already, and it seemed like it was starting again. She sighed heavily, as she went down the stairs in the home she'd come to love. She looked back at the hopeful yellow door she'd painted as Dean locked it carefully. She walked ahead of them down the path and entered the kitchen quietly.

"Hey," Lindy said, surprised. "What's going on?"

"Layla's going to sleep over with us a couple of nights," Dean explained.

"What happened?" Libby asked, taking a step toward Layla.

"I think someone was in the house," she said quietly.

"Noah," Lindy said in a flat tone, glancing up toward the

bedroom where she'd just put Maya down.

"Maybe," she agreed.

"We're changing the locks tomorrow, over there and here," Dean explained. "She'll stay here until then. I'm installing a security system and making sure our cameras cover all the doors on her place," he told them, typing into his phone. "We should be able to get it done in a day," he said, looking up at Layla. "Two, tops."

"I appreciate it. Of course, I'll pay for whatever it costs," she said, feeling embarrassed and exhausted in equal measure and wondering how much new locks and a security system would cost her.

"Not at all. Don't even think about it," Lindy said sharply. "We're family after all," she told her fiercely, moving over to stroke her arm.

"We'll make it a sleepover tonight," Libby said brightly, looking over at Lindy for confirmation. "How do you feel about Julia Roberts?"

"Um …" she wasn't sure how to answer.

"We don't *have to* watch *Pretty Woman*," Libby said with a smile. "I just want to."

"I call *Notting Hill* after that," Lindy replied. "Call Presley and see if she wants to come back and join us."

"She can't. She's on shift tomorrow," Layla said, feeling tears welling up.

"Tell her about this though, okay?" Dean reminded her. "I'm going to make a few calls."

"And you need to get that restraining order," Seth told Layla, following Dean out of the room.

"I'll make the popcorn," Lindy offered.

"I'll get Seth to grab me a few things from home," Libby said, touching Layla's arm gently. "Are you okay?"

"I'm … better now," she said, surprised. "This helps."

"I just need to get this out, and then we can continue with this sleepover. I hate your rat-bastard ex," Lindy said with feeling. Layla choked out a laugh.

"Yeah, I'm not a fan either," Libby agreed.

"To put it mildly." Lindy snorted.

"I can't say I'm a fan. I just feel so stupid," Layla admitted.

"Well, you shouldn't. You're smart. Coming to get Dean like you did was the smartest thing you could have done," Lindy told her.

"I almost didn't," Layla admitted. "But I was more afraid than embarrassed." She shrugged, feeling the panic again and that sense of a disturbance in her home.

"You don't need to be embarrassed about this," Lindy told her.

"But I am," Layla argued. "I know that it's not my fault, but it's still humiliating."

"You're entitled to feel that way," Libby said softly. "But we're going to do our level best to distract you. We should have this sorted in a couple of days, and you'll feel a little safer."

"I already feel a little safer," Layla admitted. "Can we add *Runaway Bride* into this mix? I feel the need for a Richard Gere double feature."

"I think that can be arranged," Lindy said.

"Let's make this a pajama party," Libby enthused.

"That's what I like to hear," Dean said with a grin in the doorway.

"Not you," Lindy told him. "Pervert."

"Fine, I'll just stay in my man-cave and have a drink with Seth," he said, rolling his eyes at his wife. "Sexist."

"I'm not saying you can't watch the movie," Lindy returned. "I just don't think we're going to have the kind of pajama parties of your adolescent fantasies."

"Too bad," Seth commented, as he walked in. "I do like a good pillow fight."

"With your sister?" Lindy asked wryly.

Seth made a face. "Gross," he said. "Okay, you made your point. Regular movie night then."

"I could go for a pillow fight," Dean muttered, as they walked into the living room. Lindy picked up a pillow and hit him with it.

"There," Lindy told him with satisfaction. Layla laughed, and they looked over at her.

"You guys are cute," she told them. "I'm going to go change, and then I'll be ready."

"I'll go with you," Lindy said easily. "Seth, go grab some clothes for Libby."

"I'll go with him and be back in five," Libby said.

"You can sleep in the guest room," Lindy suggested, heading up the stairs. "It's just down the hall from us."

"I appreciate it," Layla told her sincerely.

"Well, you are my sister now," Lindy said with a grin. "So, naturally, I'm going to give you a hard time about Jude later."

"Oh, that," she said, relieved and annoyed in equal measure. "There's nothing going on."

"You sure about that?"

"Yeah, pretty sure," Layla said. "I'd know, wouldn't I?"

"Well, I didn't. Dean hit me like a ton of bricks," she admitted. "He was just supposed to be sex. Actually," she amended, "he wasn't supposed to be anything to me. Just Seth's friend. Then it was supposed to just be sex. The relationship thing? That was not expected."

"That's sweet," Layla admitted. "But this isn't like that."

"Why? He's hot, even with the bun, which is saying something."

"I'm not saying he's not attractive," Layla began. "Are you going to watch me change?"

"Yes. I told you, we're sisters now." Layla shrugged and stripped down to her underwear, grabbing pajamas from the bag. "So, you admit he's hot. What's the problem?"

"I've kind of dated his type before," Layla said shrugging. "I'm not trying to repeat my mistakes."

"He's nothing like Noah," Lindy pointed out.

"No, I mean, the guys before Noah. All my relationships have been garbage, and I'm the common denominator," she explained, shrugging.

"So, how's he like the others?" Lindy asked. "Single dad? I mean, you didn't even know about that."

"No, not that. That doesn't bother me," she said, wondering if that was entirely true.

"Then what?"

"You really are nosy," Layla said. "You're worse than Presley."

"I'm not offended," Lindy said with a grin. "So?"

"You know, blue collar. Diamond in the rough," she shrugged and then pulled the shirt over her head. "You know the type."

"We're talking about Jude, right?"

"Well, yeah."

"Huh," she grinned at Layla suddenly. "Okay."

"Why are you looking at me like that?" Layla demanded, shooting Lindy a questioning look as she pulled on the pajama pants.

"No reason," Lindy said innocently. Layla didn't believe that for a minute and said as much. "I just don't think he's what you think he is."

"Well, that's your opinion," Layla told her. "We're just friends, me and Jude."

"Okay," Lindy agreed, and Layla rolled her eyes.

"You say okay, but you don't mean okay," Layla told her, as they headed downstairs.

"Okay," Lindy said with a grin.

"God, you're annoying," Layla said, only half-joking.

"That's how you know we're family," Lindy replied, throwing an arm around her.

Chapter 14

Layla woke up tired and disoriented. She reached one arm up to cover her eyes and cracked them open slowly. The guest room, Lindy's house, she reminded herself. The sun was filtering in through the lace curtains, and she might have enjoyed the play of the light on the pale celery-toned walls, if she'd been a morning person. Which she wasn't, she reminded herself with a groan. She sat up slowly, stretching her arms above, and then brought them down quickly at the thought that struck her. She'd had nightmares. She could remember them now. She had a moment to feel embarrassed that she might have called out in her sleep when she heard Lindy come striding down the hallway.

"If you want to get your lazy ass up, there's breakfast."

Layla smiled as she heard Dean's muffled reply. "Lindy, let the woman sleep! Don't be rude," followed by a rude suggestion from Lindy and a laugh from Seth. Well, Layla thought, the gang's all here.

She got dressed quickly, relieved she'd managed to find a matching outfit when she'd just thrown everything together. She walked down the stairs and tried to shake off the ominous feeling that had stayed with her since she'd gone into her house and realized something was off. She walked into the kitchen and put her hands on her hips.

"I wouldn't have set an alarm if I'd known there was a wakeup call scheduled," she said, a smile playing at her lips.

"Yeah, sorry about Lindy," Dean said with a grin, taking a sip from his coffee and looking impossibly sexy leaning back against the counter. She tried not to notice how his shirt stretched across his well-muscled chest, but she must not have been successful because she could see Lindy smirk behind him where she was pulling plates out of the cabinets. He ran a hand through his hair, and Layla worried that she audibly gulped. She remembered Naomi talking about Dean's hair, how it was the silkiest—and sexiest—hair she'd ever had her hands in. Not a productive line of thought, Layla thought, as she turned her attention to Seth.

"Where's the wife?" she asked with a smile, walking over to select a mug from the counter. She read the side of it and smiled. "Feminism is my second favorite F word," it read. She grinned. Typical Lindy.

"She's already out for a run," Seth explained. "Did you sleep okay?"

"Yeah, I slept okay," she lied.

"Liar," Lindy muttered. Layla shot her an annoyed look at the same time as Dean rolled his eyes.

"I'm off work today. I'm doing the locks first thing, and we've got the security installation scheduled already. I've adjusted the cameras. There really wasn't anything to see from last night, but there were areas the footage just didn't cover. We've got you covered now though," Dean told her reassuringly. "You're welcome to stay here as long as you need to, though. We have plenty of room."

"And plenty of other rooms to use for sex," Lindy said with a wink.

"Can you not?" Seth asked, exasperated. "I'm just going to head out to the truck and wait for you, Dean. When y'all are done talking about all that, we can go get those locks." He headed out, and Dean stood up with a grin. He sauntered over to Lindy and planted a kiss on her so hot that Layla wasn't entirely sure she hadn't swooned when it was done.

"Nice seeing you, Layla," he said with a grin as he sauntered out of the room.

"I know you just checked out my husband's ass, but I don't blame you," Lindy said, coming up to stand beside Layla, where she was pretty sure her mouth was hanging open.

"It's a reflex," Layla said with a grin and shrug.

"No worries," Lindy said. She turned to Layla with a serious look. "You had nightmares." It wasn't a question.

Layla closed her eyes and sighed heavily, embarrassed and strangely defeated all at once. "Yes," she answered. When she felt Lindy's hand on her arm, she opened her eyes

"If some asshole had been creeping around my house, I'd have nightmares, too." Lindy told her. "Have you been having nightmares? I mean, before this?" When Layla only nodded, she continued. "Does anyone else know?"

"Presley," Layla answered honestly. "And Naomi. Presley heard when I was living with her. Naomi ... I told her."

"Of course you did," Lindy replied, heading to the French press to pour another cup of coffee. "She'd understand." Lindy poured a cup and held it out for Layla, who stepped forward gratefully. "So, what did she say?"

"She wants me to get therapy." At Lindy's even look, she protested, "I don't need therapy. I could use some sleeping pills though."

"That won't fix anything."

"But it'll help me sleep," Layla said, peeking in covered plates to see what was for breakfast. She grinned when she saw bacon. "I'm dealing with it."

"Well, you don't have to deal with it alone. You have a bad night, just come over, okay?" Lindy told her, sliding a key across the counter. "Just come in. I'll give you the alarm code, and the guest room is just yours. Just don't complain if you walk in on us naked," she said with a laugh.

Layla felt incredibly touched, but she managed to smile in reply, "If there's a chance to see Dean naked, I may have to do that."

"You'd be seeing me naked, too."

"Oh, well, damn," Layla said, picking up the key. "Thanks."

"I don't have time for this mushy nonsense," Lindy told her, although Layla could see she was just trying to put her at ease. "My baby's going to wake up hungry."

"I'm surprised she's not already up," Layla commented, as Lindy started out of the room.

"Well, she's been a night owl lately," Lindy explained. "I'll be down in a sec, and then if you need anything next door, we can head over."

"Dean said to wait for him and Seth," Layla reminded her.

"We are *not* waiting for the men," Lindy countered hotly. "I'll be locked and loaded, if that eases your mind."

"That's actually kind of terrifying," Layla called as Lindy mounted the stairs. She looked down at the key in her hands and smiled. I guess we really are family, she thought.

***

Jude came home to have a quick bite to eat in peace. He took it out to the backyard and settled on the bench under a tree, hoping to enjoy the quiet. It was rare enough, between the constant renovations and his work. When he kept hearing voices from Layla's, he stood up, puzzled. She should have been at work. Curious, he headed over.

"Hey, what's all this?" he asked, as he saw Dean and Seth holding the yellow door open and messing with the lock.

"Changing the locks," Dean said briefly. "Come on up."

"You kicking Layla out?" Jude joked.

"Some asshole broke into her place last night," Seth said.

"Not *some* asshole," Dean amended. "We pretty much know which asshole."

"Wait, are you talking about the crazy ex?" Jude asked sharply, following their conversation with ease.

"Did she tell you about that?" Seth asked, guardedly, unwilling to share Layla's secrets.

"A little," Jude answered, equally guarded. "You think he did this though?"

Dean and Seth exchanged a look. "Who else?"

"Did he take anything?" Jude asked, taking a seat on the porch swing and worrying about Layla.

"Maybe some pictures. And messed with a bottle of wine she bought," Dean explained.

"Messed with it how?" Jude demanded.

"It was in the bag when she left. It wasn't when she got back. Don't worry. I replaced it and tossed out the other," Dean told him.

"So, are you interested in Layla?" Seth asked curiously, looking up from his work.

"She's a friend. Of course, I'm going to worry," Jude pointed out evenly.

"She slept over at our place last night," Dean told him. "And I'm installing more security. If he comes by again, we'll catch the bastard red-handed."

"Did you ever meet him?" Jude asked.

"Noah?" Jude now had a name to put with the story. He nodded. Seth continued, "Yeah, we met him a couple times."

"What was he like?"

"You know, your typical sociopath," Dean said blandly. "Seemed like an all-around nice guy. Everyone was congratulating Layla on finally landing a decent guy, and it turns out he was ..." he broke off, taking a deep breath and cursing a blue streak.

"Dean's a little more pissed than the rest of us," Seth explained. "Noah was harassing a girl in town but making everyone think it was him."

"Well, I had the reputation for dating around," Dean said caustically. "And Noah seemed like this upstanding guy. It was all too easy for him to point the finger my way." He steamed as he thought about it, what it might have cost him if the ones he loved had believed it.

"How's Layla doing?" Jude asked.

"Stop by later and ask her yourself," Dean suggested. "She's a tough girl, but it was a hard night."

"You think she's tough?" Jude asked with a quirk of his eyebrow. He thought she seemed fragile.

"I think the fact that she's been through all this and hasn't broken down is pretty tough," Dean told him.

"Hmm," Jude responded noncommittally.

"You don't think so?" Seth asked, testing out one of the keys and nodding to himself.

"I think if she hasn't broken down yet, it doesn't mean she's in the clear," Jude told them.

"Yeah, the wife told me you're a shrink," Dean said with a grin. He sat on the steps and consulted a list he'd tucked into his pocket. "Locks are done. Security's gone. Anything else we've forgotten?" he asked Seth.

"Libby put together a care package for her," Seth said with a smile. "Pepper spray, an air horn, Legos, and some wine." He turned to Jude. "I thought you were in construction."

"Wait a second," Dean said, "we'll get to that. Why Legos?"

"Libby claims it's the perfect home defense system. We've stepped on enough of them with our nieces and nephews that I agree. Just wait until Maya's older," Seth told him.

"What? Is Layla supposed to *Home Alone* her house?" Dean asked with a laugh.

"There are worse ideas," Seth snorted. "Besides, I think it's supposed to lighten the mood. Anyway ..." he said, turning his attention back to Jude.

"Yes, I'm a therapist," he answered with a shrug.

"So why does Layla think you're in construction?" Seth asked.

"Misunderstanding."

"But you haven't told her what you really do?" Dean asked. "Man, you're going to get yourself in some deep shit if you don't."

"I've tried to tell her—"

"Try harder."

"Point taken," Jude said with a sigh. "Think it'll freak her out?"

"Oh yeah," Seth agreed. "But tell her anyway."

"So, what are we going to do about this Noah asshole?" Jude asked.

"We're trying to talk Layla into filing a restraining order. She doesn't think it'll fly because we don't have any proof," Seth told him.

"And we're going to keep an eye out. I haven't really been reviewing the security footage we set up. There hasn't been a reason to. Now there is," Dean said.

"You could get a dog," Jude pointed out. "Just as an added layer of protection." When Seth winced, Jude looked at him quizzically.

"Dogs aren't really security. They're dogs," Seth told him.

"Don't listen to him. He's thinking about surprising Libby with a dog, and she's pretty vocal about people who use dogs as security systems rather than pets," Dean explained.

"I didn't mean it like that, exactly," Jude said, although he had in a way. "I mean, it would give her a sense of not being alone."

"Like a therapy dog?" Dean deadpanned.

"I know you're messing with me, but yes. But also, a dog that might bark if someone comes around when she's here by herself. I mean, there will be times she'll be alone here," Jude pointed out.

"Maybe she can help me pick out a dog for Libby," Seth suggested.

"And then you think she'll want one for herself?" Dean asked. "You're devious."

"The word you're looking for is clever," Seth pointed out with a grin, getting up with a nod and heading to his truck. "I've got to get back to the shop."

"And I've got work," Jude told them. "I'll stop by later and say hey to Layla."

"Come over for dinner. JP is welcome, too," Dean told him, as Seth headed out.

"JP has plans, but I'm in," Jude told him. "Thanks for the heads up," he told Dean who only nodded. "Maybe she should see a therapist," he added before he walked away.

"Like you?" Dean asked with a wink.

"No. I mean, really. I can be her friend, but I can't be her therapist. She might need the help with this."

"Hey, you don't have to convince me. Layla's going to be the hard sell there. Good luck with that," Dean told him, striding back toward the house with another glance at his list. "Dinner's at eight," he called back.

***

Layla took a bite of her pizza and watched Naomi process what she'd told her. Her brow was furrowed, and she'd abandoned the slice of the vegetarian and gluten free pizza she'd been so eager to try. "Dean thinks I should get a restraining order," she finished.

"I agree with Dean," Naomi said honestly.

"I don't have any proof. What am I going to tell a judge? That I left the door unlocked and someone messed with my wine and my pictures? That doesn't even sound dangerous," Layla said, taking a sip of grape Fanta and wincing at the sickly-sweet taste. Naomi was right, Layla thought. She should have gotten a regular Coke. She thought about a meme she'd seen earlier in the week about how Grape Fanta didn't taste like grape, but it sure as hell tasted like the color purple. She reflected that nothing she'd read had ever been so accurate.

"The fact that someone was in your house when you weren't home sounds dangerous," Naomi pointed out, picking up a fork to slice her pizza. Layla grinned at the action. She'd been shoveling her own straight into her mouth.

"Well, yeah, but I can't prove it was him."

"I'd go with you," Naomi said calmly. "If I need to file charges for what happened to me, I will."

"I thought you didn't want to do that," Layla said, feeling confused.

"I didn't. I just wanted to put it behind me. But lately I've been wondering if he's dating anyone new," she admitted. "I don't like the thought of it."

"Yeah, I've considered that, too," Layla admitted. "But it won't stop him from dating just because you file charges."

"It might make it harder for him to do to someone else what he did to us," Naomi said. "And maybe it was selfish of me to keep quiet. I was so worried about what everyone would think and my parents finding out, but then I think about it happening again and don't know if I could live with myself knowing he's out there doing this to other people."

"I don't want you to do this for me," Layla told her honestly, wiping her hands on a napkin.

"I wouldn't be. It'd be for them," Naomi answered. "And for me, really. It'd be nice to see a little justice in this whole situation."

"It might not feel like justice," Layla said, and they were both quiet as they thought about all the public trials where the women were dragged through the mud while the defendants got a slap on the wrist for assault. "But it might back up the need for a protective order."

"Then let's do it," Naomi said evenly. "Want to try this?" she offered, holding out a piece of pizza.

"If I'd wanted a salad, I would have ordered one," Layla said blandly. "I'll just stick to my carnivore pizza."

"Suit yourself," Naomi said. "It's a thing I'm trying. I just want to be healthier right now. Like overall healthy. I thought this would be a start."

"I thought your counselor was the start," Layla pointed out.

"Yeah, him, too," Naomi agreed. "Have you reconsidered seeing one?" she asked. "After yesterday and everything?"

"No. I don't really want to talk about it to a stranger," Layla said, and then amended, "except to get a restraining order if I have to. Though I wish I could avoid that mess, too. What if it's not him, and it makes it worse?"

"Is there any part of you that thinks it's not him?" Naomi asked, leveling a glance at her as she took a drink.

"No," Layla sighed. "It's going to put me off wine," she joked lamely.

"Well, that would be a damn shame," Naomi agreed. "Look, why don't I come over tonight, and we'll make margaritas and watch movies."

"Just no Julia Roberts,"

"What's your problem with her?"

"I love her, but Libby and Lindy decided we were having a sleepover, and we ran through some of her hits."

"That sounds like fun."

"I'd have called you, but I wasn't thinking," Layla told her, realizing she might have made her friend feel left out.

"No worries. I had a date," she answered with a twinkle in her eye. "Much as I love a good look at Lindy's eye candy, I'd rather go shopping for my own."

"With the same guy?"

"No, of course not," Naomi said, waving a hand. "I scared him off good. New guy. Met him on this new site. He's cute. A little nerdy." At Layla's look, she corrected herself, "Not like Noah was.

Nothing like that. I mean more full-geek but hot with it."

"I don't think that's possible," Layla pointed out.

"Yeah, well, I didn't think so either. We'll see," Naomi said with a shrug. "So, margaritas tonight?"

"I'm having dinner at Lindy's, but if you can do a late night, I'm game," Layla told her.

"Text me when you're done, and I'll head over," Naomi replied, and then with a glint in her eye continued. "Maybe I'll catch a glimpse of the hot neighbor."

"I never said hot," Layla pointed out.

"You didn't have to," Naomi said. "I inferred. Or is it implied? I always forget the difference?"

Layla rolled her eyes. "Ask your hot geek."

"I may do that. Second date this weekend," she said with a cheeky grin. "Think Ryan Gosling with geek glasses."

"Huh." Layla thought about that. "I need to see pictures. Come on. I know you have some."

Naomi pulled out her phone and scrolled through the app. "Are you ever going to date again?"

"God, I hope so," she said with a sigh. She looked at the picture. "This is more Ryan Reynolds than Ryan Gosling."

"That's what I meant," she insisted. "Still hot."

Layla grinned at her. "Okay, so tell me everything."

Chapter 15

Presley twirled the spaghetti around on her fork and tried to focus on what Donovan was saying. She was admittedly distracted but was trying to cover it. After all, he'd made the effort to make reservations at the little Italian place downtown she'd wanted to try forever. She wanted to enjoy it, but she kept wondering about Layla.

"So, are you going to tell me what's going on with you tonight?" Donovan asked, reaching for his glass of wine and meeting Presley's eyes. She focused in on him, pulling her thoughts back abruptly.

"Sorry," she told him. "I'm distracted."

"I noticed. I'm trying not to take it personally."

"What do you know about restraining orders?" she asked him bluntly, coming out with the thing that she'd been worrying over since Layla called.

Donovan sat up straighter. "I'm a little worried about why you're asking. What's going on?"

"There was a guy my sister used to date who was … well, we'll leave it at a real piece of work," she said, her face tightening. "Anyway, he used to bother her, but then he stopped. Anyway, she called and said they think he broke into her place last night."

"Who's they?"

"Dean, Seth, Lindy, Libby," Presley said, rattling off names. She's already filled him in on the overlapping relationships. "We were all over there for dinner, and then when she went home, things were out of place."

"And you all think it was him," Donovan concluded.

"I have no doubt," Presley said seriously. "It's not beyond him. At all."

"And she wants to get a restraining order?"

"I don't know if she does, but we all think she should," Presley said. "He's scary, Donovan. I mean, really sick."

"I believe you," Donovan said, reaching for her hand. "You're worried."

"Yeah, I really am," Presley admitted with a sigh. "I thought it was over."

"So, what do you want to know about restraining orders?"

"Can she get one if we can't prove it's him? Or if we don't know where he lives now? I guess I just want to better understand the process, so I can explain it to her."

"Would it help if I talked to her?"

"You wouldn't mind?"

"Not if it helps you feel better. Besides, I'd like to meet your sister," he said honestly, squeezing her hand. She looked at him closely.

"That sounds serious," she told him, raising an eyebrow.

"Would that be so bad?"

"I guess not," Presley said with a small smile, realizing that she hadn't really thought about where this was going. It had been such a whirlwind that she hadn't had time to think about where they were headed or what she wanted.

"You're not still hung up on Elevator Guy, are you?" he asked pointedly, gesturing with his fork.

"Derrick? Don't be ridiculous."

"Well, you've got enough on your mind that I think we'll leave it for now," he said, stroking her hand with his thumb in lazy circles. "Would it make you feel better to stop by and see your sister tonight?"

"I'd feel better if we did."

"We can go over after dinner."

"You don't mind? I know it's a drive, and we'll probably get back late."

"Don't worry about that," Donovan told her. "It's worth it if it makes you feel better."

"So, you want to meet my family?" Presley asked, her eyes narrowing speculatively. Derrick had tried to avoid family events and had mostly moped around when forced to attend.

"I wouldn't mind it."

"They're a little much."

"That's not a no."

"I guess it's not," she admitted. "And do you want me to meet yours? I mean, other than Vashti?"

"Maybe I do. Problem?"

"I'm thinking about it," she told him with a grin. "You haven't said much about your parents."

"What do you want to know?" he asked, turning her hand over and threading his fingers through hers.

"I don't know. Just tell me about them."

"Alright. Dessert?" She nodded, and he flagged down their server, putting in an order for cannoli. "So, I already told you my dad married Vashti's mom."

"Yeah, I think that's been made pretty clear," Presley said, rolling her eyes at how monumentally she'd misunderstood his relationship at the start.

"Well, my parents were divorced when I was a teenager. They fought a lot, so it was kind of a relief," he said with a shrug. "My mom remarried straight away. Decent guy, I guess. I lived with them a while, but they wanted to relocate. I didn't want to change schools, so I moved in with my dad. He was dating Vashti's mom, and then they got married. Anyway, I still see my mom and Joe, the guy she married. They're back in Georgia now, but they were in Florida for years."

"You were a teenager, and you didn't want to move to the beach?" Presley asked, her eyebrows quirking.

"They were pretty well inland from the beach," Jude said with a laugh. "It was cool for a visit, but I had a girlfriend at the time."

"Yeah, I figured. Love is the only thing that trumps the beach."

"Well, lust," he countered with a grin, squeezing her hand. "For instance," he said, taking a bite of cannoli and chewing for a minute. "If I were given the option of going to the beach right now …" He let the sentence hang and winked at her.

"You know you can have sex at the beach, right?" Presley pointed out with a laugh.

"You want to go to the beach?"

"Want to go back to my place?"

"Thought you'd never ask. How about after we go see your sister?"

"That could be arranged. You don't happen to have your handcuffs on you, do you?" He laughed.

Presley knew he was trying to take her mind off Layla, and for a few minutes, it had worked. They were easy enough with each other now. After all, he was regularly sleeping over at her place or vice versa. At least, when they weren't on shift. She was relieved that their schedules were synced up right now. She'd had a lot of relationships flounder purely because of scheduling. She concentrated on her cannoli but kept his hand in hers.

"We could swing by my mom's sometime," he said. "But my dad is in town now. To see the baby."

"Oh?" she asked, feeling nervous. Meeting families seemed like rushing things.

"Or we could wait until the next visit," Donovan said easily, sensing her nervousness.

"I'm okay with meeting him now," Presley told him, meeting his eyes. "And I've already met Vashti."

"I should warn you though," he began with a grin. "Vashti's already told them how we met."

"Of course she did," Presley muttered. "I'll never live that down."

"Never," Donovan agreed. "Want to take the rest of that to go and get on the road?"

"Let's."

***

Layla felt weird about coming home from work and going to Lindy's instead of her own place. She opened the door with the key and still felt like an intruder. She sighed. There was no helping it, after all. Dean was pretty adamant that she avoid going back home by herself until everything was done. It did give her a little peace of mind, but it still felt strange.

She came in and went upstairs to change out of her work clothes. She'd paired a button up and tie with a pencil skirt and heels for work, and she'd braided her hair intricately around her head. It made for a professional look, but she'd spent the last hour thinking about slipping into something a little more comfortable. She pulled on leggings and a dress with pockets and headed downstairs. She stopped short when she heard the back porch door open, but then breathed easy when she saw Dean.

"Hey, there. You want to go next door for a second?"

"Sure," Layla said, feeling nervous. "I wish you'd let me pay for everything."

"Don't worry about it. It's our property, and we want it safe. Not just for you."

"I feel like I've put you all in danger," Layla admitted, darting a look at him.

"Do you think he's dangerous? I mean, you don't think he's just fucking with you?"

"I think he can be very dangerous."

"Well, you'd know better than I would. But none of this is your fault. Anyway, we've changed the locks. I've got a key, and we made a couple for you. I wouldn't hide one outside. If you ever get locked out, come get one of us, and we'll let you back in. The security company came by and got your alarm set. I'll give you the code, and we'll have it, too, just in case. I'll show you the whole set up." Dean unlocked the door and stepped over to the security panel on the wall where he entered the code. "We set one up in the main house, too, but I turned it off when I got home. We'll use the same code to make it easier to remember."

"I appreciate you doing all this," Layla told him as she looked around.

"Do you notice anything else different?"

"I don't know. It's so hard to say. I just feel like things have been moved around."

"I don't doubt it. How'd Presley take it?" he asked, following her back outside and over to the main house.

"Okay, I guess. She's worried, of course. But she said she'd stop by later. She's dating this cop, and he's going to talk to me about my options," Layla said with a sigh and then caught Dean's major eye roll.

"A cop?" Dean looked disgusted. "If she's hard up for a date, I could introduce her to someone."

"You don't like cops?"

"Firefighters and cops don't generally see eye-to-eye," Dean explained, holding open the door to let her go in first.

"Okay. That's weird, but okay," Layla said with a grin.

"What's weird?" Lindy asked. She walked into the room bouncing Maya on her hip.

"Dean's pissy because Presley is dating a cop."

"Ah," Lindy said with a nod. "Yeah, they're weird about that. We're likely to hear donut jokes and references to speeding tickets." She shared an equally amused look with Layla and then turned her attention to Dean. "Women don't think like that."

"So, you've said before. It's just a rivalry." He shrugged. "I just don't see why she'd want to date a cop."

"Uniform," Layla pointed out.

"Handcuffs," Lindy added with a wink.

"I've seen a cop or two I wouldn't mind frisking me and maybe checking to make sure I wasn't concealing anything dangerous," Layla said with a grin, taking a seat at the counter with a mischievous look on her face.

"Mmm hmm. Read me my rights," Lindy agreed.

"I'm standing right here," Dean told them.

"Hey, you've got the whole firefighter thing," Layla pointed out. "You know ..." She looked at Lindy.

"Fire pole. Uniform. Dangerous job. It's a thing."

"Okay, you ladies need a cold shower," he told them, reaching for Maya. "We're going to go play, and the two of you can cool off."

"He's cute when he's annoyed," Lindy told Layla when he walked out of the room.

"He's pretty cute when he's not. I hope you don't mind if Presley stops by later. She thought he could give me a breakdown of my options. It might be good for Naomi to hear, too. She was going to come over and watch a movie with me if I can go back home."

"You don't even have to ask. I'll be interested in hearing what he has to say. So ... how hot is this cop of hers?"

"I just want you to know I can still hear you," Dean said from the living room.

"Mind your own business," Lindy called back and grinned at Layla.

Chapter 16

Layla wasn't sure how she felt about Jude coming to dinner. It was weird, she thought, as she looked over to where he was seated across from her. No one had mentioned what had happened last night, but she knew it was only a matter of time before they did. She wondered if she'd be able to get him to leave early, before Presley and Donovan showed up to go over things with her. She fiddled with her food until Lindy kicked her under the table.

"Ow," she complained, giving Lindy a dirty look. "What is your problem?"

"Stop playing with your food and eat it," Lindy told her. "If you're worried about Jude here finding out what happened, you should probably know Dean already told him." Layla shifted her annoyed look from Lindy to Dean.

"He saw us installing the new locks," Dean said, defending himself. "Besides, we didn't say anything about Noah. Turns out he'd already heard about that," he said, giving Layla a pointed look. Lindy looked at her curiously.

"It just came up one day," she muttered in the direction of her plate.

"I can't say that I'm not worried," Jude said, speaking up and getting Layla's attention. "How are you doing?"

"I'm," she paused to find the words, "okay, I guess. It helps to know there's security in place. I don't think he'd be stupid enough to try anything now."

"Not at your house," Jude pointed out.

"Right," she agreed, meeting his eyes. "But I have a lot of other people at work, and it's not like I'm ever really alone."

She shrugged and turned back to her food. She really wanted to enjoy her meal in peace, but she was worried. She didn't like people knowing her business, and the story was spreading faster than she could manage it. Still, she admitted to herself, maybe it was better to let more people in. After all, keeping to herself hadn't helped with Noah before.

"Still, you think he's starting back?" Jude asked.

"Looks like it. But it could have been a one-off." She shrugged as if it didn't really matter.

"Bet that's your sister," Dean said, hearing the doorbell. "I'll get it."

"I hear we're just in time for dessert," Presley said, as she came into the room.

"We just had dessert," Donovan pointed out.

"So, it's dessert, the sequel," she said, before turning to the assembled group. "Okay, I'm going to do this once." She took a deep breath and went around the room: "Dean, Lindy, Maya, Layla, Jude. Jude's the neighbor," she explained. "This is Donovan."

"I really want to say *hey, Jude*," Donovan told the new arrival with a grin.

"Please don't," he replied with an answering smile.

"Sit and let us know what you think about all this," Lindy said, as Dean stood up to go grab dessert.

"I just want to know if I can file a restraining order if I can't prove it's him," Layla said, meeting Donovan's eyes. She had to admit he was just as attractive as Presley had said, although she was a tiny bit disappointed he hadn't worn the uniform. Of course, he was off-duty, she reminded herself.

"You have to have more than a suspicion and some circumstantial evidence," Donovan explained.

"I could have told her that," Dean muttered.

"You're a firefighter, right?" Donovan asked. When Dean nodded, he rolled his eyes. "Anyway," he said, turning back to Layla, "you can get a temporary order of protection. It'll last you a couple of weeks, but then you'd have to go in front of a judge and explain why you think it's him. He'd be there and could defend himself. It'd be up to the judge as to who to believe."

Layla's eyebrows drew sharply together, as she thought about having to see him again. "I talked to Naomi, and she said she'd come forward with her story if it would help." She broke off when she saw Donovan shake his head. "What?"

"That looks like collaboration. I'm sorry, but that's not going to help. If she wants to come forward on her own, that's one thing. But it's going to look like you're targeting him. I know that's not fair, but that's the way it is." He looked over at Lindy who was scowling in his direction.

"So, if some asshole abuser goes around harassing women no one can come forward without looking like it's a set up?"

"It's complicated," Donovan agreed with a sigh. "The temporary protection order is going to be the only thing you can do, from a legal standpoint."

"But then I'd have to see him?" Layla asked. She could feel Jude watching her and wished he'd excused himself and gone home. She couldn't see why this was his problem. "I don't know if I can do that."

"Presley told me you're getting the full security set up here. What else do you have by way of protection?"

"You mean, do I have a gun?" When he nodded, she shook her head. "No, I wouldn't even know how to shoot one. But Libby brought me some goodies on my lunch break. Pepper spray and an air horn. Stuff like that."

"That's not a bad idea. Where is it?"

"Up in my room, in my purse," she told him with a quizzical look.

"That's just it. Until this is over, it needs to be on your person at all times," Donovan said.

"She's eating with family right now," Presley pointed out.

"Yeah, but if she walked off and he was waiting?" Donovan asked, looking around and assessing them. "I'm not trying to scare you."

"Well, yeah, you are," Dean pointed out evenly. "That's kind of the point."

"Okay, I'm trying to scare you enough, so you'll be smart about it. He hasn't done anything violent, but he is flying under the radar, which worries me a little."

"How do you mean?" Jude asked, speaking up for the first time. "You think it's more dangerous that he's leaving so little evidence?"

"Your typical crazy ex might send text messages and make phone calls, even key your car. But this? I don't know. It doesn't sit right with me," he admitted, turning to look at Layla who had gone pale. "That's what you've been thinking, right?" She nodded.

"It might not hurt to have someone stay over at your place for a while," Donovan told her. "Or you stay over with someone else."

"I don't want to be forced out of my home," Layla returned. "Besides, Dean put in new locks and security."

"Alarms?" Donovan asked, looking at Dean.

"Cameras, too. It should cover the whole property," Dean told him.

"You going to get offended if I ask to see them?" Donovan asked blandly.

"Well, yeah," Dean said, exasperated. "But you can see them anyway."

"I appreciate it," Donovan said. Presley nudged his shoulder.

"I could do a walk-through of your place with you and look for any weak points, maybe give you a couple of tips," he told her. "But from now on, you record everything. Any weird call or text message, anything that seems even a little off."

"The glass," Presley said suddenly, looking at Layla. Layla nodded.

"Wait—from the driveway?" Jude asked.

"Are y'all going to tell us what you're talking about?" Lindy asked, exchanging baffled looks with Dean and Donovan.

"There was broken glass in my driveway a week or so ago," Layla said, shakily. "I got it cleaned up, but I couldn't see what could have broken like that. It was all around my car."

"Okay, could have been kids messing around," Donovan pointed out. "But I don't like it. Anything else?"

"He used to call a lot when I lived with Presley. Crazy calls, the occasional text message. No, I didn't keep them," Layla told him with a sigh.

"And he, uh, stopped by once," Presley admitted. The entire table turned to look at her. "I was home by myself, and I stepped out into the hallway when I saw who was at the door."

"I cannot fucking believe you opened the door to that psycho," Dean said from across the table. "What is wrong with you?"

"Let her finish," Lindy said sharply. "What'd he do?" she asked, curious to see where this was going.

"He demanded to see you," Presley told Layla, hesitantly. "It got ugly. Anyway, I got really loud, and a few neighbors came out in the hall. He went away, and then the calls and texts stopped."

"Why didn't you say anything?" Layla asked.

"Honestly, I thought I had made it worse," she admitted. "When he quit altogether, I thought maybe I was wrong."

"But now you think you weren't wrong," Jude said quietly. Presley nodded. "You think you made it worse." She nodded again.

"I had the right to know," Layla said angrily.

"I know," Presley said quietly, meeting her eyes. "I just didn't know how to tell you. When he went away, I didn't want you to worry."

"But you've been worried, and this is why," Layla said, a questioning note in her voice. "Did you even stop to think about how dangerous that was to open up the door to him? What if no one else had been home?" Dean started to speak up, but Lindy put up a hand to motion him to stop. "Do you have any idea how crazy he is?" Layla asked. "I'm going to need a minute," she said, abruptly pushing back her chair and walking out.

"You neglected to mention this," Donovan told her.

"I wasn't sure it was important," Presley told him, watching the door where Layla had exited. She started to stand, but Jude reached over and touched her shoulder.

"I've got this," he told her. "Give her a little space."

***

In the kitchen, Layla was leaning against the counter looking out at her little house. He could be watching her now, Layla thought. For all she knew, he could have bugged the place, she thought anxiously. And Presley had been sitting on this secret all along.

"She was trying to protect you, you know," Jude said, as he went over to stand beside her, looking outside.

"I know," Layla admitted. "But it wasn't fair not to tell me."

"No," Jude agreed. "She's worried about you."

"I'm worried about me," Layla said. "Look, you don't have to stay here for my drama."

"Let me worry about me," Jude said. "Anyway, there's something I should tell you, while we're talking about keeping secrets. Although it's not exactly a secret."

"What are you talking about?" Layla asked, confused.

"You seem to think I'm in construction, and I guess I let you think that," Jude said, turning to meet her eyes.

"Okay, so what do you do?" Layla asked, wondering if this was the appropriate time to have this conversation. At the moment, she didn't really care what he did, she thought in frustration.

"I'm a therapist. Psychologist," Jude added.

"I'm sorry, what?"

"I'm doing some renovations on the house, but I'm a therapist," he explained. "It occurred to me that you should know that."

"Is that why you've taken such an interest? Professional curiosity?" she asked, affronted. "Look, I don't want to be analyzed."

"And I don't want you to do my taxes," he retorted. When she looked at him in shock, he continued. "Do you really think I go around analyzing people all the time? You've got some strange ideas about therapy. I talked to you because I'm your friend. And because you were having a full-blown panic attack, which I'm pretty sure you haven't mentioned to your sister."

"You're still having them?" Presley asked from the doorway, her face as white as Layla's. "Why didn't you say?"

"Why didn't you tell me about Noah's little visit?" Layla retorted.

"Touché." Presley nodded. "The nightmares, too?"

Layla darted a glance at Jude and then just sighed, nodding.

"I wish you'd told me."

"You can't do anything about it."

Presley looked at her, hurt. "Yeah, well you thought that before, too," she told her. They both held a look that was filled with years of hurt. Layla remembered suddenly her mother's illness and how far she'd pushed Presley away then. She could see Presley remembering it, too.

"We're going to go. Good seeing you again, Jude. I'll call you tomorrow, Layla." She turned on her heel and went back into the suspiciously quiet dining room where Layla suspected the others had been listening.

"Nightmares, too?" Jude asked, quietly. "You're going to need to start trusting the rest of us to be there for you."

"You don't even know me, Jude. You're just the neighbor."

"Is that all?" he asked, letting the question hang there between them. "I hope you can consider me a friend."

"So, you're a therapist," she said, looking at him closely. "And you've got kids. Anything else you want to tell me?"

"No, I think that covers it."

"I'm just going to head up with Dean and check out the security," Donovan interrupted.

"Not that I need the help," Dean retorted behind him.

"Yeah, I get it," Donovan said, annoyance creeping into his voice.

"Take the pissing match upstairs, guys," Lindy said from the dining room. "Presley's ready to go."

"I think I should go talk to my sister," Layla told Jude.

"Afterwards, I'd like to walk you home. And if you'll allow it, I'd like to sleep on the couch."

"I have a friend coming over later," she told him, uncomfortable at the idea of having him in her house in such a casual way. He misunderstood her discomfort.

"A friend," he said blankly. "Well, I'll leave you to it. I'll be next door if you need anything." Layla could tell he'd misunderstood but thought maybe it was best that he had. After all, she had nothing to offer except drama right now.

"Thanks," she told him and headed into the dining room.

"I'm sorry, Presley," Layla said simply, sitting down beside her. "I've gotten used to doing things my way, on my own." Lindy stood up and took Maya out of the room to give them privacy.

"You never had to," Presley told her honestly. "You always had the choice to go through it with me."

"Well, it doesn't seem like either one of us has been good at that lately," Layla pointed out. "But I'd like to try again."

"Okay. We should tell Dad what's going on.

"But his heart?"

"He's been good lately. And he might hear it from the others. We could tell him together."

"Yeah, we can do that."

"Why'd you send Jude home? You know he thinks you've got a booty call later, right?"

"Yeah, I got that," she said wryly. "It's just professional curiosity anyway."

"You think so?"

"I'm not ready for anything else."

"Fair enough. I'm sorry I didn't tell you about Noah."

"What did he say? Really?"

"It was pretty awful," Presley admitted. "I lost my temper, too. Look, I'll give you a blow-by-blow tomorrow, but suffice it to say that I thought I'd made things exponentially worse or gotten him to leave you alone. I was hoping for the latter, but now ..."

"This isn't on you, Pres. If he started back, it's not because of that. It's been months."

"I know. I just don't feel good about it."

"Thanks for bringing Donovan by to help," Layla said. "He's hot."

"He is. Sweet, too," Presley added, glancing toward the door.

"You're not still missing Derek?"

"No, not anymore. I mean, every now and then, it sort of hits me, but that's more because of the work gossip. But lately, the work gossip has been in my favor," she said smugly.

"I take it you're not the butt of jokes anymore."

"Not at all. It's pissing Amber off to no end."

"Thanks for being here," Layla said, reaching out for Presley's hand. "I'll do the protection order, but I'd like you to be there. Please."

"Okay. Just tell me when. I'll go with you to file it, too, if you want."

"I appreciate it."

"Everything good?" Presley asked Donovan, as he walked in with Dean.

"Yeah, it's good. For a firefighter," he said with a grin.

Dean merely shot up a finger. "Presley, this guy's okay—for a cop," he sneered. "But you decide you want a real man, I've got a few friends I can introduce you to," he suggested with a wink.

"I'll keep it in mind," Presley said, rolling her eyes. She hugged Layla tight and then grabbed Donovan's hand. "We're going to get home. I'll call you in the morning."

"After your run," Layla suggested. "Not before. I'll be asleep before."

"Deal."

Chapter 17

Layla paused on the doorstep, looking up and down the street. She wanted to walk, but then she wondered if that was the safest choice she could make. After all, if Noah had been in her house, he could be anywhere. He could be staying in town or driving by. She wrapped her arms around herself, torn between wanting to dispel his power over her by walking and wanting to keep herself safe by driving. She shifted her purse to her shoulder and considered.

"Did your friend go home?" Jude asked from the driveway next door. He began to walk over, keeping to his side of the property.

"No, um, still asleep," Layla said, nodding to the house. "I have to go to work."

"Can I drive you?" Jude asked carefully, wondering what kind of friend would let her go out by herself after everything without even making sure she was okay. After all, he thought, she clearly wasn't okay.

"That would be great," she told him, feeling relieved that the decision was taken out of her hands. "Thank you."

"No problem," he said, nodding to his truck.

"Nice ride," she told him, taking a look and trying to reconcile the truck with the profession.

"Thanks," he said, opening her door for her. "It's come in handy with the renovations."

"So, can I ask you a nosy question?" Layla asked, before he could ask her about how she was doing or ask anything about Noah.

"Sure," Jude said with a nod, starting the truck. "What's up?"

"Why don't you see your kids?" she asked, wondering why she needed to know. After all, she'd always been a big fan of everyone minding their own business. It just didn't seem to fit: this man with kids he didn't see.

"My ex has gotten really good at being somewhere else when I go to pick them up. Or generally making things tough for them. Last year, she took them to Disney when I was supposed to have them for the week. Of course, they wanted to go to Disney," he said, frustrated. "Somehow I came out of it looking like the bad guy again." He looked over at Layla who was considering him. "I hired the lawyer to try to get her to comply with our parenting agreement. When that didn't work, we decided it might be best if I went after full custody. Since I filed, it's gotten pretty ugly. She's conveniently forgotten my last few weekend visits, and when I call, she doesn't answer."

"So, what's her problem?" Layla asked, mystified.

"She didn't want the divorce," Jude admitted with a shrug. "We weren't happy, but she still didn't want things to change. It started to spill over to the kids. We argued more than we talked, or we just ignored each other completely. When I filed for divorce, it got worse, though."

"Do you regret doing it? Since it made things harder?"

"I regret not seeing my kids every day. But I couldn't stay in that marriage. I don't want to normalize that kind of relationship for them. Anyway, it's done now, and I just want to see my kids." He looked over at Layla. "Are you doing okay today?"

"I'm alright," she said with a sigh. "I just wish this was over already."

"What, the TPO?"

"That, but whatever fallout is going to come with it, too. I just want him to leave me alone," she said quietly, looking out the window. "You're going to turn up here. It's the building on the end."

"Until he does, just make sure you take precautions. If you're hanging out at home alone and Dean and Lindy aren't home, give me a call. I won't get in your space, but I can be a little more aware."

"I kind of hate the idea of everyone hanging around watching me," Layla admitted. "This whole thing is creepy enough."

"It's nice that you have so many people who care about you, though."

"Why do you?" Layla asked, turning fully in the seat to face him suddenly.

"I told you, we're friends. I hope we are anyway."

"And you're not just trying to get in my head?"

"I've got plenty of clients, Layla," Jude said wryly. Layla wondered if Naomi was one of them. After all, she said the guy was hot. She looked at him speculatively. "Though I don't think it would hurt if you talked to someone else about all this. It might help with the stress."

"The only person I really need to talk to is whatever cop will help me with the protection order. Even then, I don't know how much it will help." She shrugged, swallowing the lump in her throat. She knew what Noah was capable of, after all, and he was just a little too smart to get caught.

"It's a step," Jude told her, taking off his seat belt and shutting off the truck. "And you have a lot of people who care about you who are going to keep an eye out as long as we need to."

"What are you doing?" she asked him, taking her own seat belt off.

"I'm walking you in," Jude said easily, opening his door and coming around the truck. He opened the door for her, and she turned toward him, not exiting the vehicle.

"Jude," she said his name with exasperation. "We're all of six steps from the door."

"Well, then it won't take long, will it?" he asked her with a smile.

"That's not the point," she told him, frustration in her voice. "I don't need an escort."

"Just look at it this way," he told her. "If he's watching, he'll see that you're not alone going to work. He'll see you have people around you who aren't going to let down their guard."

She considered that, cocking her head to the side and looking at him. Despite the man bun, which she had to admit sort of suited him, Jude looked quite professional today. He had on a suit, minus the tie, with the top button loose. It was a dark gray that made her think of Libby's wedding and the charcoal colored suits of the men. It was a good look for him, she thought. The pale blue of the shirt beneath it worked, too. She slid forward in her seat, coming in to his space a bit, and was amused when he jolted but held his place. She put a hand on his shoulder and slid out of the truck, glad of the help since she'd chosen another pencil skirt with a sweater. Her heels touched the ground in front of his shiny shoes, and she slowly allowed her gaze to travel up, up, up to meet his eyes.

"You have a good point," she admitted, liking the closeness but suspecting she was playing with fire here. Still, it was nice to be cared about, even if he was totally not her type, she thought.

"What are you doing for lunch?"

"I'm meeting Presley and filing the TPO."

"So soon?"

"I want it over with," she said with a shrug.

"And after work?"

"Just heading home," she told him, adjusting the purse strap on her shoulder.

"Text me when you're ready to leave, and I'll come over to drive you."

"You sure? What if you're in a session?"

"I won't be. I have a clear space at the end of the day to work on my files. It's not like I'm not heading your way."

"I guess that's true," she said. He stepped back, and she fell in step beside him.

"That was eight steps," he pointed out with a grin. She rolled her eyes, holding the door with one hand.

"Thanks for this."

He nodded. "I'll see you after work."

She went inside and counted to herself how many seconds it would take before the nosy receptionist asked about Jude. She didn't even make it to ten, and she smiled to herself as she glanced back to see Jude climbing into his truck. She put her phone in her purse and answered the questions vaguely, heading to her desk.

***

After work, Layla walked outside only after she saw Jude's truck pull up. She was pretty sure he'd have something to say about it if she waited outside on the sidewalk. It had been a long day. Dana, the receptionist/office manager, had spent the better part of it on extended coffee breaks, gossiping with the staff. Layla hadn't seen her do much actual work since she'd been in the office, but she didn't spend a lot of time thinking about it. She just wanted to concentrate on her own workload.

Dana popped over to her desk a number of times during the day to inquire after Jude, which Layla successfully deflected, to her increasing annoyance. Layla didn't want any problems at work, but the last thing she needed was the office gossip and general mouth-of-the-South knowing about her problems with Noah. Once she filed the TPO, the news would probably make the rounds soon enough.

She sighed as Jude pulled up, grateful she wouldn't have to walk home in her heels and happy that she didn't have to worry about being alone for a walk or a drive, vulnerable to Noah if he was out there. Jude slid out of the truck, as she'd known he would, and came around to open the door. He looked tired, and Layla wondered if he was thinking about his kids or just having a tough day. She wasn't sure, so she asked him.

"A little of both, to be honest," he told her. "Tough day with clients, and then Michelle called to rant about how the latest hearing date conflicts with her plans."

"I take it Michelle is the ex?"

"Yeah." Jude rubbed a hand over his face. He looked stressed, and it reminded Layla that she was hardly the only one in the world with problems. She knew she could be a little self-involved; after all, Presley accused her of it often enough.

"Do you have plans tonight?"

"I was just going to grab dinner, maybe watch a little TV," he said, putting the truck into gear and backing out, one arm stretched across the back of the seat and nearly touching her shoulder.

"Do you feel like grabbing a pizza, maybe watching a movie?"

"It depends," he said, glancing over at her sharply.

"On?" she asked, catching his glance.

"Is this a date thing or a friends thing?"

"I was thinking friends. You said you wanted to be friends, right?"

"Okay, then. How about we run by the house so I can change and then go out? Then you can tell me about how it went at lunch on the drive."

"Fair enough."

"I'd appreciate it if you'd come inside and wait while I change, and then we could go back to your place if you need anything. I know Dean put in security, but it would make me feel better."

"Fine," Layla said, choosing not to argue about it if she was going to try to take his mind off his troubles. "Do I get to pick the movie?"

"I figured that's how it would go. Does that mean I get to pick the pizza?" When she grinned over at him, he amended the statement, "Or the pizza place?"

"It's a deal," Layla told him. "Would you mind if I asked Presley and Donovan to join us? I'd kind of like to get a better sense of him. Her last boyfriend was a real ass."

"That might be a pot calling the kettle situation," he pointed out, pulling up at his house and getting out his keys. "But sure. Wouldn't that kind of seem like a double date though?" he asked her, unlocking the door.

"It's not a date," she reminded him. "Where's JP?"

"Out with friends—and so you say."

"I'll let you pay though, if it means that much to you," Layla said cheekily, sinking into a couch while he turned toward the stairs. When he glanced around the room, Layla's smile faded. "I'm not going to move from this spot until you get back. I'm not going up to watch you change, Jude."

"I wouldn't mind," he told her, with a grin she had to admit was pretty sexy. "I'm not shy."

"I'm sure you're not," she said with a laugh in her voice. "Maybe I am."

"I don't believe that for a minute, but I'm going."

Layla watched him walk away. The backside was as pretty as the rest of him, she admitted. Of course, she reminded herself, she wasn't interested in him that way. Maybe he wasn't the blue-collar guy she'd thought, but being a shrink might just be worse. Of course, he told her no one used that term anymore, but she couldn't help feeling like he was secretly diagnosing her. She probably seemed neurotic as hell, she thought in annoyance. And helpless to boot, a feeling she absolutely despised.

"If you're done scowling, do you need anything from your place?" Jude asked with a smile. She looked at him in the faded jeans and Guns N' Roses T-shirt and smiled widely. If he'd had flip flops on right now, he'd look like such a stereotype, but he was wearing sneakers instead.

"I'd like to change into something a bit more comfortable," Layla told him, dying to get out of her heels. They walked next door companionably, their shoulders brushing. "I'll just be a minute," she said, after she disabled the alarms.

He nodded and sat down on the couch. She left him sitting there and went upstairs. She gave her closet a cursory glance and pulled out a tunic top and pair of leggings. She discarded her skirt and sweater on the floor and remembered to grab a cardigan from the closet before she headed down. She slipped her feet into the ballet flats she'd left at the bottom of the stairs and then walked into the living room where Jude was waiting. "Presley said they could meet us for pizza but would skip the movie after."

"Well, that works anyway. You can inspect him over dinner. Though he seems like a decent guy."

"Well, appearances can be deceiving," Layla said, rolling of her shoulders, feeling the pinch of anxiety that practically lived there now.

"You can't compare everyone to Noah," Jude pointed out, as she reset the alarms. He reached around her to turn on the porch lights.

"I don't," Layla said defensively. "Okay, I do, but I think I'm in a better position to see some of the signs."

"Are you seeing them with me?" Jude asked, walking her to his truck.

"No. But we're not dating either."

"So you've said," he told her dryly. "I'm starting to wonder if I should be offended."

Layla laughed and bumped against him affectionately. "I do appreciate having a friend right now. But I think maybe I shouldn't date for a while. Not while all this is going on."

"You don't have to explain. But I'm just going to let you know I'm paying tonight. It'll save us an argument later."

"Fine. But it doesn't seem fair to make you drive, too."

"I don't mind," Jude said, opening the door for her again. She looked at him quizzically.

"You always do that?"

"I try," he said with a grin. "Fill me in on the TPO."

"Well, the officer was relieved that my expectations were based in reality so I have Donovan to thank for that. It was pretty straight-forward, but a little embarrassing, too. I think he believed me, but he didn't offer a lot of hope that it would go anywhere. Anyway, I'll get a notification in the mail when he's served, and I have to go to court in a couple weeks."

"I'd like to go with you."

"I don't have a date yet. You might be busy."

"I won't be."

"I'm really trying not to assume you have motives here, but it's hard."

"I care about you, and I don't want you to go through this alone. Let's leave it at that, okay?"

"Okay," Layla agreed. Jude reached over and turned the radio on, automatically adjusting the volume to a bearable level for company. It was tuned to a classic rock station. "If I sing, will it bother you?"

"You're going to sing anyway, aren't you?" he asked with a grin.

"You're right; I am."

It was starting to get dark already, and Layla relaxed completely for the first time all day. She hadn't even realized how stressed she'd been until her shoulders relaxed. She belted out Heart and then a little Pat Benatar while Jude grinned and occasionally joined in. It wasn't over. She had a feeling Noah wasn't done yet. But for tonight, she wasn't going to let him live rent-free in her head. She could see Jude relaxing, too, and was glad she'd been impulsive enough to suggest the night out.

Chapter 18

Presley kicked her feet up on the table and wiggled her thick sweater socks. She grinned when Layla puffed out an annoyed sigh but didn't move.

"Quit that."

"Fine," Presley said, withdrawing her feet from the table and curling them under her. "You haven't been watching *Jessica Jones* without me, have you?" she asked, narrowing her eyes at her sister.

"No," Layla said, shifting restlessly in her seat. "We can watch it, but I don't want to watch more than one episode. I need to read a few chapters of the book club book tonight."

"Okay," Presley agreed, and then leaned back to stretch her arms overhead. "So, what's eating you?"

Layla got up, not for the first time, and went to the kitchen. Presley could hear her fiddling around in the cabinets and then running water. She came back after a couple minutes and sat down with a sigh.

"Well?" Presley asked, still waiting.

"Why aren't you out with Donovan tonight?" Layla asked, clearly avoiding the question.

"He had to work," Presley said with a shrug. "And we don't spend all of our time together anyway."

"You spend a lot of it," Layla said, inclining her head toward her sister.

"You're not flipping this on me. We're talking about you and whatever is wrong with you tonight,"

"It's just someone is constantly here," Layla said with a one-shouldered shrug. "It's not that I don't appreciate it, but there's been constant foot traffic to my door over the last couple of weeks. I'm feeling a little cagey. Or just a little caged." She sighed and sat down, then hopped up again when she heard the shrill whistle of the tea kettle. Presley followed her into the kitchen. She pulled the tea kettle off the eye of the stove and continued as she poured the boiling water over the tea bag. "I feel like he's winning. I mean, I'm trapped and watched no matter what."

"I guess I hadn't thought of it like that," Presley admitted, looking at the dark circles under her sister's eyes. "But he did key your car a few nights ago, so it's not like he's left you alone. And the one camera that could have caught it was conveniently knocked down." She saw Layla's shoulders sink even lower. "We're worried about you."

"I know. And I know I sound ungrateful," she said, passing Presley a cup of chamomile tea.

"I just didn't think about how it would feel for us all to hover around. You know, we're trying to make you feel safer."

"I know you are. I know," she said with a sigh. "I just miss being able to come and go without feeling like someone is watching me all the time. I wish it made me feel safer, but I feel like a bug under glass."

"Look, we've got court in a week, and maybe that will stop him," Presley said, although she was actually unconvinced that it would do anything but inflame the situation.

"You don't really believe that."

"Maybe I don't," Presley said with a sigh. "But until he leaves you alone, we're going to keep coming by and checking on you."

"I wish we hadn't told Dad. He doesn't need the stress on his heart," Layla said, removing the tea bag and adding in a little honey. Presley reached for the sugar, and her sister pushed the honey toward her. "This is better with the chamomile."

"He needed to know, and his heart is fine. He hasn't had an incident in more than a year," Presley pointed out, sipping her tea. It wasn't her favorite, but she wasn't going to complain. "Look, we can all try to give you a little more space, but I'd be lying if I said we won't all still be watching and waiting. You being safe is more important than you feeling caged here."

"I know," Layla said, taking her tea back to the living room. Presley walked a couple of steps behind her, trying not to spill the tea and incur her neat-freak sister's wrath. "One episode," Layla reminded her, reaching for the remote.

"Two, tops," Presley offered with a grin. "We're almost done with the season."

"Fine," Layla said, nudging the bag of apple chips toward Presley.

"What's with the health food?" she asked, eyeing her sister.

"I went shopping with Naomi the other day and got a whole lecture on the mind-body connection," she said, exchanging an eye roll with Presley. "I've got regular potato chips in the cabinet, hiding behind the zero trans-fat pretzels. And cookies hidden in the tin behind the low carb tortillas in the pantry."

"Now we're talking," Presley said. "Want me to get you a Coke?" she asked, getting up and holding up her cup of tea.

"Let's make it a glass of wine," Layla said, smiling.

***

Donovan walked into the hospital feeling a little foolish. He'd been to Presley's work before, but they'd always planned it. He wanted to surprise her since he had gotten the night off. He got tired of waiting for the elevator and took the stairs instead, carrying the box of chocolates he knew she preferred. He promised himself he'd just drop them off and go. Another door opened on the floor above him, and he soon fell into step beside the guy climbing the stairs. He caught his assessing look and did the standard head nod men did with other men.

"Did your wife have a baby?" the other man asked him curiously, nodding at the chocolates he carried in their fancy box.

"No, uh, no," Donovan answered, feeling awkward. "Just surprising my girlfriend. She works here."

"Nurse?" the man asked, and Donovan looked at him with interest. He was dressed casually, with a ballcap, jeans, and black T-shirt. His shoes were black, too, and his beard was just this side of shaggy, as if he hadn't had time to groom it. He found himself profiling the guy, and then he reminded himself he was off duty.

"Midwife," Donovan said with a smile. "How about you? Visiting someone?"

"Yeah," he said, hesitating at the door Donovan was about to open. "But I think I'll head to the gift shop. I can't have you make me looking bad by showing up empty-handed, now can I?" he asked with a grin.

"Better not," Donovan recommended. "Should I offer congratulations?"

"Not yet," he said with a grin. "Soon though," he added, turning on his heel and heading back down the stairs quickly.

Donovan got out of the elevator and went over to the desk, shaking his head at how having a baby seemed to make some men so nervy. The guy had practically been vibrating with energy. He approached the receptionist and tried to remember her name.

"Hey, Erin," he said, grabbing the name out of his consciousness. "Is Presley around?"

"Donovan, aren't you a sight for sore eyes?" she asked with a grin. "You missed her. She was in earlier."

"Oh," he replied, feeling foolish. "Well, I guess my timing is off," he admitted with a rueful smile. "Why don't I just leave these with you then, and I'll grab her some for next time?" he asked, passing over the box of chocolates. He didn't want to pass that guy still carrying the same box, though why it mattered he couldn't say. He decided to take the elevator instead. "I'll just give her a call."

He waited at the elevator and sent Presley a quick text. He sighed when he realized she'd gone over to her sister's. Well, even if she'd been at work, he might not have been able to see her, he reminded himself.

"Thanks for these," Erin said, walking over to refill her cup of coffee at the side table near the waiting rooms. "You sure you don't want me to hold them for Presley?"

"No, you enjoy them. I'll get her more. Are you having a busy night?"

"No, it's been suspiciously quiet. It probably means we'll be slammed later," Erin said with a shrug. "We had a couple we sent home earlier, but that's pretty much it. Of course, we have a few patients still here from this morning."

"Huh," Donovan wondered who the guy was coming to see if no one was in active labor. It seemed odd, but maybe he had misunderstood. After all, he'd been busy thinking about Presley and hadn't wanted to make small talk in the first place. "Well, I'll catch up with her later, but you enjoy the chocolate."

"I sure will. Thanks," she said with a smile, heading over to the desk again. "Presley sure is a lucky girl."

"That's what I keep telling her," Donovan said with a grin, stepping into the elevator.

He heard his phone ring when he was walking out to the car, and he paused by the entrance to answer it. "Hey, Pres," he said, pulling out his Bluetooth and putting it in. He noticed the guy from the stairs driving slowly by and waved at him, figuring he hadn't found what he was looking for in the hospital store. He should have told him to try the gift shop just up the street, but he hadn't thought of it. He walked to his car and listened to Presley on the other end arguing with Layla in the background.

"Sounds like you're having a fun night," he said, climbing into his car.

"She's driving me crazy," Presley told him. "Fine, we'll watch the rest tomorrow," she called, and Donovan could tell she had one hand over the phone because her voice was muffled. "Layla's just pissed I talked her into a third episode, and she won't have time to read her book."

"You're a bad influence," Donovan told her, putting his key in the ignition and then sitting back. "Well, I won't tell you that I made a complete fool of myself by trying to surprise you at work."

"You don't need to." He heard the smile in her voice. "Erin texted me to say you gave away my chocolate. I hope you plan on making it up to me."

"At the earliest possible moment," Donovan said fervently. "When are you coming home?"

"I'm staying the night," Presley told him, regretfully. He could hear Layla shout *go home* in the background and Presley's accompanying laugh. "She's trying to get rid of me, but I'm not going anywhere." He couldn't hear Layla's pithy comment in the background, but he heard Presley's answering snort. "Sorry we missed each other. But I'm free tomorrow night, if you are."

"How about breakfast tomorrow?" he asked her, starting the car. Or trying to. He turned the key and cursed under his breath.

"What's up?"

"I think my battery is dead," Donovan said, perplexed. "Car won't start."

"Did you leave the light on?"

"Pres, I was only in there for about fifteen minutes. I don't know what's up," he said, scowling at his car and turning the key again. He started a steady stream of cursing and then checked himself. "Hey, let me get off here and take care of this, and I'll call you back."

"Call me after, okay?"

"Of course. I'll talk to you soon."

He disconnected the call and then sighed. His night had not gone as planned, not in any way. He opened the door and popped the hood. He knew his way around a car, but if he needed a battery, he'd have to call a friend to come pick him up. There wasn't a parts store anywhere close enough to walk. He put his hands on his hips and just looked at the SUV with a grimace. He shook his head and started to look closer when he noticed the car from the elevator pull back up. He got out, gift bag and a bunch of yellow balloons in hand, and Donovan waved at him absently.

"Car trouble?"

"Just the battery," Donovan told him with a shrug. "I see you found a gift." He nodded at the fancy gift bag with the tissue paper peeking out and the bright bunch of balloons overhead.

"I think the balloons might be overkill," the guy said with a grin, shrugging.

"I'm sure it's fine," Donovan replied, distracted.

"You need any help? Want me to jump you off?"

"I'm good. You should get those to your wife."

"Oh, she's not my wife, just yet," he said with a grin. "But I'm hoping. Look, I don't mind helping out."

"Hey," a voice interrupted loudly. "Presley called and said you had a little car trouble," a big man in a security uniform said, coming toward them.

"Guess I'll get out of the way," the man said, nodding to him and heading inside with the balloons and bag. "Good luck."

"Thanks," Donovan replied, turning to the approaching guard. "Hey, thanks. I'm Donovan," he said, introducing himself.

"Wes," the guard responded with a quick handshake. Donovan took in his stats easily. He was about 6'3" and a few pounds shy of three hundred, if he wasn't mistaken. His grip was firm. He turned to survey Donovan's car. "You need a jump?"

"Yeah, if you don't mind. Appreciate it."

"Any friend of Presley's and all that," Wes said with a grin. "She delivered my baby a few months back. My wife gave her hell, but Presley was an absolute peach," he added with a thick Southern accent. Donovan grinned at him.

"She is a peach, isn't she? Does she have you on speed dial?"

"I told her if she ever needs anything, she just has to call. First time she has though, other than tossing out rowdy relatives," Wes said, shrugging. "Are you the boyfriend?"

"Yeah, I guess I am."

"Well, you treat her right. You don't, I got a brother who might be interested," Wes warned him with a good-natured grin.

"I'll keep that in mind," Donovan said, amused. "You tell Presley that?"

"I surely did. She said the same thing. She'll keep it in my mind. Give me just a minute, and I'll pull my truck around."

"I'll wait right here," Donovan said wryly, gesturing to the dead battery as Wes chuckled and walked off. He crossed his arms and leaned back against the truck. He got out his phone and texted Presley to thank her for the help. "My hero," he typed in with a grin that stretched wider when he got her response, "You can thank me later." He was reading all kinds of things into that and figured she'd meant it that way. He stood up straight when he noticed Wes pulling up with the truck and tucked the phone into his back pocket.

Chapter 19

Layla stood in her pajamas in the middle of the living room and blew her hair out of her eyes in frustration. It was her day off, and she would usually spend the morning lounging around or working on a project from home. Since everyone she knew had started dropping in at regular intervals, she just wanted to get away for a little while. She put down her coffee with a solid *clunk* on the end table, missing the coaster and not even caring. She headed up the stairs and opened her closet dramatically.

I'll just get out for a little while, she thought to herself, pulling out her suede pants and an olive-green shirt. She considered her shoes as she stripped off her pajamas and started pulling on her clothes. She had the perfect ankle boots for this outfit, but if she wore that, she knew it might limit her activity for the day with the sharp, high heels. Of course, she thought, she could run laps in heels, so maybe it wouldn't even matter.

She put on the shoes and went into the bathroom to do something about her hair. A few minutes later, expertly made-up and with her hair reasonably tamed, she headed downstairs. She stopped short at the alarm and considered. She couldn't leave without telling anyone. Even she realized it wouldn't be safe, and when she heard the knock at the door, she jolted. Taking a deep breath, she moved slowly to peek out the curtain. When she saw Jude there, she let out a long, relieved sigh. She hadn't seen him since pizza and a movie except in passing.

"Hey," she told him, holding the door open. "Are you coming in?"

"Hey," he said with a grin. "You look like you're going out," he noted with a nod at her outfit.

"I'm thinking about it," she replied easily, stepping back just enough that he brushed against her as he walked in.

"Going alone?" he asked with a raised eyebrow.

"Thinking about it," she replied again in an entirely different, acerbic tone. She turned on her heel and went to retrieve the coffee cup off the end table to deposit it in the dishwasher. She looked over her shoulder at him when he came in behind her.

"That's not what I meant," he told her with a sigh.

"What's not?" she asked, pretending to misunderstand.

"I'm not saying you shouldn't do things alone, though I think it's safe to say we all worry. I just was curious if you were going out on a date."

"Oh," Layla paused, looking at him. She'd been so annoyed that she thought he was checking up on her that she hadn't even considered he might just be trying to find out if she was dating someone. It wasn't the first time they'd misunderstood each other after all. "No, I'm not, actually. I just wanted out of this house. Why are you here?"

"Actually, I was thinking the same thing. It's supposed to be my weekend with Kelsey and Connor, but Michelle conveniently forgot. They're in North Carolina at a cabin somewhere," he said with a long sigh of frustration. "I was going to go for a drive, see where I end up, and I thought you might want to get out, too."

"Don't even say another word," Layla said fervently, grabbing her purse and heading over to set the alarm. "Let's just get out of here. I'll text everyone to let them know we're going out when we're on the road."

"You didn't even ask where we're going," Jude said, as they walked over to his truck.

"I don't care. Anywhere that's not here," she told him frankly. "Everyone means well, but I can't stand this. My anxiety's already through the roof with the hearing at the end of next week."

"You didn't say," he said reproachfully, opening up her door.

"I was going to," she said, rolling her shoulders and then reaching over to fasten her seatbelt. She looked at Jude who was still holding the door. "I promise. I was going to call you later and tell you. I just got the notice in. Well, yesterday, if I'm completely honest."

"Okay," he said, closing the door and walking around to the driver's side. "Those don't appear to be walking shoes," he said with a glance at her footwear.

"I could run a marathon in these," she replied with a grin, wiggling her feet.

"Comfortably?" he asked with an answering grin.

"Ha! Well, maybe not. But I'm game for whatever you are. I don't necessarily want to hike in these, but I can manage most anything else. What'd you have in mind?"

"Short road trip and a couple cool places," he said, pulling out of the driveway. "Do you mind a drive? We might get back later this afternoon."

"There's no hurry. I have no plans other than to sit around and be watched like a bug under glass until this thing ends," she sighed. "But enough about my drama. How are you? Did you at least get to talk to your kids?"

"For a minute."

"Were they disappointed?"

"Honestly, they really weren't. She's convinced them that I'm responsible for the breakdown of the family. Never mind that they're up there in her boyfriend's cabin," he said, rolling his eyes. "They didn't seem like they cared if they missed another weekend with me."

"I'm sure they do," Layla said with certainty. "They probably just feel like it's disloyal to their mom to want to be with you."

"You think so?"

"Of course. I know it's not the same thing, but I felt disloyal to my mom for liking Keely. At first anyway. I was a real brat to her the first few times I was around, and I'm an adult."

"What made you change your mind?" he asked, heading out of town on the highway.

"She just kept being herself, being nice, and I realized that my mom would never have wanted me to be rude to someone else for something outside of anyone's control. And I realized it was okay if our family got bigger. So now I've got a stepmom when I haven't said the word "mom" in a …" She paused, choked up. "In a long time," she said softly. "And I have Lindy and Seth, too, and everyone that comes with them. It wasn't bad for things to change. It was just different."

"So maybe I can get the kids to see the benefits of it?"

"Well, they're getting a trip to the mountains with their mom's boyfriend. That's pretty cool. Maybe things will be completely different, but maybe there are advantages to it. You just can't give up on them."

"I wouldn't," he said, meeting her eyes.

"I know. But you might feel like it sometimes. Just keep trying," she told him, reaching over to touch his hand softly. "You must be a really good dad."

"Why do you think that?"

"Well, I grew up with one. I know what they're like," she said with a shrug, looking out the window. "It's pretty out here. Are those pecan trees?"

"Yeah. It's a nice drive."

"So, how'd you get to be a therapist?"

"It's not a pretty story."

"That's okay. My story wasn't pretty either," she reminded him, leaning her head against the seat and facing him.

"Well, I started working in construction as a teenager. I mean, small stuff at first, but I moved up. Anyway, an older guy I worked with was real quiet. Came in, did the work, went home. Kept to himself." He paused for a minute, remembering. "Anyway, one day he came in early. Hanged himself on some beams at the work site."

"Wow," Layla breathed. "That was bleak. I wasn't expecting that."

"It was bleak. We weren't expecting it either. Anyway, turns out he had some issues at home. A lot of debt, a rocky marriage, some problems with his kids. He'd struggled with depression on and off since he was a kid, and he just couldn't take it anymore. Anyway," he said in a lighter tone, "when I went to college a couple years later, I decided to study psychology and learn a little more about what could make someone do that. I mean, he was a good guy with a family who loved him, even if life was hard right then. I liked what I studied, and I kept doing it."

"That's a good story. I mean, not the suicide. Obviously. But the rest of it."

"What about you? You do know that you look nothing like someone's idea of an accountant, right?"

"Um, excuse me," she said, reaching over and grabbing the man bun. "Look who's talking."

"Hey, therapists have a diverse vibe. In fact, when I tell people I'm a counselor, they mostly look at my hair and nod like it makes sense."

"You ever wear it down?"

"Sometimes," he replied, looking over at her slyly. "You seem awfully interested."

"Just being neighborly," she said, snorting out a laugh. "Anyway, I like numbers. Always have. Accounting made sense. So where are we going?"

"This road takes us into Macon."

"What's in Macon? I mean, specifically."

"I thought we could grab coffee at this place I know, and then I had another stop in mind before lunch."

"And after lunch?"

"A scenic walk, if you can manage it," he told her with another look at her shoes.

"I can manage anything," she said smugly, and then paused. "How long a walk are we talking about?" When he just laughed, she rolled her eyes and played with the radio.

"Are you going to sing?"

"I might. Depends on the song." They rolled into Macon finishing up *Silver Springs* by Fleetwood Mac, and Jude headed downtown, sliding easily into a spot so early in the morning.

"What are we doing here?" she asked, looking around at the mostly darkened buildings.

"The awning over there," he said, pointing to the soft teal awning that was the only thing that set it apart from the other brick buildings on the block, each more dilapidated than the last. "I need coffee. I think you'll like this place," he told her, opening the door.

She stepped in and stopped short. She hadn't expected much from the outside of the building. After all, it was a little bit of a hole in the wall. Inside, the hardwood floors gleamed with polish, and local art hung on the walls. The counter was made of stone and surrounded by pillars made from driftwood. It gave it a rustic vibe. Layla perused the lengthy menu and selected something called a Maple Leaf and stood beside Jude while he ordered. They carried their mugs over to a sofa placed across from a large stone fireplace. Jude took Layla's mug so that she could sink easily into the soft cushions and then reached up to take her drink.

"This might be bliss. I didn't realize how cold my feet would be in these boots."

"Too cold for a walk later?"

"Maybe."

"Well, I have an idea about that, but first coffee."

"And next?"

"You'll see," he told her with a smile over his mug.

***

Presley sighed as she headed down the stairs. It had already been the longest shift ever, although it was no longer than any other if measured in hours. She'd had every pain in the ass patient she could handle in the last eight hours, and she still had a few to go. She descended the stairs quickly, thinking she'd be fine if she could just grab a quick lunch. Her phone vibrated in her pocket, and she pulled it out to answer without thinking.

"Hello," she said. "Hello? Hey, I'm on the stairs, and my reception isn't great." She looked at the number, wondering why her caller ID hadn't picked up on a name. "Look, call me later," she said in frustration. The door on the floor below her opened, and Derrick rounded the corner, coming her way. She drew up short. "Hey.".

"Hey. Look, I'll start taking the elevator."

"I don't care what you do," Presley told him with a raised eyebrow. He nodded and started to walk past her but turned around a few steps above.

"I hear you're dating the guy from the elevator."

"So what if I am?" she returned with irritation. "It's my business."

"As long as you're happy."

"I am," she told him shortly, heading back downstairs. She could feel him watching her, and as uncomfortable as it made her, she had to admit there was a little satisfaction in knowing that she had thrown him off stride, as surely as he'd once thrown her. Besides, she thought to herself, she was happy with Donovan. It was weird, in a way, to have a relationship after so long, but they just seemed to work.

When Presley made it to the cafeteria, she chatted with a few of the workers while choosing the options she wanted on the hot buffet. By the time she made it to the table, her irritation at seeing Derrick had faded to a different kind of irritation. The PTO hearing was coming up, and she'd already made sure she'd have the day free to attend. She wasn't looking forward to that particular awkward encounter either, not after her last run-in with Noah. She rolled her shoulders and wished that she wasn't so nervous about it. After all, they were taking action this time, when last time they'd pretty much let him walk off Scot-free. That was progress. She speared a diced potato on her fork and hoped the rest of her shift would pass quickly, without so many complications and cranky patients.

When Donovan called as she was heading back up, she answered quickly. "Was that you who called earlier?"

"No, I didn't call. Look, I've got not-great news," he said without preamble. "My schedule's getting changed. I'm having to switch weekend rotations."

"Okay, so we'll be on opposite schedules?"

"Yeah, looks like it," he said with a sigh.

"Starting when?"

"Starting now."

"But the TPO hearing …" Presley trailed off. She knew he couldn't help the schedule change. She'd had it happen herself enough to know. But he'd promised to come with her and Layla to face Noah.

"I know," he said, clearly irritated. "I can't do anything about it."

"I know that," she returned, her own irritation rising. "Why are you mad at me?".

"I'm not," he said and then sighed. "I'm really not. I'm mad at the situation. What are we going to do?"

"What do you want to do?" she fired back, not sure if they were breaking up or what.

"Look, I—" He broke off, and she could hear background noise. "Hey, I've got to go. I'll call you later," he said, hanging up before she could answer.

Presley put away her phone and hurried up the stairs. She needed to check on a few charts and see if anyone had come in during the half hour she'd shoved food in her face. She felt an uneasiness about the day. After all, it was bad enough that she'd had another awkward encounter with her ex. Now she wasn't sure when she'd ever see

Donovan, if he still wanted to see her at all. Added to all that, she could feel herself tensing for the court date coming up. Now she'd have to face it without Donovan by her side, and she could feel her anxiety creeping up higher than she liked. She took a few deep breaths. She needed to be the professional, not the patient, after all.

She reached for the door, and it was locked. She swiped her badge against the keypad by the door and waited. When that didn't work, she shifted her ever-present tote and entered the code. Damn, she thought to herself. Still, not working. She looked up and then down the stairs. Amber was working the floor below, if she wasn't mistaken. She jogged up to the floor above and was able to enter without a problem. She waved at the receptionist at the desk and headed to the elevator. She stepped in, selecting the floor below, and wondered what else could go wrong. Of course, she thought to herself sarcastically, that was a great thought to have in an elevator, where she could get stuck for hours. After a minute, the doors opened on her own floor, and she breathed out a sigh.

"Thought you went to the cafeteria," one of the nurses called out from the desk.

"I did. Got locked out. Again," Presley answered with a roll of her eyes.

"Third time this week?" the nurse asked with a grin.

"Something like that," she said, not wanting to admit it had been the fourth. "I guess I should start taking the elevator."

"I'll call maintenance and see what we can do about it," Erin said from behind the counter.

"Appreciate it," Presley told her. "Now, what'd I miss?"

***

Layla stumbled out of the darkened theater into the bright sunlight. She blinked at Jude and grabbed his arm to steady herself.

"That," she breathed. "Was amazing!"

"Have you never been to a planetarium before?"

"Maybe a couple times as a kid, on school field trips. But it was nothing like that."

"I take it you liked it."

"You know I did. Now. Food?"

"We'll hit up The Rookery downtown. You good with burgers and shakes?"

"Do I have a pulse?" she asked with a snort. "Of course I am. Are we still walking after?" she asked, looking at him speculatively.

"Well, I did buy you sweater socks before we got here," he said with a grin.

"That's true," she said with a laugh. "I guess I'm game. Where are we walking?"

"First, food. You'll like this place. It's just a few minutes from here, downtown."

"I'll be fine with whatever. I'm starving!" she told him dramatically. "You know, this isn't a date."

"So you've said about a hundred times."

"No, I mean we both know it's not a date, but I have to say this would make a great date idea."

"Yeah, well, I'll keep that in mind."

"I don't mean for me."

"Who said with you?" he asked her with a laugh. "But I might just get my feelings hurt if you keep saying that."

"As if," she said with a laugh of her own.

"Do people still say that?"

"Not since the '90s," she agreed. "But what can I say, I'm an old soul."

"Okay, the fact that you just called the '90s old just hurt my heart," he told her, patting his chest dramatically.

"I think you're going to live. Besides, you are older than me, right?"

"We're talking a few years, not decades. So ... glad you got out of the house?"

"Yeah, I really am. You're a really good friend."

"I know that you've friend-zoned me. You don't have to keep saying it," he said in mock exasperation.

"I mean it though. I appreciate you."

"Yeah, well, it's helping me, too. At least I'm not sitting around angry because another weekend has gone by without the kids."

"You know, I bet they'd like the planetarium, too."

"Yeah, I thought about that," Jude answered honestly.

"Is this what you were going to do with them?"

"With some modifications, yes. But since they can't be here, I thought I'd just check it all out."

"I think they'll love it. And who doesn't love a shake?" she asked, as they got out of the truck to walk toward The Rookery.

"Right? That's what I was thinking. But I guess they'd prefer the cabin in the mountains."

"Okay, trapped inside with grownups or an adventure?" Layla held out her hands like an imaginary scale, weighing the options. "I think I'll take the adventure, Alex, for five hundred."

"You're too young for that reference," he pointed out playfully.

"We watched a lot of game shows when my mom was sick. It was kind of our thing. *Jeopardy*, *Wheel of Fortune*, *The Price is Right*. *Family Feud* was our favorite though. Anyway, I think I'd take a pastry by a warm fire, a trip to the stars, and burgers and shakes over being stuck with a parent and some boyfriend in a cabin when it's too cold and probably isolated to even go outside and play."

"Yeah, that's true," he said, brightening. "How are the socks?"

"Oh my God, they're the best. My toes are toasty now," she said with a smile. "I didn't thank you for that." After the planetarium, he'd pulled her into a shop and bought her sweater socks. She'd chosen a pair with gnomes, calling them whimsical.

"You didn't need to. Okay, so, I have to ask. Did you and your mom have a *Price is Right* dance? You know, the thing you'd do if your name got called?" he asked, as they approached the restaurant.

"Of course," Layla said with a snort. "We regularly practiced it. Before she got too sick anyway. We talked about going sometime, getting in the audience. My mom could eyeball anything and guess the right price almost to the dollar. I got her genes," she said with a grin.

"Alright. Let's see it," Jude challenged her.

"What?" Layla laughed. "My mad pricing skills? My dance?"

"The dance. Let's see it," Jude said, stopping on the pavement. "I dare you to do your *Price is Right* dance into the restaurant."

"You are so weird," she told him with a laugh. "Okay, fine. I'll do my *Price is Right* dance if you'll take your hair down."

"Only until the burgers come, and then I get to pull it back up."

"Fine," she said, sticking out her hand to shake his. He shook it firmly, and she grinned. "I'm going to need you to give me the intro," she told him as he reached out and pulled the rubber band out of his hair, shaking it out. She had to admit, to herself anyway, that his hair was pretty sexy.

"Layla Westerman, you are the next contestant on the *Price is Right*," Jude said dramatically, in his best Bob Barker impression. Layla grinned and did a full-blown happy dance down the sidewalk and into the restaurant with Jude laughing behind her. A handful of people on the sidewalk burst into applause, and Layla blew them a kiss, laughing.

"I'm not sure what that was about, but can I get you a table for two?" the host asked with a grin.

"Please," Jude said, then turning to Layla. "That was worth it."

"So was this," she said, reaching up to touch the tips of his hair, with his blonde curls. She felt a jolt of electricity run through her, and she met his eyes. She could see them narrow with interest and then darken, and she took a deep breath and a step back with a smile.

"I hope you know that you're the only one since my mom who has seen that dance."

"And the world is worse off for it," Jude said, taking a seat across from her. "We're going to need to start with shakes," he told their server.

"I'm going to need a double," Layla said.

"Chocolate?" the server confirmed.

"I'm going to need the Jimmy Carter," Jude corrected. "Banana, peanut butter, and bacon," he explained to Layla.

"Um, eew," she grimaced.

"You just wait. You're going to want to try it."

"Sometimes I want to try things that aren't good for me," she told him playfully.

"Sometimes you're afraid to try things that could be good for you," he pointed out, leaning back.

"Fair point. But sometimes you need to be ready," she said, looking at him evenly, a smile tugging at the corner of her lips.

"True enough. Now about these burgers ..." He shook the menu and began looking at the options with mock seriousness.

Chapter 20

After Jude shut off the truck, he made no move to get out. Layla looked at him quizzically, watching the expressions play over his face.

"What's your problem? Are we getting out?"

"I think I'm insensitive."

"Yeah, well, you're a man," Layla joked, rolling her eyes. "About what?"

"I thought we could walk at this historic cemetery. I mean, it's scenic, but I didn't think about your mom," Jude pointed out uncertainly.

"Jude," Layla said, with exaggerated patience, "I've been to cemeteries before. I even go on tours at Halloween. It's not a big deal."

"Okay, fine. I just wanted to make sure," he said, finally taking off his seat belt. "Let's just do a short walk, and then maybe we can head back if you're ready."

"Are you ready to go home?" she asked him, taking off her own seat belt and opening the door. He walked around to her side to help her down.

"I'm happy spending the day with you," he replied honestly. She looked at him skeptically, trying to read if he was saying more than it seemed. When she was satisfied that he meant just what he said, she nodded.

"We can stay as long as you like. I have no interest in going back to the cage just yet."

"You know, you could always stay at my place," Jude told her and then laughed when she puffed out a breath. "I didn't mean that way. Although …" he paused and winked at her. "But it's a big house. We have a couple of guest rooms, if you just need a change of scene."

"I appreciate that. I just hate feeling like I'm under lock and key," she complained. "*He* should be under lock and key," she muttered.

"Yeah, I wish it were that easy. Has he bothered you lately?"

"He hasn't really had the opportunity. Although we had a couple of weird calls the other day."

"We?" Jude asked. "Is that like the royal *we*?"

"No," Layla said with a grin. "You're so weird! I meant me and Presley. Couple of strange calls. No number, no one on the line that we could hear."

"Why'd you answer? I mean, don't you screen any of your calls?"

"I just picked it up without thinking," she admitted with a shrug, walking down the path beside him. She had to admit that even in winter it was pretty enough. It would be spring soon. In fact, it was strange to think that Valentine's Day was only a couple of days after the hearing. The year was already moving so fast, she thought to herself. "I mean, it could have been solicitors, but it was a few calls. One was in the middle of the night."

"You could have called me."

"And say what?" Layla countered. "That I got a handful of calls? It could have been solicitors or wrong numbers. I don't know. The number was blocked, so there's no way to prove anything." "I could have come over," Jude told her, his eyebrows drawn sharply together in consternation.

"Stop that," she told him, reaching up to forcibly smooth out his face with her hands. "Anyone ever tell you that's how you get wrinkles?" she asked him with a grin. He smiled at her, and she realized how close they were standing and that her hands were still holding his face. She brought them down and then jolted when he took her hands in his. She looked up at him curiously.

"Your hands are absolutely freezing. Didn't you bring gloves?"

"I went out so quickly I left them on the counter."

"Here," he said, slipping off one of his gloves and handing it over.

"Now you're going to have one cold hand."

"No, look," he said. He put the glove on her left hand and then tucked her right hand into the glove he was wearing. He then stuck his own left hand into his pocket. "See?" he told her with a smile.

"You're holding my hand," Layla pointed out.

"It's not cold now, is it?" he asked her with an eyebrow raised. She rolled her eyes, and he grinned.

"Fine. Thanks," she added, wiggling her fingers and admitting, to herself anyway, that it was more comfortable this way. His big hand dwarfed her small one, and his glove was roomy enough to fit her hand comfortably inside.

"We'll go back in a few minutes. I just wanted to show you the view."

"I like it," Layla said, surveying the area around her.

"In the spring, it's actually a nice quiet spot to read."

"How'd you find this?"

"Guy from my work? The one who ..." he trailed off. Layla nodded. "He's up there," he pointed up a hill. "It was the first time I came here, and sometimes I found myself coming back, just to tell him what was going on at the job site. It's really peaceful here, actually. Made me feel better about it, in a strange way."

"Yeah," Layla agreed, nodding. "The place where my mom is? It's quiet like this. And pretty. There are flowers, real ones. I know she liked it because she chose it when she was sick."

"That's tough," Jude said, squeezing her hand.

"Yeah, it was. But it was good that she got what she wanted. I mean, not to get better and to live longer, but she got to choose how she wanted things at the end," Layla explained. "Can I say a thing and you not be weird?" He'd pulled his hair back down when they'd left the restaurant, to her amusement, and it blew a little in his face.

"I make no promises," he told her with a small smile.

"You've actually been a pretty great friend," she admitted and then looked at him sharply to see if he was going to misread her.

"So have you," he said with a wide smile. "And I got to see your game show contestant dance. Might have been the highlight of my day."

"Shut up," she laughed, bumping against him playfully.

"Ready to go?"

"In a minute," she said, motioning to a bench and sitting beside him. She leaned her head against his shoulder and sighed. "This was a good idea."

"Getting better and better," he grinned into her hair.

"I can feel you smiling."

"It's the view," he said with a laugh in his voice.

***

Presley got off work and eyed the stairs. She wondered what the odds were that she would (a) lock herself in the stairwell again; or (b) run into Derrick for a second time that day. She assessed the probabilities and decided the odds were likely against either eventuality, but she headed for the elevator anyway. She grabbed her tote and swung it over her shoulder. Her laptop clunked heavily against her hip, and she winced. She was angry, she admitted. Or maybe *frustrated* was the better word, she thought to herself. She didn't know what Donovan had been planning to say, but she could just bet she wasn't going to like it one bit.

She stepped into the elevator and impatiently pressed her button multiple times, as if it would make the elevator magically hurry up and descend. When the elevator opened a floor below, she couldn't believe it when she saw Amber waiting, although her back was turned to the elevator bank.

"Look, can we just ..." she hissed into the phone, trying to keep her voice down. "We're going to talk about this when I get home," she warned the caller and then looked at the phone in shock when whoever was on the other end obviously hung up. Presley had a pretty good idea who she'd been talking to and suppressed a smile, keeping her face as neutral as she was able.

Amber spun toward the door and caught it with her hand, tossing her phone in her bag and entering without even noticing Presley—at first. When she did, Presley decided that her face must not have been set completely in neutral after all. Amber took one look at her and rolled her eyes.

"You don't have to look so smug," Amber said with irritation. "It's nothing."

Presley shrugged, saying nothing and facing the door, leaning against the opposite wall from Amber. She finally said, "Not my business."

"No, it's not," Amber agreed, crossing her arms in front of her. She looked at Presley a couple times.

"Something on my face?" Presley asked blandly, observing from her peripheral vision the repeated looks.

"I hear you're dating that patient's brother," Amber said, not minding her own business. Presley shrugged. She wasn't even sure if it was still true, and the last person she wanted to talk to about that was the woman who had done everything she could to wreck Presley's last relationship. "You're not supposed to date patients."

"Last time I checked, Donovan doesn't have a vagina. He could hardly be my patient," she said smoothly, a twitch of a smile playing on her lips. She was impressed that she'd come up with the perfect reply in real time instead of hours after, but she was still probably riding the wave of irritation she'd been on since Donovan had called. Amber sighed dramatically and pushed the button to the lobby again.

"Was—" Amber began and then cut herself off.

"What?" Presley asked, wondering how long it took an elevator to descend. It usually didn't seem this slow.

"Was Derrick always so …" Amber tried to find the word.

"Conflict avoidant? Passive aggressive? Selfish? Unfaithful?" Presley listed, adding some heat to the last item on the list. "You're going to have to be more specific."

"Ugh," Amber groaned aloud. "All of that, I guess. I mean, was he like that with you?"

"Yep," Presley said shortly.

"But you seemed so ..." she broke off, realizing what she was saying.

"Yeah, well, he could also be really sweet, when he wanted to be. And smart. And funny. Anyway, it wasn't perfect," she explained, shrugging.

"But the rest of it?"

"He was those other things, too. If he hadn't started up with you, I'd have figured that out and got gone. Eventually," Presley admitted, realizing that it was actually true. She felt a weight lift that she hadn't realized was there. Amber, unbeknownst to her, had actually saved her some time she'd have wasted with Derrick. "Is he cheating on you?"

"I don't know," Amber said with a shrug. She paused, eyeing Presley and then admitted. "He keeps his phone face down, when he's with me."

"Then you know."

Amber sighed, long and loud. "You must be happy. To know he's doing to me what we did to you," she said, as the elevator doors opened and they both headed to the parking garage.

"Actually, I'm not. Believe it or not, Amber, I wouldn't wish on anyone else what you both did to me," Presley said honestly, meeting her eyes, and seeing for the first time a little shame enter them. "This might be one of those *be careful what you wish for* situations," she continued with a shrug. She started to walk away, heading toward her car, then she turned back. "Hey," she called.

"What?" Amber asked, frustrated.

"Don't take any shit from him," she warned, and then headed to the car.

"I won't," she heard behind her. Amber's tone was grim. She would have laid pretty good odds that Derrick was going to pay for hanging up on her earlier. Presley grinned, a little surprised at herself that she'd be Team Amber for any reason. Well, she admitted to herself, they did kind of deserve each other, but maybe one of them would grow up from it.

She walked to her car and looked up annoyed at the busted lights in the parking lot. She took out her phone and called Wes. "Hey, sorry to bother you," she said when he answered. She spent a few minutes catching up on the family before she finally made it over to her car, walking gingerly through the darkened parking lot and cursing the fact that she wasn't one of those handy people who carried a flashlight on her. "Look, I just wanted to give you a heads up that there are lights out on the south side parking lot. I mean, it's pitch black out here," she told him and then listened to his response. "No, I'm good. I'm not scared. I just wanted to give you a heads up." She listened again and nodded. "I appreciate you, Wes. Let's all grab lunch when you have time. I want to kiss that baby."

She chuckled as she hung up the phone. Wes was a good guy, and if he said he'd send someone out to fix it right away or come into work to do it personally she believed him. She fumbled in her bag for her keys and kicked herself that she hadn't gotten them out earlier. She admitted that the whole encounter with Amber had been unprecedented and more than a little distracting. She found the keys and then dropped them, cursing aloud. A car pulled up an aisle or so over, and she caught a glimpse of her keys in the flash of headlights.

She felt really stupid as she remembered that her phone actually had a flashlight function, so she was, in fact, one of those handy people who carry one around. She turned it on and easily made her way to her car, sighing when the door lock function wouldn't work correctly. She braced herself for the alarm, as she stuck her key into the door. She quickly entered and put her key in the ignition to cut off the sound. She knew security wouldn't even come out and check and would likely tease her about it on her next shift, but she hadn't had time to get the key fixed. Hey, she thought to herself grimly, if Donovan breaks up with me, I'll have plenty of time for stuff like that.

She headed home, trying to ignore the tension headache she'd been fighting since she'd grabbed a bite to eat. Today was just—too much, she decided. She just wanted to take a long bath and go straight to bed. When she pulled up and saw Donovan's car waiting, she saw her plans for an early night evaporating. She could admit that maybe she slammed her car door a little harder than strictly necessary.

"You don't exactly look happy to see me," Donovan noted, leaning up against his car. It wasn't the police cruiser anyway, so he must have been home to change already, she thought.

"I'm just tired," Presley said shortly, not sure how to handle this. She nodded toward the stairs and headed up them without going to him first. She could feel his frown behind her, but she wasn't sure what it meant.

"Bad day?"

"Something like that," she said, opening the door and cutting on the lights. She went inside and could hear him following behind. She went straight for the fridge and pulled out a Coke. If she couldn't have an early night, she'd take the caffeine instead. "Want anything?" she asked him from the fridge.

"You ever going to look at me?"

Presley stood up slowly and met his eyes over the door of the fridge, taking out a Coke and slowly closing the door. "What?"

"So that's it? We're just done?"

"I don't know. You tell me," she said evenly, stepping around him and heading to the adjoining living room.

Presley handed him the Coke and then went to the couch. She immediately kicked off her shoes, curled her feet under her, pulled a blanket up to her chin, and put the Coke against her forehead rather than opening it. She could feel him sit down carefully at the other end of the couch.

"Headache, baby?" he asked her. She kept her eyes closed and was grateful that he couldn't see the tears that would have welled up in her eyes at his tone.

"Mmm hmm," she murmured.

"Come here," he said, reaching and pulling her head into his lap, grabbing a pillow to prop up her head. She could feel him taking the blanket and covering her up, tucking it around her. She tried to stop the tears leaking from her eyes but couldn't. "That bad?" he asked softly.

When she shook her head no, he brushed her fringe of nearly jet-black bangs back. She knew she needed to get them trimmed again. He kept stroking her head.

"You thought we were over? Just like that?"

She nodded, keeping her eyes shut tight and the Coke pressed against her head where the headache was starting to ease up.

"Well, you're not getting rid of me that easily," he told her, and she could feel him kick his feet up on the coffee table and stretch out. She nuzzled her head toward his chest and reached out for one of his hands. "Give me a few minutes, and then I'll run you a bath. Then we can call it an early night if you want me to stay."

She nodded, squeezing his hand.

"I'm going to need you to say it," he told her gently.

"Stay," she told him shortly, opening her eyes and feeling more tears spill out.

"We'll work it out. We'll just have to find a way," he told her, bringing her hand to his lips and kissing the back of it before turning it to place a kiss in her open palm. "You've got to have a little more faith in us."

Presley sat up slowly and put the Coke on the end table. Then she moved the pillow and climbed into Donovan's lap, placing her head on his shoulder. He cupped the back of her head and started stroking her hair.

"Better?"

"Yes," she said softly. "Can we talk about everything tomorrow?"

"Yeah. Let's get you in that bath. No funny business, I promise. You can relax and maybe tell me a little bit about your day."

"Well, I thought my boyfriend was breaking up with me," she said with a raised eyebrow.

"I mean, other than that. I told you, I'm not going anywhere," he reminded her, leading the way to the bathroom. He turned on the water as hot as it would go, just like she liked it, and dumped in probably a little too much bubble bath. She smiled at him, wiping away the tears on her cheeks.

"Are you getting in with me?"

"I don't think I'd quite fit, and I don't know that I can be trusted to keep my hands off you if we're both slippery," he pointed out with a wide grin.

"What if I don't want you to?" she asked him saucily, feeling a little better.

"Quit," he laughed. "Tell me about your day," he continued, sitting down on the floor and stretching out his legs. He whistled as Presley undressed, and she laughed.

"Okay, I'll start with the babies, but then I need to tell you about my two awkward encounters. Oh, and I got locked out on the stairwell again," Presley said, stepping gingerly into the bath and adjusting to the heat.

"Presley, that's, what, five times?" Donovan asked with a laugh.

"Four," she said, defending herself. "Anyway ..."

Chapter 21

Noah James looked around the empty bathroom at the courthouse with a quick assessing gaze. He made sure to check underneath the stalls for telltale shoes signaling occupants. Satisfied that he was alone, he walked over to the mirror and looked at himself critically. His dark red hair was conservatively cut. He consciously smoothed out the frown line at his forehead. He'd never liked the red, but he found that it made people think of him a certain way that was helpful. He wasn't sure why it made him appear so affable, but he wasn't going to question the success of it.

He looked at his face and made sure that it showed what he wanted. He'd always been good at this. He'd learned the technique of clearing his emotions in an early theater class his mother later regretted taking him to. He could make them play across his face on command, and he had an uncanny way of sensing which would work. He tried a few now, and then he cleared his face carefully when he heard the door open.

He washed his hands, taking care not to acknowledge the other man who entered with anything more than a nod. As much as he hated observing social niceties, he knew it was necessary. Sometimes it was even entertaining to see just how far he could go and just how much they would believe. He thought about striking up a conversation but thought better of it. After all, he was sure Layla was anxiously waiting on him.

He exited the restroom calmly, his face betraying little more than mild concern and boredom. He selected a seat in the back of the courtroom where he could see all the players easily. He hadn't expected this particular move. Noah admitted that he'd experienced one wave of rage after another when he'd first been served the TPO.

Had he been a less careful man, he might have betrayed that anger in front of the officer. Luckily, he'd been ready with a look of confusion and concern, had even managed to shake his head and express the difficulties of having dated such a vengeful woman. He'd nearly smiled at that. Layla had been a mouse but one he could mold so easily. He looked at her now and saw her fidgeting. She was nervous alright. She would never have had the guts to file if it hadn't been for her sister.

Noah looked Presley over with disappointment. He'd been sure they had a connection. In fact, he was hoping to be able to exploit it a little further down the road. He'd been entertaining himself with Naomi in the meantime, but he'd had plans for Presley. She'd proven to be so much less pliable than her sister and much more suspicious, although not at first. He watched her out of the corner of his eyes while calmly turning the pages of a newspaper he'd brought as a prop. When he was done with that, he'd brought a book of Sudoku to amuse himself as needed.

He looked at the man seated next to Layla and wondered if he was going to need to do something about that. He wasn't surprised Presley was alone. He'd anticipated that, but it did surprise him that Layla would bring a plus-one when she knew how jealous he could be.

Noah looked at the conservative picture she made in her frilled white collar and plain gray skirt and wondered if she thought that disguised the kind of whore she was. He could still feel her writhing beneath him, her hands reaching up to try to pull his hands off her throat, her body bucking with pleasure. He looked down, shifting the newspaper carefully over his lap. He knew her well and would know her better before this was over. He wondered if the man she'd brought with her had enjoyed her body already. He knew that he could find out easily enough. They weren't the only ones who could set up cameras, and he'd been the first to think of it, after all.

He watched their little tableau, how they leaned together to talk.

He knew the exact moment when they became aware of him and calmly completed the Sudoku, as if he had no other care in the world. He let them observe him, even waved at the asshole beside Layla. She didn't turn, not that he'd expected her to, but he'd known that Presley couldn't resist. Her reaction couldn't have pleased him more, or made him more coldly furious. He let the delight and rage twist inside him and wondered if they had any idea what was coming next.

***

Layla sat in the dress she'd selected for the hearing and fidgeted. Libby had stopped by to help her pick something out. It had a high frilly collar that was a little old-fashioned, and the gray skirt fell just below her knees. Even her heels were conservative, charcoal pumps with the tiniest bow. She'd paired it with pearl earrings and felt like she was impersonating someone else entirely. Presley, she thought, looking at her sister, looked entirely like herself in jeans and a sweater. Of course, she was just moral support, so no one was going to be focusing on her.

"Quit it," Presley hissed. "You're making me nervous. I'm nervous enough as it is."

"I can't help it," Layla said, shifting in her seat and crossing and uncrossing her legs. She glanced at the door again, until Presley smacked her leg.

"Are you worried about seeing him?"

Layla swallowed, hard. She'd forgotten about Noah, for just a minute. She'd been thinking about Jude, and as if she conjured him, he walked through the door and immediately met her eyes. "Of course I am," she told her sister absently. "Hi," she told Jude.

"Sorry I couldn't get here any earlier," he said, sitting down to flank Layla's other side.

"At least you're here," Presley said, leaning back in her seat with a sigh.

"Are you okay?" Layla asked him, sensing something off.

"Guess I forgot to get gas. Almost didn't make it," Jude said shortly, obviously not wanting to talk about it. "I took JP's car."

"How's he getting to work?"

"He's not going in until later. Is the asshole here yet?"

"Not yet," Layla said, just as Presley said, "Yep." Layla and Jude shot her a look.

"What?" she asked them. "Look, I saw him sitting in a car outside when I pulled up, and then he came in just a second ago. Don't look now, but he's sitting in the back corner, watching us."

"How do you know if you're not looking?" Jude asked her suspiciously.

"My lip balm fell out of my purse, and I caught a look at him when I turned to get it," she said with a shrug. Jude ignored her advice and turned to look in the back of the room, his arm casually around Layla's shoulder. Layla didn't dare look at Noah, but she turned to look at Jude, scooting closer to him.

"Well?" she asked quietly.

"He looks more normal than I expected," Jude admitted, meeting her eyes. "But I'm thinking sociopath normal. He just waved at me when I looked at him." Layla felt her mouth go dry and the color leach out of her face. "Hey," he told her, tapping a hand to her shoulder. "It's going to be okay. It'll be over soon."

"I just have a bad feeling about this," Layla said quietly, feeling like she was going to be sick. "I think I'm going to be sick."

"No, you're not," Presley hissed over at her. "If you do that, you have to walk past him, and one look at your face will let him know he got to you. Don't you dare give him the satisfaction." She turned nonchalantly in her own seat and appraised him. He looked up from whatever he was doodling on and smiled at her. She lifted a single finger and turned back around in her seat.

"Presley," Layla breathed. "You'll make it worse."

"Well, fuck him," Presley said, louder than she'd meant to. People turned in their seats, and she calmed herself down. Or at least made her voice quieter. "Seriously, Layla, fuck him. Don't let his weaselly ass get to you."

"Your sister has some fire in her," Jude said with a grin.

"It's a family trait," Presley told him, reaching out to squeeze Layla's hand.

"It's about to start," Jude told them, nodding as the court reporter filed into the room and took a seat. "Are you ready?"

"No," Layla said quietly, and then, "Yes. Yeah, let's get this over with."

***

About an hour later, Layla managed to stumble out of the courtroom and into a bathroom with Presley right on her heels. She hit the first stall and was vomiting before the door closed behind her. She felt her sister enter the stall with her and close the door. Presley's hands scooped her hair back, but she didn't say a word. When she was done, she sat up with a tear-streaked face and met Presley's eyes, wide in her own pale face.

"I can't fucking believe it," Presley said. Layla considered that this was the most profanity she'd heard her sister use since the whole Derrick situation, and before that when their mom died.

"I can," Layla said roughly. Noah had wiped the smile off his face and approached the courtroom looking properly somber and concerned, aggrieved even. Layla watched him slide on the mask and felt a weight drop into her stomach. She'd thought she'd have a full-blown panic attack, only she needed to observe everything she could. She, more than maybe anyone, knew his tells.

He'd gotten up and produced proof of work schedules and letters from his boss and colleagues showing that he had been working over an hour away in Atlanta at the time in question. He even nodded to a man in the back who he could bring up as a witness. The judge seemed satisfied. By the time Noah was done, it sounded like she was an ex out for revenge, not the victim of a clear attack. Noah even made it sound like she'd likely made the whole story up, something he claimed she'd done in the past for attention. Even though they'd scored a female judge, Layla knew how effective and disarming he could be when he tried. By the time she left the courtroom, she'd been summarily dismissed and made to feel ashamed for causing trouble. The case was dismissed, and there was no protective order left between her and Noah now.

"Don't let them make you think you're wrong. You know he did this," Presley said fiercely, crouching down to look her sister in the eyes.

"I know he did. Pres, I know it," Layla said, tears spilling out. "It's going to get worse."

"I honestly thought Jude was going to get up and punch him. I'd have paid to see it."

"Yeah," Layla let out a shaky laugh. "He'd have flattened him, too." They both paused to think about the well-built Jude effortlessly laying Noah out. Noah had come in wearing a suit, his dark red hair conservatively styled. He looked like your typical boy-next-door, fresh-faced and unassuming. But Layla had seen the evil in his eyes up close. She knew what she was up against. She just had to decide what she was going to do about it.

"Jude's going to worry," Presley told her, helping Layla up.

"I know," Layla said with a sigh.

"You sure you don't want to date him? I mean, he showed up, which is more than I can say for my boyfriend."

"I know, but I just can't ... not with all this. Just go out and tell him I'll be out in a sec? Please? Pres, I need a minute." Presley hugged her and went out without another word.

She looked in the mirror and wondered what was worse, Noah's airtight alibi and the way he'd easily turned the judge on her or the way he'd smiled and winked as he turned to go. She didn't think anyone else had seen it, but she knew that she was going to pay for this day. She looked in the mirror and wondered how high the price might be, and if it would spill over to the ones she loved.

***

Presley had seen the look, but that was because she was sure it was directed at her. She didn't know what to make of it. She guessed that she probably shouldn't have flipped him off right before court started. Once again, she'd reacted, and it might have put Layla in danger. She sighed and wondered why she didn't think of that sort of thing before reacting.

Her phone vibrated, and she looked down to turn it back on while she stood with Jude waiting for Layla to come out. She'd actually thought something good would have come of this, despite Donovan telling her it likely wouldn't go in Layla's favor. She looked at the message from him and fired one back. It had gone to shit, she admitted. He replied to say he'd call her when he could, and she shrugged, sending an okay and then tucking the phone into her pocket.

"Everything okay?" Jude asked, leaning against the wall beside her.

"Not really. That was just Donovan checking in. I don't know how to protect her," she said, nodding toward the bathroom.

"It's not really your job" W.hen Presley opened her mouth for a fierce rebuttal, he lifted a hand in the universally accepted gesture of peace. "I know you're the big sister. I get all that. I'm just saying it might take all of us. Including Layla. She's going to have to be extra careful, and she's already having a hard time with that."

"I know," Presley said with a sigh, relaxing next to him. "You own a gun?" she asked him with an appraising look.

"Why?" he asked her evenly, meeting her eyes. "You think I'm going to need one?"

"Layla doesn't carry. Maybe she should. But I'd feel better if somebody close did. Look, before she comes out, I hate to ask this, but can you stay with her tonight?"

"Are you pimping out your sister?" Jude asked with raised eyebrows.

Presley rolled her eyes and continued, "You know what I mean. I can't tonight. I've got to go into work to sub in for someone who's out sick, and I don't know where the hell Naomi is because she was supposed to be here and didn't show up so I can't count on her. Hey, if you can't, I'll call Lindy. Or Libby. Somebody."

"Hey, as long as Layla's good with it, I can occupy the couch. And, yeah, I carry. Let me talk to her about it though. I don't want her to think we're ganging up on her."

"Even though we are."

"Oh, hell yeah. Until this bastard stops or someone stops him."

"Whichever comes first."

"Do you carry?" he asked her, curiously as Layla stepped out and looked down the hall to find them.

"No. But maybe I should," she said quietly, waving to Layla to get her attention.

Chapter 22

Layla carried blankets and pillows down the stairs and wondered how she'd been talked into this. It's weird, she thought to herself. She wasn't sure if she'd ever had a male friend sleep in her home. Friends with benefits, sure, she thought. But not a friend she was attracted to who wasn't a friend with benefits or someone she was dating. It felt strange. She came downstairs where Jude was still standing by the window, looking out, a duffle bag by his feet. He'd even insisted she wait with him while he packed the damn thing, she thought with frustration. She walked over and set the pile of blankets and pillows on the couch.

"Bird watching?"

"If you've got things to do, you don't have to keep me company," he said, sensing her discomfort.

"My things to do actually involve this TV. Unless I want to go to bed right after dinner, I guess you're just going to have to put up with me."

"Your place," he pointed out easily with a careless shrug. "Why don't I make dinner?"

"I know how to cook," she said sharply.

"How about I go one better, and we just order in. Do you even feel like cooking tonight?"

She'd mentioned to him once that Noah had taught her how to cook and then later used it as part of the abuse. She'd cook, he'd throw it on the floor or against the wall and make her clean it up or dump it straight in the trash and have her start again. That was toward the end, when she knew she had to get out but wasn't sure how. She could see Jude remembering that, and she knew that she really didn't feel like cooking today. Noah had ruined the kitchen for her. One day, she'd take it back. Not today though.

"No. No, I don't," she answered softly, deflating.

"What would you like? I'll order."

"I want Noah to go away and stay gone," Layla began, closing her eyes. "I want to never have met him. I want to feel like a whole person and not a broken one."

Jude stepped forward and pulled her in for a hug. When he stepped back, still holding her shoulders, he looked into her eyes and said, "I meant to eat." He smiled at her, brushing a tear from her cheek, and she offered a weak smile in return.

"Chinese?"

He nodded. "Now that I can do." He found a menu online and took down her choices. After he hung up the call, he looked over at her and said, "You're not broken."

"I feel like I am." She headed to the kitchen and took out a bottle of wine. She took down two glasses and filled them up.

"What you did today was brave," he reminded her, taking a glass and not saying a word about how much she'd poured into it.

"What I did today was probably stupid," she corrected him. "He's going to hit back harder than ever now."

"But he was always going to hit back hard. You just showed him that you're not going to keep quiet about it anymore," Jude told her evenly. "He hits back hard, and you report it. Until he gets the message, or someone stops him."

Layla considered. "I hadn't thought of it that way." She was quiet for a minute, sipping her wine, and then nodded. "I can do that."

"Not broken."

"Maybe not."

"I need to tell you something, since I'm staying here," Jude began. Layla tilted her head and motioned for him to continue, lifting the glass to her lips again. "I'm licensed to carry concealed. I did bring my gun. Just in case."

Layla took a sip and paused, considered. "I think, under the circumstances, I'm okay with that. You any good with it?"

"I hope we don't have to find out. But, yeah, I'm good at a shooting range."

"I asked Donovan to show me a little hand to hand combat," Layla admitted. "I haven't said anything to Presley yet, but I will. I just thought it might be good to know—how to protect myself, I mean."

"Smart."

"Necessary."

"You think he'll come after you like that?"

"It would be in character. He didn't start out hurting me physically. He did everything else first," she admitted, shrugging and looking down into her glass. She noted it was empty and poured another one, her hands a little shakier than she liked, then held the bottle toward Jude who shrugged and held his out to be topped off. She sloshed just a little over the edge, and he reached over to take the bottle, setting it down on the counter.

"I hated him before, but now I'm hoping for a chance to shoot him," Jude said hotly. Layla laughed, and then clapped a hand over her mouth, surprised. She started giggling and then full out laughing, and Jude just grinned at her uncertainly.

"I haven't lost my mind," she said when she finally calmed herself. "It's just … you shooting Noah. God, I'd pay to see that. You're just the sweetest," she told him with a smile, feeling the best she had all day.

"What is it we're watching tonight anyway?" he asked her, glad the laughter had brought color back into her cheeks. She'd been looking wan all day.

"Well, I can't watch the rest of *Jessica Jones* or Presley will be pissed," Layla said regretfully. "But maybe something like that."

"We could do Daredevil," Jude offered. "Or go old-school."

"What'd you have in mind?"

"Maybe a little Buffy. Or Alias."

"You'd watch that with me?"

"Yeah, why not?"

"We can do a Buffy marathon," Layla offered. "I've always wanted to see it."

"Wait," Donovan interrupted. "You've never seen *Buffy the Vampire Slayer*? What planet are you from?"

"Planet I-Was-Born-After-You," she pointed out with a grin.

"Says the girl who's seen every episode of every game show ever," he pointed out. "And the original versions, not the new ones."

"Well, that's why I didn't watch anything else," she explained with a shrug. When she heard the doorbell, she started to move to answer it, but Jude reached out a hand to stop her. "Chinese," she pointed out. "I'm hungry."

"We're going to check. Since I've got the gun, can I get the door?"

"Yeah, but don't scare the dude with the food," she told him wryly.

"I wasn't going to draw it on the delivery person," Jude pointed out, but heading to the door with one hand near the holster. He peeked out the peep hole and then waited a second to open it.

"Hey, Jude," the young girl sang out, her mop of curly blue hair twisted up in a top knot as she held out the bags of food.

"Haha, Avery. That's hilarious every time," he said, grinning at her. Layla noticed Avery looked all of fifteen but might be older. Layla was just a little surprised that she even knew who The Beatles were.

"You move houses?" she asked him, handing over the bags.

"Nope, hanging out with my friend here. Layla, meet Avery." Layla stepped over beside Jude and said hello. "Your dad waiting in the car?"

"Every time," she said, rolling her dark eyes in a face that was free of blemishes but accented in heavy cosmetics for a goth look. "I asked him what good it is to hire me as a delivery driver if he's going to come with me every time."

"I'm sure he just wants you to be safe," Jude pointed out. He waved to the car, and Layla saw the man inside wave back.

"You want to check it?"

"Nah. You never get it wrong. Which is why you make the big tips," he said, handing over a $10 bill and grinning. She rolled her eyes but tucked it in her pocket.

"Thanks," she smiled, then turning to Layla, "Don't let him eat all the egg rolls."

"Would I do that?"

"JP says you do," she tossed over her shoulder. "Don't worry," she called back to him. "I put in a couple extra."

"I appreciate you, Avery," he called back and then waited until she got in the car before he stepped inside.

"She seems nice," Layla said quietly.

"You seem sad," Jude replied, a questioning tone in his voice.

"Do you think I'm putting other people in danger? I mean, maybe I shouldn't call for delivery with all this going on?" Layla was twisting her hands together again and made herself stop. "She's a sweet girl. I just …" She let the thought dangle there.

"You can't help what he does. You need to worry more about yourself. Avery's dad doesn't let her out of his sight. I've seen the pizza guy. He can take care of himself. Dude carries, though you didn't hear it from me."

"You seem to know all the delivery people," Layla said, cocking her head and looking at him.

"I didn't always feel like cooking after pulling some of the longer days over there," he said, nodding to the constant renovation of his house. "And I order for lunch when we have meetings. You be careful, and let the rest of us worry about ourselves," Jude told her, taking the bags over to the counter and unpacking them.

"Are you really going to eat all the egg rolls?" Layla asked, to change the subject.

"That happened once," Jude objected. "God, maybe twice."

"Well, good thing I don't like them," she said with a grin, snatching up her box of lo mein. "So ... Buffy?"

"Yeah, you're going to love it."

Chapter 23

Presley hung up the phone in frustration after another argument with Donovan. Apparently, he'd taken Valentine's Day off, but she'd already taken over another midwife's shift since she'd thought Donovan would be working. She hadn't wanted to spend the evening alone, and now he was pissed that he'd managed to get the time off only for her to be working. She shook her head and wondered why it had to be so hard. She couldn't exactly read minds, she thought to herself.

"You look fierce," Erin commented, looking up from the desk. "Trouble in paradise?"

"We're on opposite schedules now, me and Donovan. It's frustrating."

"My boyfriend lives four hours away," Erin pointed out. "If we can manage it, you can."

"But how *do* you manage it?"

"A lot of phone sex." When Presley laughed, she continued, "Actually, we just make sure what time we have is appreciated. We don't talk about the distance when we're together—or argue. We just enjoy one another. We leave everything else for the times when we're apart. We just try to make it count."

"But for how long? Is it going to be long distance forever?"

"I don't know," Erin answered, honestly. "I hope not. But he has to be where he is for grad school, and I have a job here. When he gets out of school, one of us will move. Or both of us," she considered, shrugging. "But it's been a couple years already, and we're okay."

"I don't know if I can do that. I mean, I'm working every hour he's off, and vice versa. Unless we're sleeping."

"So sleep together," Erin said, and then waved her hand. "Not like that. Or not *only* like that. Just be together. God knows schedules are bound to change."

"Yeah, I guess so."

"We've got another one coming in, by the way."

"Alright, how far out?"

"Maybe in about fifteen?"

"I'll grab coffee real quick. Buzz me if they get here early. And thanks."

"No problem. You'll work it out," Erin said, reaching to answer the phone. "Grab me a coffee?" she mouthed. Presley nodded, knowing Erin's favorite without asking.

Presley decided to take the stairs on the way down. It'd be quicker, and she could take the elevator once she had the coffee. She got into the stairwell and nearly collided with Amber who was on the way up and looking pissed.

"Whoa—what's your deal?"

"Look, you need to quit calling us," Amber said. "I know I vented about Derrick the other day, but we're still together, and you need to stop."

"I don't know what you're talking about," Presley said, edging by her with her hands lifted in a gesture of peace. "I haven't been calling you. Or Derrick. Hell, I deleted his number."

"You can block your number, but we know," Amber said, incensed.

"Hey, maybe it's some other woman he's dated or has been dating, but it's not this one. Boyfriend, remember? And if I called, I'd admit it," Presley told her, starting to get irritated. So much for being cool now, Presley thought.

"This is your last warning," Amber called, spinning on her heel and heading back down to her floor.

"This was my first one," Presley called after her and then headed down. "I'm not following you either," she called loudly. "This is how you get to the cafeteria," she said with heavy sarcasm.

Amber turned around. "It really wasn't you?"

"Why the hell would I do that? I don't want Derrick anymore. That's been done for ages," Presley said, shrugging and heading down. She heard Amber go back to her floor, the door slamming behind her. It did that though. Slam, Presley thought. Maybe Amber believed her, and maybe she didn't, but she was getting really tired of drama everywhere she went. When she got to the bottom floor, she sighed when the door opened. All the doors had been tricky lately, and she was about to have it out with maintenance. But coffee was the priority.

***

Jude sat up in the middle of the night and reached for the gun on the table beside him. He paused, wondering what had woken him when he heard it again. A scream, then crying. He grabbed the gun and headed up the stairs quickly. He burst into Layla's room and saw that she was covering her eyes, crying, curled into a fetal position.

"Hey, Layla, hey," he said softly, going to sit on the edge of the bed and setting the gun on the nightstand. "Are you okay?"

"Nightmares," she said sleepily, her face still covered. He could see she was trembling and touched her shoulder but then took his hand away when she jerked back. "Sorry," she told him. "Reflex."

"Are you going to be able to get back to sleep?" he asked, making sure not to touch her even though he wanted to offer comfort.

"Eventually," she said, taking her hands away from her face. He could see it was tear-streaked. "Sorry I woke you up."

"Don't apologize. Look, I'll be right back," he said and then jogged downstairs. He came back up with a blanket and pillow and threw them in the floor beside the bed. "I'll just stay here, okay? That way if you have another one, you won't be alone."

Layla sat up in bed, and Jude tried not to notice how the over-sized T-shirt fell off her shoulder. "You don't have to do that."

"Would it help?" She paused for a minute, looking at him, and then nodded.

"Can you just …" she let the words trail off. He just looked at her, giving her time. "Could you just hold me until I fall asleep? Please?"

"Yeah." She scooted over, and he slipped into the bed where it was still warm from her body. "Do you want to talk about it?" She shook her head and then lay down and turned away from him.

He settled carefully and then pulled her back against him. He kept an arm around her, and with the other arm, he stroked her shoulder softly. "Just go to sleep. I'll be right here." When she finally fell asleep, he didn't move his arm although he knew that it would fall asleep soon. Instead, he wrapped his other arm around her and fell asleep, too. Eventually.

She woke up twice more in the night, and he reached for his gun once when he heard some noises outside. He had to admit that he was a little more concerned after seeing the guy. It wasn't the tough looking ones you had to worry about. He'd had one client like Noah, years ago when he was just an intern. Jude looked out the window and remembered how the kid had seemed perfectly normal unless you looked at his eyes. He could turn emotion on at will, but it was never real. He'd been glad when his internship ended, and he'd never had to see the kid again. He wondered sometimes what he was doing now, and if he even wanted to know. He looked at Layla where she slept, half on her side and half on her stomach. She whimpered in her sleep before the screaming started, and he wondered how she functioned at all and what nightmares haunted her.

He put a hand to the gun he held and looked down the street. He couldn't be sure, but he thought he'd seen a flashlight down the block. Of course, he told himself, it was likely a late-night dog walker or an insomniac. There was no reason to think it had anything to do with Noah. Only the light had made its way to her house a time or two more than Jude liked. He crept back over to the bed and put the gun down on the bedside table. He climbed in with Layla and wrapped an arm around her. In her sleep, she moved to fit her body to his and sighed. He thought her face relaxed a little, and he finally allowed himself to relax as well. He lay awake for a while and then slowly drifted off to join her.

***

Noah was tempted to whistle as he walked. He'd gotten a lot done in a single evening, not that anyone appreciated his work, he thought to himself. He knew most men would keep a low profile right now, but most men were fools. He didn't bother to wear a ball cap, but he'd added temporary color to his hair and styled it differently. Just a little stage makeup made his face look different, and he'd added a few pounds with careful padding, easy enough to do in the winter. His shoes added just a little more height and were nearly a size too big, and he'd dressed casually. He didn't look suspicious. He'd even offered to pet sit his neighbor's dog, so that his walk wouldn't seem at all suspicious. He hated dragging the dog around, but it was a quiet breed at least, if perhaps the dullest creature on the planet.

He hadn't had to wait for long, and he'd been sure not to stay in one spot for too long. He knew exactly which bedroom to shine the light on, and he'd only cursed under his breath a little when he'd noticed through the binoculars who was at the window. He'd have to get to know a little more about him. Noah knew that even the smallest piece of information could be useful if you knew how to use it. He let the light linger there before he turned it toward the street, walking the stupid dog back to the car parked in an old lot nearby.

He wasn't ready for the next step yet, but he was definitely putting all the pieces into place.

Noah got into the car, letting the dog in the back instead of shoving it into the trunk like he wanted. He put on his seatbelt carefully and then turned on the phone. He watched a man slip into bed beside a woman sleeping restlessly beside him. He wondered if he'd have to wait long to hear her scream. That was his favorite part, after all. Then he wondered, with some distaste, if he'd have to watch them fuck first. Still, he stroked himself thoughtfully, and knew even watching could have its entertainment value. *She* would have to pay for every indignity he suffered, but he turned up the volume anyway as he drove, waiting to see how it played out. If anything interesting happened, he'd pull over to watch.

***

Presley almost went straight home. She just wanted to go to bed, but then she thought about what Erin had said. Donovan was off tonight, but he'd be back on in the morning when she was off. She wasn't sure if he'd even be home. After all, he hadn't exactly mentioned what he was doing after their Valentine's Day phone call earlier. She pulled up at the house. She saw the minivan and realized she'd forgotten about Vashti and the baby. She knew Donovan was subletting his apartment for the first six months so that he could help out. She hadn't thought about that when she decided to drop by unannounced. At the knock on the other window, she jolted. She looked over and saw Vashti and rolled down the window with an awkward laugh.

"Didn't mean to scare you. Just wondered if you were going to go in or sit out here all night," Vashti asked, leaning through the window.

"Um, I just realized that I shouldn't just drop by," Presley pointed out.

"Why not? Donovan's been a bear all day. Now you can deal with him," Vashti said with a grin. "Make him quit."

"I can't make him do anything. What are you doing outside? It's getting dark."

"Natalia likes the stroller. She was having trouble sleeping, so I go up and down the block a couple times until she calms down."

"By yourself?"

"No," Vashti giggled, nodding toward the street. A couple of other mothers were waiting with strollers parked. "There's a group of us. We won't be out long, but it gives us a chance to catch up. Go on in, and we'll be back shortly."

"Okay, thanks," Presley said, turning off the car and getting out. She thought she saw the curtain twitch, but then she was sure of it when the door opened as she approached.

"What's up, Presley? I told you I'm working tomorrow," Donovan said shortly. Presley looked at him in the low-slung jeans and henley shirt and felt her mouth water. Then she paid attention to his tone and stepped back.

"Sorry, never mind," she said, retreating toward her car, feeling that sharp taste of disappointment.

"Wait," Donovan said, with a frustrated sigh, reaching out to take her arm. "Come in. But I can't stay up long. I've got to go in early."

"Actually, I wanted to see if I could stay the night," Presley said, feeling awkward despite all the nights they'd spent together.

"Is this a booty call?"

She shook her head, feeling her throat tighten. He just looked at her and then seemed to relax, the anger draining from him.

"Okay. Okay, Presley," he said, stepping forward to hug her. She wrapped her arms around him and then with a leap, her legs. She curled into his arms and put her head on his shoulder, her favorite place. He tightened his grip and carried her over to the couch. "You okay?" She nodded, not saying anything. "Are we're still making this work?" he asked into her hair.

"Yes," she said, her voice muffled in his shirt.

"Okay," he said, stroking a hand over her thick, short hair. "I wasn't sure earlier."

"Me either."

"Mind if I watch the game?"

"No," she said softly, "Mind if I just stay right here?"

"I was hoping you would." He smiled and planted a kiss on her hair.

Chapter 24

Naomi knocked on the door, hoping it wasn't too early. She shifted from one foot to the other and wished she felt better about what she'd done. She took deep breaths, remembering what her therapist had told her about calming her anxiety. When the door opened, she nearly leaped out of her own skin.

"What are you doing here?" she asked Jude, taking a step back.

"I could ask you the same thing," he said with a grin. "Come on in. Is Layla expecting you?"

Naomi came in slowly, confused. "No, I just thought I'd drop by. Is Layla around?" She looked around the empty living room and kitchen and wondered what was up.

"She's just getting up. Come on into the kitchen. Want some coffee?"

"Sure." She set the bakery box down on the counter and nodded to it. "Donuts, if you want any." She looked up the stairs and started to feel nervous. "Maybe I'll just run upstairs and check on Layla."

"No need," he told her, nodding to the stairs. They could hear footsteps coming down.

"Hey," Layla said, stopping short and then slowly descending. She looked from Jude to Naomi and back again. "What are you doing here?"

"I needed to talk to you," Naomi said. "Didn't really expect to see him here." She paused and then grinned. "When I said you need to see a therapist, this isn't exactly what I meant."

Layla blushed to the roots of her hair, and Jude grinned. "It's not like that."

Naomi looked from Jude's pajama pants and T-shirt to Layla's freshly washed hair and raised an eyebrow. Jude glanced over at Layla and then poured a cup of coffee, passing it over to her. Naomi didn't miss the brush of their fingertips or the way Layla looked up at him. Hmm, she thought, definitely something going on.

"I stayed over after the court thing," Jude explained. He nodded to the couch with its stack of blankets and pillows.

"Oh. About that," Naomi said.

"It doesn't matter," Layla said quickly, cutting her off.

"It really does."

"Should I just ..." Jude gestured toward the door.

"No, I mean, she'll just tell you in therapy anyway, right?" Layla asked bluntly.

"Naomi's not a client."

"But I thought ..."

"I see one of the other doctors in the practice," Naomi said with a shrug. "That's how I recognized him. But he isn't my therapist."

"Oh."

"Can we sit down? I brought donuts."

"Sure," Layla said easily, glancing at Jude who was taking one out. He passed the box over to her, and she selected one coated in chocolate and sprinkles. Naomi was relieved to see that she seemed okay, all things considered.

"I want to explain what happened to me yesterday, but I also want to know what happened," Naomi admitted. She'd pulled her brown hair up in a careless topknot and had gone with the bare minimum for makeup. She'd been too anxious to do much else and had pulled on yoga pants and a tunic sweater, not caring how she looked.

"He did what he usually does," Layla admitted, looking down at her coffee. "He lied, and he made me look like a vengeful ex." She shrugged, as if it didn't matter, but Naomi knew better.

"Yeah, I thought that would happen. Look, I really wanted to be there, but I, um, had a massive panic attack in the car when I got there. I saw him going in, and I just ..." She lifted up her hands but then dropped them and laced them together in her lap. "I kind of fell apart. I went straight over to see Charlie." She looked up at Jude.

"My partner," he explained to Layla.

"I was there the whole time. He squeezed me in for an emergency session, and I didn't get back to normal until it was too late to go." Naomi looked down at her hands, squeezed together.

"It's okay," Layla told her, moving over to the couch and sitting down beside her.

When Naomi looked up, tears fell from her eyes. "I didn't realize how afraid I was until that moment. I haven't seen him since …" Her words trailed off, and Layla nodded. Naomi knew she could understand the terror. She'd lived it. She still lived with it. Layla put an arm around her shoulder and leaned her head against Naomi's. They both just sat there for a minute. When she sat up, she looked at Jude. "What did you think of him?"

"You want my personal or professional opinion?"

"Both. Either," Naomi said, shrugging.

"Personally, I think he's an asshole. Professionally, I think he's a sociopath."

"Yeah," Naomi nodded, understanding. "He doesn't look like he'd be scary, but …" She looked over at Layla.

"Definitely scary," she agreed with a nod.

"Anyway, I just wanted to say I'm so sorry I wasn't there with you," Naomi told her. Jude got up to get the donut box from the kitchen counter, and she lowered her voice. "And later I want to know when you started sleeping with the shrink."

"I heard that," Jude called back.

"I'm not sleeping with him," Layla objected.

At Jude's muttered, "Liar," Layla amended her statement. "I'm not having sex with him," she corrected herself.

"Why not?" Naomi asked, taking a donut for herself and looking at Layla with interest. "I mean, you're not seeing him professionally."

She looked over at Jude, "I keep telling her she should go to counseling, but she won't do it."

"Sitting right here," Layla pointed out.

"I'm just saying. He's hot, so why aren't you?"

"Thanks," Jude said with a grin. "Yeah, why aren't you?"

"You're both impossible," Layla muttered into her coffee, a smile teasing at the corner of her lips.

"Are you okay?"

"Yeah, I'm okay."

"You had a bunch of nightmares last night," Jude said.

Layla glared at him. "I thought therapists were supposed to be discreet," she said in frustration.

"I'm not your therapist," he returned with a shrug. "She had a bunch of nightmares."

"Again, I'm sitting. Right here," Layla told them, reaching for another donut.

"I didn't think you were still having them," Naomi said, her eyebrows drawing sharply together in concern.

"Sometimes, I do," Layla replied shortly. "I'm fine."

"She will be fine. We're going to be extra vigilant until he stops," Jude told them.

"If he stops," Layla pointed out.

"That's the spirit," Naomi said, rolling her eyes. "He's got to stop, right?" she asked, looking at Jude. "I mean, he can't do this forever." There was a note of question in her voice, as she looked at him, and she heard him sigh heavily.

"He'll stop, or he'll be stopped," Jude said, shrugging. "It's one or the other, but we're going to keep an eye out until that happens." He looked at Naomi. "Do you have someone watching out for you?"

"Yeah, I do," she said with a nod. "I moved back in with my parents, after everything. They have a fully furnished apartment over the garage, and I just pay utilities. It's a good setup for me right now.

Plus, it's got two bedrooms, and I got a roommate."

"Someone you trust?"

"My cousin. I'm rarely alone."

"She does online dating though."

"Yeah, you might want to quit that, at least until this is over," Jude agreed.

"Well, I'm kind of seeing someone."

"Since when?" Layla asked.

"Since that last date. Anyway, it's kind of a regular thing now," she said with a shrug.

"Still, be careful," Jude advised. "And maybe tell him what's going on."

"Oh, he knows. I got that out of the way early, just to make sure I didn't freak out and leave him wondering why I was acting that way. He's cool about it," Naomi said with a small smile. *Jailhouse Rock* abruptly started playing, and Jude and Naomi looked over at Layla with a grin.

"I need to take this. It's Presley," Layla said, standing up with her phone and heading out of the room.

"As if we didn't know," Naomi said. She looked at Jude in appraisal. "So, what's really going on here? You just friends or is this something more? Because you should know better than anyone that she's vulnerable right now," she said with some censure creeping into her voice.

"I'm interested, but she's not ready. I'm going to be her friend. Maybe that changes later, and maybe it doesn't, but I'm not trying to complicate anything. I'm just worried about her."

"Yeah," Naomi said with a sigh. "Me, too." She looked back at him. "So … a lot of nightmares?"

"A few. It really scared her, but it scared me, too. She woke up screaming, and I thought for a minute …" Jude let it trail off, shaking his head.

"Yeah, I can imagine," Naomi said softly. "We've got to keep her safe."

"You, too."

"Yeah, me, too. But I don't think he's really focused on me. If it wasn't me, it would have just been someone else. It's Layla he's obsessed with. I was just—an amusement for him," she said with a shrug. "He pretty much said so."

"I'm sorry."

"It is what it is. I just don't want him hurting anyone else." They heard Layla coming back in.

"Fine, I'll call you later," she said into the phone. "Yeah, yeah, I know. Love you, too," she said. "Go bother Donovan," she added, ending the call.

"Everything okay?" Jude asked.

"Peachy," she said with a sigh. "I'm just tired." She looked at the clock. "And I'm scheduled to be at work in another hour, so …"

"I've got to go anyway," Naomi told her, standing up. "I promised Beth I'd walk Mr. Darcy and Lizzie at least three times a day while she's out of town. I'm dog sitting," she explained to Jude.

"The dogs are Mr. Darcy and Lizzie?" he asked with a grin.

"Yep. Cute story for another day," Naomi told him.

"Where are Beth and Jamie?"

"Oh, they're on a cruise. If they could have taken the dogs, they would have," she told them with a grin. "Anyway, I don't mind dog sitting and stopping by to check on the house."

"Just don't do that alone," Jude said.

Naomi's smile faded. "I'll start asking someone to go with me," she agreed with a nod. "And, yeah, when I walk the dogs, too."

"Okay, then." Jude nodded.

"Well, I'm out of here," Naomi said. "Text me later," she told Layla. "And you remember what I said," she told Jude as she headed out.

Naomi could hear Layla asking him what she'd said as she went out the door and closed it behind her. She took out her phone and texted her parents, hoping one of them was home. She'd been walking the dogs alone, but she realized just how stupid that had been. She got a reply from her dad and grinned. He'd been told to exercise more anyway. She'd just give him a good excuse to do it.

Chapter 25

Layla heard a sound that was unfamiliar coming from next door. She sat up in bed and looked at the time. It was early, hours before she wanted to be awake on a weekend, particularly as she hadn't slept well that night. Or the night before. Or the night before that. She sighed. She grabbed a robe, and threw it on over her pajamas, slipping her feet into the cozy bunny slippers she'd gotten at the office as a door prize at a company meeting. She wiggled her feet and smiled a little. They were ridiculous, but cute.

"Did a daycare open up next door?" Presley asked with a groan from the couch.

"I was wondering the same thing," Layla answered, going over to peek out the kitchen window. "I think maybe Jude finally got to see his kids," she said with a tone of wonder in her voice. If she was honest with herself, she'd started to think that the kids weren't even real. After all, in the few months he'd lived next door, Layla hadn't seen them. Of course, Jude showed her pictures on his phone, but it wasn't the same. She heard the sound of laughter and grinned. It sounded liked it was going well.

"That's nice for him," Presley muttered, rolling over to her other side. "But can't they play inside?"

"I'm not going to complain," Layla told her, putting on a pot of coffee. "But I might go say hello, later." She looked out the window and saw one of them run by. "I have to admit I'm curious."

She heard Presley sit up and shuffle into the bathroom. When she joined her in the kitchen, her sister looked a little more awake. "What do you have to eat?"

"One stale donut," Layla said, picking up the bakery box with a roll of her eyes and tossing it in the trash after a look of disgust. She'd had such a revolving door of guests lately that housekeeping had fallen by the wayside. "Or not. I've got cereal, and bagels if you want them. Fruit in the fridge," she said with a shrug. She looked at her sister and softened. "You don't have to keep staying here. It's hard enough for you and Donovan to see each other without having to work around my schedule, too."

"I'll stop when Noah does," Presley returned evenly, looking in the fridge for the fruit. She pulled out the container and slowly sat down on the stool at the counter to open it. "Have you heard from him lately?"

"I had Donovan here, then Naomi. Now you. He hasn't had a lot of opportunity."

"That's the point," Presley said. "We don't want him to have the opportunity. You're not bait, and we're not trying to prove anything. We just need him to stop so we can all move on."

"And until he does, you're going to babysit me?"

"Wouldn't be the first time," Presley said with a smile, stabbing a cube of pineapple with the fork Layla passed over.

"So how are things with you and Donovan? Really?"

"We're—good. Surprisingly. We're making it work. But if one of us can get our schedules changed, it would be so much easier."

"Are you trying to? I thought you hated nights."

"I do, but I also hate never seeing him. Maybe nights would be easier if our schedules lined up," she answered, and Layla wondered if she knew she was frowning. "Let me ask you something. What's up with you and the sexy shrink?"

Now it was Layla's turn to frown. "He's just a friend. We've covered this."

"Fine," Presley told her, spearing a piece of honeydew melon this time. "What's the plan for today?"

"We need to have lunch with Dad, and then afterwards, I thought I'd do some projects here. Before you ask, Dean will be home, and so will both guys next door." Layla heard a burst of laughter outside. "And maybe some kids, too."

"Alright. You might want to put on a little more concealer before we go to Dad's," Presley observed with her head cocked to one side.

"At this point, I need hemorrhoid cream for the bags and concealer for the dark circles," she admitted, rolling her eyes.

"I didn't hear you scream last night," Presley said, a look of concern in her eyes. "Did I sleep through it?"

"No, I didn't scream," Layla answered evenly but didn't tell her sister how she'd woken up whimpering, which was worse for her. "I just didn't sleep well."

"Well, wake me up next time. We'll put in a movie."

"Yeah, sure," Layla agreed easily, knowing she wouldn't. "I'm going to get dressed so we can head to Dad's."

***

Noah was glad he'd hung back a little today. The park was isolated enough that he could stand out just by loitering. He'd walked a couple of laps, surreptitiously checking his fitness tracker at regular intervals, as if he cared what it said. When he heard the dogs, he'd crouched down to tie his shoes. Naomi wouldn't be able to see him from here, but he had a clear view of her. He sat back on his haunches when he saw the tall man beside her. He shook his head. He was starting to think that she had been encouraged to take precautions, too. He didn't think she was smart enough to come to it on her own.

He stood up and took a different path. He was familiar enough with the hiking trails to know which one he could take that wouldn't intersect her own. He walked briskly, eager to get back to the parking lot. He'd never intended to include Naomi in the game. After all, she had just been something to play with, but he realized that shaking her up would certainly get back to Layla. He needed her anxiety high. He couldn't execute his next move without her heightened fear.

He knew he was close. After all, he'd been watching when she'd woken up whimpering and crying. He wasn't sure if he liked that or the screams best. It was a toss-up, he thought with a small smile. His empty eyes scanned the path, looking for any branches that could trip him up. He was careful, always. Of course, he'd seen Presley, too, and knew she'd slept through the whole thing. He'd watched them both and wondered why they couldn't see how close he was or how little time was left in the game.

He walked quickly, adjusting the pack on his back in frustration. He wouldn't have carried so much gear in if he knew he'd only be hiking. He made a mental note to change his shoes in the car, to ones that actually fit. He didn't miss a trick and never had. Well, he hadn't expected Layla's betrayal, not that it was her fault really. Still, she'd come back. She'd have to. She wouldn't have a choice.

***

Layla grabbed another ham and cheese slider from the stove where her dad had left them to warm. She felt the glances exchanged behind her without even having to look. She calmly turned back and went to sit at the wide farm style table in the kitchen and looked over at Presley, her dad, and Keely.

"I know you're all worried. You can talk *to* me instead of *about* me," she pointed out, taking a sip of the sweet tea her dad had made with his signature honey. It was different than what she was used to, but she was acquiring a taste for it. She suspected the higher quality tea was Keely's doing. She did own a tea room after all.

"We were just thinking it wouldn't hurt for you to spend a few nights out here," Keely said gently.

"No offense, but I don't think I'd be any safer here than where I am," Layla pointed out. "For one, it's more secluded here. There are more places to hide on the farm. And then there's just the two of you. At home, I've got Dean and Lindy, Jude and JP next door, and someone constantly staying over. Plus, Dean's got the security system in place. And I haven't even heard from him since court."

"To be fair, that hasn't been long," Presley said.

"Could you get Jude to stay over more?" Theodore asked, and Layla's mouth dropped open.

"What are you suggesting?" Layla asked before turning to look at Presley.

"I just told him that Jude was taking turns on your couch, too. He carries. He's *useful*," Presley insisted innocently.

"Also, he's easy on the eyes," Keely pointed out. Theodore rolled his eyes, and Layla let out a huff of exasperation.

"He really is," Presley agreed. "Although he could lose the man bun."

"I'm fine. Things are fine," Layla insisted. "I'm surrounding at all times, and Dean put in good security, too."

"We just worry about you, honey," Theodore said, reaching across the table to pat her hand.

"I know you do, and I'm doing everything I can, but it looks like things are blowing over so maybe don't worry so much," Layla answered, trying to reassure them and lying through her teeth. She knew better than to think Noah was done just yet. If nothing else, he'd have to lob a parting shot her way. She was bracing for it.

***

After lunch, she came home and heard the surprising sound of barks mixed in with laughter as she got out of the car. Instead of heading toward the house, she turned toward Jude's. Curious, she headed for the gate next door, letting herself in.

"Hey," Jude said in surprise, as she rounded the corner.

"Hey, yourself," Layla replied. "What's going on here? And

236

who's this?" she asked with a smile at the kids and the dog currently rolling in the grass. She didn't think kids actually did that anymore. Mostly, they were giggling, as the dog stepped around them on the ground and licked their faces.

"Well, this is Connor, and this is Kelsey. And this boy right here is … Wait—what did you decide?" he asked, looking at the kids.

Kelsey and Connor looked at each other and nodded. They looked at the dog and then at their dad and said together, "Gryffindor."

"Gryffindor?" Jude asked, and Layla smiled. "Why?"

"Because he's *brave*," Kelsey declared.

"Okay, could we shorten it to Gryffin? Or Gryff?" he asked.

"It's Gryffindor," Kelsey said seriously. "But we can call him Gryffin sometimes."

"It's a *nickname*," Connor said knowingly.

"You know, sometimes people call that a *pet* name, and he is your pet," Layla said solemnly.

"Yeah," Connor agreed, nodding vigorously.

"Yeah, he's our *pet*," Kelsey said with glee. They went back to playing with the dog, and Jude gestured to the porch swing he'd put in the yard. They went over and sat down, watching the kids.

"What kind of dog might that be?" Layla asked. "Or is that a bear?" she added with a grin.

"That is a Newfoundland," Jude clarified. "He's a rescue."

"He's enormous."

"Yeah, well, he's the one that the kids wanted."

"How's JP feel about the dog?" Layla asked, glancing toward the house.

"Oh, he's a big kid himself. He's going to start in complaining about shedding, but don't pay him any mind. He's a bigger softie than they are, and he's always wanted a big dog," Jude told her, stretching his hands over his head and then settling them on either side of the back of the seat.

"Your kids are cute," Layla told him, leaning back and stretching her legs in front of her. Of course, her feet barely touched the ground.

"Thanks, I think so," Jude told her. "Michelle had something to do, so she actually let me have them when I went to pick them up. That hasn't happened in months."

"Are they staying all weekend?" she asked him, laughing when the big dog ran around the yard with the kids.

"Yeah," Jude said with a smile. "They'll actually get to sleep in their rooms for once."

"Where's Gryffin going to sleep?"

"Ostensibly, in his dog bed, but we both know he'll end up sleeping with the kids—or me."

His hair was starting to fall down on one side where Layla guessed he'd been playing with the dog, too. She reached up and brushed it back, and he turned in toward her. Her eyes met his, and she felt something move between them.

She took a deep breath, careful not to move. It wasn't just heat. Or just butterflies. There was connection here, and she ached to explore it but knew it was a bad idea. After all, she had enough going on without that. Still, she felt herself leaning toward him, just a little, when the screen door on the house slapped behind them, and she jolted.

"Did we get a dog?" JP called from the porch. "Oops," he muttered to himself with a grin, looking at Jude and Layla, their faces nearly touching as they turned to look at him. Layla eased back, putting a little distance between them and avoiding Jude's eyes.

"His name is Gryffindor," she called to JP.

"He's going to shed everywhere," JP declared, his hands on his waist but a smile starting to form on his face. Layla glanced at Jude and tried not to laugh.

"Uncle JP!" Connor squealed. "We got a dog."

"I'm just going to head home," Layla told Jude quietly.

"You sure? You're welcome to stay," he said, looking into her eyes.

"I know. But you can see me any time, and you need to spend time with them. I'll see you later, okay?" She touched his arm gently and briefly before calling out her goodbyes to JP and the kids who were busy sitting on the grass playing with the dog. "Bye, Gryffin," she added, patting the dog's head and smiling at the group.

***

Layla had the key in the lock and the alarm turned off before her smile faded. She slowly backed out of the house, reaching behind her to open the door and then close it. She glanced at Jude's house and knew that she couldn't get him for this. She locked the door quickly and sprinted to Lindy's. She reached to open the back door of the screened-in porch but found it locked. She kept her eyes on her own place and her back to Lindy's as she started dialing the number.

"Are you home? Is it just you and the baby?" she paused, listening. "I'm standing by the back porch. Can you let me in? Please? Please let me in." She kept repeating those words, *please let me in,* until she heard the door open behind her and nearly stumbled getting through it.

"Hey, hey," Dean said, putting his hands on her shoulder. "Get inside, and we'll talk," he told her, glancing at the carriage house over her shoulder.

Layla knew she was shaking but couldn't stop. She stepped inside the house and felt the panic attack hit. She doubled over, trying to get air in.

"Maybe I should get Jude," Layla heard Lindy say from somewhere in the room.

"Stay inside," Dean told her, a warning note in his voice.

"Don't. His kids," Layla gasped, struggling to breathe.

"Did you call the police?" Dean asked. When Layla shook her head, he continued, "I'll do that. I'll take care of this," Dean told her, pulling out his phone and heading to the window to look out.

"You're going to need to breathe, Layla," Lindy told her, taking her by the arm and leading her to the couch, a room where she could no longer see her own carriage house sitting out back. "Breathe. Come on."

Layla took shuddering breaths and knew that tears were leaking out of her eyes when she felt them pool in the collar of her shirt. She took one breath and then another while Lindy rubbed her back and talked her through it. Lindy leaned in, her forehead nearly touching Layla's as she spoke softly, reassuring her that she was safe.

"I'll get you some water," Lindy said and started to stand when Layla grabbed her hand.

"Stay. Please. Stay," Layla said, struggling to get each word out. Lindy sat but didn't let go of her hand. After a few minutes, she got through it and could breathe again. Lindy was still there, and Layla shut her eyes in shame.

"Don't," Lindy told her. "I know what you're thinking. Don't. This isn't your fault. Now you're going to tell us what happened, and then we'll deal with it together."

Dean stood in the doorway watching them. "The police are on their way. What are they going to find?" he asked, coming in to sit down across from them.

"My ... house ..." Layla paused, trying to gather her thoughts. "He's been in there."

"Like last time?" he asked. She shook her head, no.

"No, he made sure I knew this time," Layla said quietly. "The first thing I saw were the pictures," Layla explained. "There are pictures of me everywhere. Not just pictures of me outside but in the house. He has pictures of me inside the house," she said as her breath started to come fast again.

"Keep breathing. Talk me through this," Dean told her. "There were pictures. What else did you see?"

"Pages of a book?" Layla put it as a question, trying to piece together what she'd seen in those few moments before she'd run back out. "Ripped out pages with ugly words scrawled across them. I don't know what else. It was a wreck." They heard a car door slam, and Dean stood up.

"I'm checking that, and then we'll deal with this," he said, heading for the door.

"Where were you today?" Lindy asked softly.

"Went to have lunch at Dad's with Presley. And then I went home and decided to go over to Jude's first. He had plenty of time," she admitted.

"Well, I'll take a look at the security footage while they're looking at the house."

"Where's Maya?" Layla asked, just now curious about where the baby had gone.

"Libby's watching her for a bit. I was going to head into work in a little while."

"Oh, I'm sorry," Layla began before Lindy cut her off.

"Don't do that. This isn't your fault. But you're probably going to need to walk the officer through it," Lindy told her, squeezing her hand. "You can do it."

"Looks like I'm not going to have a choice," she said quietly as an officer entered with Dean. She looked him over and thought he looked a little young and inexperienced for this, but she didn't exactly get to choose. Dean seemed to think he was alright, so she stood up and went with them out the door and toward the little house.

Chapter 26

Jude had noticed the police car pull up as he was giving the kids a bath. They were making more of a mess than getting clean, but he was enjoying it. He'd stood up to stretch when he saw the car parked outside Layla's. He stepped toward the door and called out, "JP, can you come up here a sec?"

"What's up? Can't handle the two wild ones on your own?" he asked with a grin.

"Look out the window," he said quietly. "Can you go see what's up, make sure she's okay? I don't want to leave the kids."

"Yeah," JP told him, nodding, a look of concern on his face. "I'll check it out."

"Tell her … tell her I'll call, and I'll try to get over there when I can," Jude told him and then turned back just in time to get splashed. "Hey, guys, pretty sure there's not going to be any water left in the tub," he told them with a laugh.

He finished up their baths and got them in their pajamas, Gryffin shadowing them from room to room. Every now and then he glanced out the window to see what was taking JP so long. He thought about shooting Layla a text but figured she had enough going on at the moment. A second police car had pulled up behind the first, and he was really starting to worry. He tucked the kids in bed and read a chapter from the Harry Potter book the kids had been reading at home and made a mental note to go back and read it from the beginning, so he'd understand what was going on. It had been years since he'd even seen the movies.

He turned off the light and crept quietly from the room, grinning when Gryffin opted to stay behind. He was on the floor, but Jude guessed he wouldn't stay that way for long. He went downstairs and saw JP sitting in the kitchen, his face pale.

"Hey, I didn't know you were back. Why didn't you come up?" Jude asked, pulling a beer from the fridge.

"I needed a minute. I don't know how you deal with crazy fuckers day in and day out," he told him shakily.

"First of all, most of my patients are far from crazy. Just normal people going through some shit. But if you're talking about Noah, he is crazy. Straight out sociopath," Jude told him and handed JP the beer, choosing another for himself. "Is Layla okay?"

"I mean, as okay as she can be, considering."

"I need you to be a little less cryptic right now," Jude replied with steel in his voice.

"She left here and went home to her entire place trashed. But not like anything normal. The place is covered in pictures of herself. I mean, walking outside, in the house, sleeping, in the shower." JP colored a little and shrugged. "Hard not to see he's had her under surveillance, and they're trying to pin down for how long. I tried to fill in the dates on the ones that were taken outside. It was hard to remember. I mean, she hasn't been able to check the mail without photographs." He shook his head. "They couldn't find any cameras, so he probably took them when he left this little surprise or else he moved them. I don't know. Then there were the books."

"The books?"

"He tore pages out of her books and wrote all over them. Just nasty stuff. Anyway, they kept me over there, asking if we'd noticed anything, where we were, how long we've been home today, and if I recognized any of the pictures to identify a timeline."

"Fuck," Jude breathed out.

"Yeah," JP agreed.

"And Layla's okay?"

"Well, okay isn't the word I'd use, but yeah, she's not been physically hurt. She's a mess though. She went next door and got

Dean and then just fell apart. I ran into Lindy outside, and she filled me in. They'd have called, but Layla didn't want them bothering you because ..." JP let off and nodded toward the kids upstairs.

"Can you keep an eye on the kids while I run next door?"

"Yeah, she'll be over at Lindy's if the police are done. And I'm getting my gun out of the safe, in case you were wondering."

"Just don't leave it where the kids can get it," Jude reminded him.

"Hey, this isn't my first rodeo," JP said with a roll of his eyes. "Check on the girl. I'll keep an eye out here."

***

Jude walked briskly next door to where Layla was standing on the porch with a couple of officers. A photographer headed in, stepping neatly around them, and Jude waited to get her attention. When the officer turned gimlet eyes his way, Layla explained, "This is JP's brother, Jude, my neighbor and a good friend."

"We need you to look at some pictures, see if you can help with the time line. You're in a few of them," he mentioned casually, watching Jude and Layla closely.

"Sure," Jude said easily. He didn't know what he was expecting, but it was worse than JP had said. Definitely creepier. He was hoping they'd found fingerprints but would be willing to bet they wouldn't find anything. Anyone who could record this much of someone's life wouldn't make a rookie mistake. This was experience here. Jude looked over at Layla who looked embarrassed. He reached over and took her hand, not caring about the knowing looks the cops were shooting each other. "Walk with me?"

"Jude, there are pictures of me in the shower," she told him quietly, deeply humiliated.

"Well, anything you don't want me to look at, just steer me away from, okay?" he told her, squeezing her hand. He walked through the room and was able to pinpoint a lot of the days that he saw, since he'd spent a lot of time with Layla lately. He knew the officers were looking at him closely, as if he was becoming more of a suspect with each date he could accurately place.

"Seems like you've been paying attention," one of them commented quietly.

"Well, wouldn't you if a pretty girl moved in next door? Besides, we're friends."

He walked through the house with her, sickened by the number of pictures that he saw. He looked at her pale face and realized what she had; Noah was letting her know she wasn't safe anywhere, even at home. He could feel the tremor in her hand and guessed what was next before she did.

"In here," he told her shortly, pulling her into the bathroom where pictures of her bathing were all over the room. He kept his eyes on Layla and not the images of her spread throughout the place. She vomited once and then sat back on the floor. He pulled her over into his arms and talked her through the panic attack she was clearly fighting.

"We can stop, if it's too much."

"Let's just finish this, so I can go to sleep," Layla told him shakily. "I'm just so tired, Jude," she said, pressing her forehead to his chest.

"I know. Come stay with me," he told her softly.

"Can't," Layla said. "Not with your kids there."

"Dean and Lindy have Maya," Jude pointed out. He felt her stiffen and cursed, "I didn't mean it like that. I just meant that I can keep you safe, too. I don't want you sleeping alone tonight."

"I can't risk anyone else," Layla told him, pulling back to look in his eyes. "I'm putting you all in danger."

"Just look on the bright side. If he tries to get you at my place, Gryffin will eat him, or I'll get to shoot him," he said, rubbing her arm. She let out a short mirthless laugh. "Come on," he said, pulling her to her feet. "Let's see the rest of this shit show."

They did the full walk-through, and Layla stopped near the book that had been demolished near the front door. "This one isn't even mine. Presley forgot it here."

"Have you called her?"

"No, I'll call her tomorrow. She just got off a shift so I'm not bothering her with this," Layla told him. "Anyway, she'll be with Donovan right now. They need the time together."

"Do you need to pack anything?"

"Honestly, I don't want anything from here. Lindy's packed me a few things I can borrow. But I'd be happy to burn everything I own right now."

"You'll reclaim it later, once this little exhibit comes down. But for now, you can come to my place. Get something to eat, take a bath if you want, and come to bed." He looked at her and knew she was thinking what he was, how none of her life had been private for as long as she'd been there. He'd even managed pictures before she moved in. Most everyone in her life had ended up in the pictures, too. He'd even made sure that a picture of the two of them sleeping together was placed directly on her pillow. He thought that was a little over the top, but he had to admit that the theatrics had garnered a significant reaction.

"I just need to tell Lindy," Layla told him.

"Already did," Jude said, holding up his phone.

"Thanks," Layla said. She stopped to speak with the cops for a few minutes, and they walked them as far as the door. Layla started shaking the moment the door closed behind them, and Jude simply plucked her up and carried her into the kitchen.

"You should probably eat a little something if you can," he told her, going to the fridge.

"Can't. But I'd love a drink. Strictly medicinal, doc," she said with a small, strained smile.

"Wine? Beer? Something stronger?"

"Beer is fine, honestly. I'm just so tired." She laid her head on the counter, and Jude walked around and put his hand on the back of her neck, massaging it. He slid the beer into her other hand, stretched out on the counter. "I just want to take a shower and go to sleep."

"Hey, we've been worried about you," JP said, as he came in the room. "Are you staying with us?"

"Yeah," she said, looking at Jude who nodded.

"She's staying in my room. I don't want her alone."

"If you don't mind, I want to stay in the kids' room. There's a trundle under the bed anyway," he told him. "That way they don't wake up and walk in on you in the morning."

"It's not like that," Jude told him. "But you have a point. And I appreciate it."

"You could take the dog," JP offered.

"You just don't want him shedding on you," Jude said with a grin.

"We'll take the dog," Layla told him. She gave Jude a beseeching look. "It might help."

"Fine. Dog's in our room, you're with the kids. Locked and loaded?"

"Locked and loaded," JP agreed. "I brought the little safe in, and I'll lock the door for good measure."

"Alright, we'll see you in the morning. Bring the beer with you, Layla," Jude told her, giving his brother a pat on his shoulder as they passed him and headed up. They said their good nights and climbed the stairs.

When Layla got to the door of the master bath, she froze. "I don't want to be weird, but I really don't want to be alone right now. I just need a shower after the day I've had," she admitted, a shudder running through her.

"How about this? You get in the shower and then tell me when to come in. The glass is frosted, and I'll face the other way, catch up on my reading. You won't be alone, but I can give you privacy, too."

"Okay."

***

When Layla climbed into the shower, stepping into the hot spray, she called out for Jude. She watched him walk in, his eyes down, and then he sat against the counters, facing the door. She watched him pull out a book and start reading. It felt strange for him to be in the room, but then she decided her whole life was strange. Noah had watched every moment of her life that she'd assumed was private and then practically papered her walls with her most personal moments. It was humiliating and terrifying, and she knew that it could only get worse. She looked over at Jude and hoped that he wouldn't get caught in the crossfire. Noah had already let her know that he knew she'd slept with Jude, even if he had to know that no sex had been involved. That wouldn't matter to him. After all, he was all about control.

She turned off the water and grabbed a towel, drying off inside the small shower and watching Jude still. He was a good man, she thought to herself. Not once had he done anything but step up for her. She saw him sit up when the water went off, and he told her he was just stepping outside the door, although he left it cracked a little. She got out and got dressed quickly, opening the door wide before she began combing her hair. She dried it quickly, as Jude got into bed with his book, reading still and leaving her to her routine. Layla noticed he'd changed into pajama pants and a T-shirt but wasn't sure when he'd had time. She was pretty sure he hadn't been wearing that earlier, but she couldn't be sure. After all, she'd had a lot on her mind.

She walked into the room slowly, glancing around to make sure the curtains were closed. They were thick, the kind meant to darken the room. Jude rolled the sheets down and patted the bed. She climbed in awkwardly and then just sat there beside him. He scooted closer to her, and she leaned her head against his shoulder. She sat up abruptly as a thought hit her, "The dreams will probably be worse. I don't want the kids to wake up and hear screaming."

"Don't worry about that," Jude told her, pulling her head back to his shoulder gently. "There's pretty good sound proofing between rooms in this house, and I'm right here if you do." He paused for a minute, rubbing her shoulder and then her arm in long, even strokes. "Are you okay?"

"I honestly don't know if I'll ever be okay again," she told him with a sigh. "But thank you for this. I don't know if I had the courage to sleep alone."

"You're all courage, Layla, but you shouldn't have to be," he told her. They slid down into the bed, and Jude wrapped his arm around her. She turned to face him and reached up to trace the outline of his face. He let her, watching her eyes curiously.

"Can I?" she asked him, reaching around to pull at the rubber band holding his hair. He nodded, and she pulled it, running her hands through his hair as it fell. He reached up, running a hand through hers, too, softly. "Thank you," she said, leaning over to kiss him softly on his nose. He smiled.

She snuggled a little lower, tucking her head just beneath his chin. She wrapped her arms around him and took a deep breath. Moments later she was asleep and didn't even remember when she rolled her back toward him, and he wrapped his arms around her. She only knew that every time she woke during the night, he was holding her still. She had nightmares, but each one ended with her waking right back in his arms. She wondered if he guessed that she was already a little in love with him, but she fell back asleep before the thought fully formed and forgot it.

Chapter 27

"They won't find me here," Noah said out loud, liking the sound of his voice in the room. He walked around the little cabin with a smug grin. He admired the craftsmanship of the renovations and decided that he could stay here as long as was needed to finish up. He hadn't thought far beyond the plan, but he took out his notebook and made a few notes, checking a few things off the list he'd made. He'd wanted to leave the cameras up, but he knew that it was best not to. It would be easier for them to trace him if they found his equipment. Besides, he didn't have to see the reactions to know what would happen. He could practically hear the screams of her nightmares from here, he thought as he opened a bottle of wine and poured a glass. He looked at the red, admiring it in the light.

He had to admit that Dean had good taste, in wine and in women. It was too bad he hadn't been able to finish his plan the first time. Noah sat down in the chair he was sure Dean preferred and made himself comfortable. All that security at the other house and none in the lake house, Noah thought with a shake of his head. It had been all too easy to come in and make himself at home.

Now, he just needed to bide his time a little longer. He'd be comfortable enough here. The pantry was well-stocked, and he'd brought a few provisions of his own. He was careful to leave things just as he'd found them and had even taken a picture of every room and closet in the place, just in case. It helped to have a backup plan in the event that anything went wrong.

Noah's face changed as he sipped the wine and thought about everything that had gone wrong. The smug smile he'd worn slipped off. His life had been perfect. He'd had the job he wanted, a good stepping stone to the one he had his eye on after that. He'd had a girlfriend that had been easily trained and willing to do whatever he wanted. He'd had time to amuse himself with Naomi at Dean's expense, with no one the wiser for months. He would have moved on from that eventually and married Layla if the others hadn't gotten involved.

He finished the glass and got up to pour another, filling it nearly to the top. He didn't notice when some of it dripped on the counter, spilled on the hardwood floor, and pooled there. He thought about Layla and wondered who was staying with her tonight. She was probably staying with Dean and Lindy. He'd wondered a time or two if something wasn't going on there. With Dean. Or maybe with Dean and Lindy both. He knew what kind of girl Layla was before. He just thought she'd be easier to control, to make into who he wanted her to be. She had been for a while.

He finished that glass, poured another, and turned on the big-screen TV, careful to keep the volume manageable. There were no close neighbors, but he wasn't about to get caught out by a dog walker or anyone else for being too obvious. Although, he thought to himself, if anyone stopped by, he'd claim he was house-sitting or that he was friends with Dean.

He smiled, imagining himself saying that so easily, as if it were true. They might have been friends, if he'd married Layla. Sharing a beer, talking about their wives, admitting their indiscretions. He flipped through the channels absently. He could still have that. After all, Layla would come back to him soon. She'd see it was the only way.

***

Layla rolled over in bed and eyed Gryffin who had settled on the floor, his massive head resting on his front paws. He was looking at her reproachfully, as if she had excluded him without regard to his feelings. She wondered how long he'd been huffing and sighing to get her attention. She scooted back toward Jude and nodded, and he bounded up beside her, settling in. She almost rolled into the weight of him but felt Jude's arm securing her. Even in his sleep, he held her close, and she reached out to pet the dog and wondered why she had the worst timing when it came to love. Gryffin settled down into sleep, and she comforted herself with the man on one side and the dog on the other.

She was sure that Jude was probably exhausted. Every time the nightmares had woken her up, she'd woken him up. It had been a long night for both of them. She could feel his deep, even breath against her neck, and she wanted to pretend that it was a normal morning waking up together rather than the nightmare that it was. She thought that, under different circumstances, this could have been her life. She could have had a boyfriend like this with a nice brother and sweet kids. Healthy. Normal. She sighed.

"You think too loud," Jude muttered into her hair, nuzzling her neck.

"Sorry if I woke you up," Layla offered softly, stroking his hand. He intertwined his fingers with hers.

"More bad dreams?" Layla liked the sandpaper rasp of his voice in the morning and wished things were different. She didn't want reality creeping in, not yet.

"No, the dog woke me up. He wanted up," she said softly, moving her thumb in circles around Jude's.

"You're going to want to stop that," Jude warned, his breath sending shivers down her spine. "It's bad timing, and I'm really trying to be on my best behavior here. But you're making it hard."

"Literally," Layla said, then giggled. Once she started laughing, she couldn't stop. She was sure it was probably just the shock of everything, but she could feel tears running down her cheek that had nothing to do with grief for once.

"I'm trying not to be offended right now," Jude told her wryly, starting to pull away from her.

"Don't you dare," Layla warned him. He rolled anyway, and she rolled with him. She curled up to his side while he lay on his back. She moved closer and put her head on his chest. "I didn't think I could laugh today."

"I'm glad I amuse you," Jude said.

"You're right though. It's bad timing. Really, really bad timing."

"Yeah, I know," he told her with a sigh.

She waited and then said quietly, "I wish it wasn't."

Jude wrapped his arms around her, their legs intertwining. He pulled the covers up around them and felt the huge dog shift in annoyance at the disturbance. "When this is over, we should try this again. Only next time I'd like to join you in the shower. And wake up with just you and not him," he said, nodding to Gryffin who snuffled in his sleep.

"He's a good dog," Layla said softly, wondering when all this would be over.

"You're doing it again."

"Doing what?"

"Thinking too loud. They'll find him."

"Or they won't. They haven't so far."

"Yeah, but they didn't really think he was a threat before," Jude reminded her. "It's hard not to see yesterday's exhibition as anything other than a threat." Layla didn't respond. "If they don't find him, we will."

"And what then?" Layla demanded. "A little vigilante justice?" Now Jude was silent. "It has to stop. I can't live like this."

"You won't have to, not forever. It'll stop," Jude assured her. "He probably just wanted to scare you."

"Well, mission accomplished," she said grimly.

"After breakfast you should probably call your sister before Lindy or someone else does. And your dad."

"Yeah, I know. She's working today, but I'd love to get Donovan's take on all this. I think he'll want to see it."

"We should probably walk through again, after the kids leave, and see if we missed anything," he suggested, starting to sit up. "You think there's any chance JP made omelets?"

"I was thinking pancakes, but let's go see. I'm hungry." She sat up and stretched, and then looked over at Jude who was standing there watching her with a curious expression. "Yeah, I know my hair is a mess," she said, huffing out a self-conscious sigh. "I don't exactly look my best first thing in the morning."

"You're wrong," Jude told her seriously. "You're perfect."

With that he headed toward the bathroom, and she just sat back against the headboard and watched him go. She had to admit, it was a pretty nice view. She petted Gryffin thoughtfully. "Well, what do you make of that?"

***

Presley woke up a little early just to watch Donovan sleep. She knew she'd be tired later, but she wasn't getting nearly enough time with him lately. She just wanted to memorize his face. She traced it with her eyes, those fierce eyebrows and full lips, the straight line of his nose, and the square, strong chin. He needed to shave, and his eyelashes rested softly against his cheeks. She moved in closer, studying him.

She hadn't meant to fall in love with him. After all, their schedules couldn't be worse right now. She wasn't even sure if they could make it last. Plus, she had all the drama with her sister going on. It was the worst timing. But she was definitely in love with him. She knew what that felt like. And whatever she'd felt for Derrick was nothing like this, which meant that this could hurt more. She closed her eyes tightly, feeling that familiar ache of fear and loss.

"You okay?" Donovan asked softly, pulling her close.

"I didn't mean to wake you up."

"It was the staring," he muttered.

"What?"

"You were watching me."

"I thought you were sleeping," Presley told him, rolling her eyes in annoyance. He was a little too observant for his own good.

"I was, but then there was the staring," he reminded her, those full lips quirking up at the corners in a smile. He opened his eyes and looked at her.

"I was admiring your pretty face," she told him with a grin, snuggling closer and reaching out a hand to trace his face the way she'd wanted to do when he was sleeping.

He closed his eyes and smiled, letting her, and then when he opened his eyes again, his expression had changed. He caught the hand tracing his face gently in his and brought it to his mouth where he kissed the open palm. Then he took his hand and stroked from her hair down her back before pulling her firmly against him. Their mouths met, and the mood seemed to move from that quiet sweetness to an intensity that Presley was sure she'd never experienced before. Not like this.

He was touching her, and she was moving against him, but it wasn't the mindless early morning sex she'd had before. It felt like her clothes were melting off rather than being gently pulled from her body, and they seemed to have slowed everything down. Long, drawn out kisses. Bodies moving and shifting together slowly, drawing out the heat and friction. The first orgasm came fast, and the second started on the heels of the first. Her eyes found Donovan's, and Presley could feel the love she felt for him mirrored there. He wrapped his hands in her hair at the back of her head, his face close to hers, and rasped, "I love this," and Presley felt her breath catch, as he yanked her hair suddenly and drove into her. She dropped her head to his shoulder for a minute, barely holding on, before she began moving again, slowly and then more quickly, barely aware that the moans she heard were being pulled from her own throat.

Afterwards, she was glad she'd woken up early to look at his pretty face because she'd have had to skip that little interlude to make it to work on time. Particularly since they went at it again in the shower, though that time had been more playful. She looked over at him across the breakfast table and saw his eyes darken in a way that made her sure he was thinking about their morning, too. She reached across and squeezed his hand, glad they'd decided that sleep and breakfast together could be enough for now.

"It's not enough," Donovan said, softly. Presley's smile slid away. He squeezed her hand. "I don't mean that. I just mean I want more time with you. I'm falling in love with you more every day. It's not enough."

"I know," Presley told him, her eyes holding his.

"That's all?" he asked her, raising an eyebrow.

She let go of his hand and stood up to come around the table. He turned toward her, and she slid into his lap, framing his face with her hands. She kissed his forehead and then leaned her own to rest on his. "I love you, too," she said finally, and felt his arms wrap around her.

"Oh my God, it's too early in the morning for this," Vashti said in disgust behind them, as she came into the room with the baby attached to a breast. "I'm going to get a coffee pot for my room, so I don't have to see this," she told them grumpily. "I'm getting jealous and having relationship goals at the same time, and I don't like it."

"I made coffee," Presley offered with a grin.

"Yeah, that's the only reason I didn't interrupt earlier. Besides, I wanted to see if you'd say it back," Vashti said with a smirk.

"Anyone ever tell you you're nosy?" Donovan asked with a roll of his eyes.

"Yeah, you, every other day," she said with a grin, taking her cup of coffee out of the room with her. "Just let me know when it's safe to come back out now. And if you have kitchen sex, clean up after."

Donovan looked at her speculatively, and Presley laughed. "No. Don't even think about it. I don't have time."

"I could make it fast," Donovan offered.

"I know you could," Presley said with a laugh. "But I'd rather take my time with you later."

"God, that sounds promising," he told her with a wide smile.

"I'll get off work after you go on shift, so I'll see you when?" They both grabbed their phones to check their messages when Presley sat up straight. "Shit. Shit. Shit. I shouldn't have turned my phone off." She jumped to her feet and started looking for her keys and then stopped. "I've got to go to work. There's no one to cover for me today," she looked over at him helplessly.

"Okay, what's going on?" He got up and took the phone out of her hands and read the message from Layla. "Shit. Okay, look, I'll go to Layla's. I know you're going to call her anyway, so tell her I'm coming. I'll check everything out, and I can call you after. She's fine. She's with Jude anyway, right?"

"Yeah, and Dean's still home. JP should be there, too," Presley sighed. "Okay, thanks. Wait—you need to get some sleep before work tonight."

"You know I don't need much sleep. Look, I'll try to come home and catch a few hours before I go in, but for now, you need to go to work and call your sister," he kissed her softly. "I love you. And the keys are by mine by the door."

"Thanks," she told him, heading to the door. She stopped and called back, "I love you, too," before the door closed behind her.

Donovan grinned and headed to the sink with the coffee mugs and plates. The last thing he needed was Vashti bitching about the mess, he thought with a grin. He was worried about Layla, but he still felt the lift of that *I love you* as he loaded the dishes into the dishwasher.

"Well, that was cute," Vashti told him from the doorway. "You know, up until the family emergency."

"Mind your own business," he told her, flicking the towel at her with a grin.

"Hey, I like her. Just try to keep your heart eyes to yourself. There are single people living here," she told him, sticking her tongue out as she rooted around the fridge for something to eat.

"Oven," he told her, as he headed out of the room.

"What?"

"We put you a couple of cinnamon rolls in the oven to warm up," he explained, heading to the door.

"Aww—never mind everything I said. Be as loved up as you want to be. Clearly, I hadn't considered all the benefits," she said, eyeing the fat, iced cinnamon rolls with a combination of lust and greed. "Thank Presley for me. I know you didn't think of this," she said with a laugh as she reached for the tray and Donovan headed out.

Chapter 28

Donovan pulled up in Lindy's driveway, knowing already that Layla's driveway would likely be taken up by her own car and any investigators. He jogged up to the door and knocked. He figured it would be quicker to go through the house and then jog around it. Plus, he figured he could ask Dean and Lindy a couple of questions on his way through, maybe take a look at the security camera. When Dean opened the door, Donovan's intent expression immediately turned to a smirk.

"Well, if it isn't the cop," Dean drawled. "I guess better late than never," he said with a smirk of his own.

"When the two of you finish your pissing contest, it's your turn to change Maya," Lindy called from inside the house. Donovan laughed, and Dean puffed out an exasperated sigh and opened the door.

"Sounds like there's a job for you to do after all," Donovan said, enjoying Dean's annoyance.

"Hey, Donovan," Lindy said, passing the baby into Dean's outstretched arms. She watched Dean walk out and then turned to Donovan. "One officer's already taken the security footage, and Layla's next door with Jude. His kids are over there, and they're doing what they can to keep them inside and out of the way until the police are gone."

"Thanks. Good to see you, Lindy. You look good," Donovan said with an easy smile. And she did look good. More chestnut brunette than Presley's nearly black locks and artfully twisted up into a messy bun that would have looked unkempt on almost anyone else.

"Get your own girl, Clairmont," Dean said, coming back into the room with the baby and making no move to pass her back to Lindy.

"I've got one," Donovan countered easily. "Keeping her."

Lindy looked at him speculatively but let it go. "She found it last night when she went home. She had the cops in there until late and then back again this morning. It's … I have no words for how bad this is. It's the creepiest thing I've ever seen outside of the movies. It's like that, a horror movie," she said with a shudder.

"I'll want to see it for myself. She didn't tell Presley much."

"A picture is worth a thousand," Dean said seriously, passing Donovan his phone.

"Shit," Donovan said under his breath. "Sorry," he said, remembering the baby and glancing at Lindy apologetically.

"She's heard worse this morning," Lindy said philosophically, taking Maya from Dean. "Go show him."

"Want to talk to Layla first?" Dean asked him.

"No, let's go see it, and then I'll check in with her. Presley's going to want to know everything," Donovan told him, following him to the back of the house and through the kitchen. They headed out onto the screened porch and then into the backyard.

The door that Layla had painted so hopefully was propped open, and Donovan could see an officer walking through the house, talking on the phone. He turned when he saw them approach, and annoyance flickered across his face.

"This ain't a home tour, Dean," he said after he got off his call.

"I'm the homeowner," Dean said. "Besides, this is Layla's sister's … boyfriend," he continued after a pause. "He's also a cop, and he wants to look it over and give her sister an update."

"Well, I guess if it's her cousin's sister's daughter's boyfriend then …" The cop let the words trail off and sighed heavily. "You're lucky we're friends, Walton."

"You're friends with a *firefighter*?" Donovan said with a smirk, pronouncing his occupation like an insult.

"Yeah, it takes all kinds," the cop said with a grin. "I'm Reese.

Went to school with this asshole," he said with a nod to Dean who only grinned. "Alright, look around but don't touch anything."

"Donovan Clairmont," he said introducing himself easily. "You got it."

"Creepy fucker, huh? You know the guy?" Reese asked curiously, watching Donovan take in the destruction.

"No, and he's not someone I want to know either." Donovan looked at all the pictures plastered around the room. He averted his eyes from the most personal, uncomfortably reminding himself they were of his girlfriend's sister. "Though I'd like to have a talk with him about this."

"Get in line," Jude said, leaning against the door and watching. "I only have a minute. Layla and JP have the kids doing an art project. They wanted to take the dog over to the dog park, but I don't want them outside right now. Not until we know …" he let his voice trail off.

"You know anything about where this guy is?" Donovan asked, looking at Reese and Dean.

"Not as yet," Reese said with a shrug. "You ever meet him?" he asked Jude.

"Not exactly. I saw him when she took him to court for the restraining order," Jude said with a shrug. "Looks normal, but he's not."

"I met him once at Christmas, a year ago," Dean said. "Honestly, I thought he was cool. I mean, a little reserved but not …" he gestured to the display around him. "Not psycho."

"It just seems …" Jude paused, looking around the room. "Over the top. Like he's demanding her attention. Our attention. I don't know," he sighed. "Something is off about this, and I don't just mean that he's crazy. He's clearly that."

"I know what you mean," Donovan said with a nod. "It's too much."

"What do you mean?" Reese asked, looking at both men curiously.

"He seems like a planner," Jude said. "From what Layla's told me this is a man with a plan. So, what's the plan? What's the next move?" A car door slammed loudly outside, and Jude had a bad feeling. "Shit, I've got to get back next door. Come over when you're done," Jude said to Donovan, nodding at Dean and Reese before sprinting out. The raised voices came in short order.

"Who's that?" Donovan asked, raising an eyebrow in Dean's direction.

"I'm guessing the ex-wife. She's a bit of a nightmare," Dean said with a shrug. "Do you agree with him? That there's a plan?"

"That's my read on it. Whatever it is, it's not going to be anything good." Donovan walked upstairs and then came to a stop when Dean stood in front of the bathroom door. "What?" he demanded.

"Lindy asked me to head you off here. Hey, she did the same to me. Apparently, this particular exhibit is a study of the nude form, mostly in the shower. Layla would prefer that we not all go traipsing in there," he explained, crossing his arms over his chest as if Donovan were going to argue.

"Hey, I'm good with that. This is my girlfriend's *sister* we're talking about. I don't think we're close like that," he said, walking away. "What do you think about this?" he asked Dean nodding to the picture of Jude and Layla resting carefully on her pillow.

"It's definitely a threat," Dean agreed.

"Yeah, looks that way. Are they dating?" Donovan asked. "Presley said no, but this doesn't look like *not* dating," he nodded again to the picture.

"They're friends, but I think it's only a matter of time," Dean admitted. "There's definitely something there, but she's not in a hurry. Noah did a real mind fuck on her."

"But he seemed normal to you?" Donovan asked, as they headed back downstairs.

"I mean, I was a little busy at the time, but yeah. He just seemed,

I don't know, *nice*. Kind of average guy. Red hair, quiet, just generally unassuming." Dean shrugged, but Donovan stopped. It was ringing some pretty uncomfortable bells, but he wasn't sure why. He tried to think why it seemed so familiar, but then he let it go. It would come to him later.

"Think it's safe to go next door?" he asked, glancing out the kitchen window. It sounded quiet enough, and the car seemed to be gone.

"You go ahead. I'm going to check back in with Lindy and Maya. I'll be over later, or stop by before you go," Dean said, heading back to the house. He glanced at Donovan, "I mean, I know Lindy has a gun, and she's a shoot-first-ask-questions-later type, but I don't like to leave them alone long with all this going on."

"Yeah, anyone could be a target," Donovan said with a nod, thinking maybe Dean wasn't that bad, but then cringing at the idea. Next thing you know, he thought, I'll be friends with a *firefighter*. He gave a mock shudder and headed to Jude's place, instinctively cutting across the yard and going to the back door the way he'd seen Jude do.

He hadn't liked seeing all those photos, particularly as he'd found himself in one of them and Presley in more than he liked. In fact, she'd been everywhere that Layla was. There'd even been pictures of her sleeping over. He could feel the anger spreading through him and tried to keep it in check.

He heard voices before he even knocked. "I'm sorry. I'm so sorry, Jude." Donovan recognized Layla's voice and paused, not wanting to interrupt whatever this was.

"They're my kids, Layla. I can't do anything that will jeopardize me seeing them," Jude said in a slightly raised voice, more anguished than angry.

"Look, we'll talk to the attorney," JP said. Donovan figured if this wasn't a couples' argument he might as well go in. He went up to the door and knocked, waving through the glass. Come on in," JP told him. "Maybe talk some sense into these two while you're here."

"What's up?" Donovan asked, going to sit down in a chair at the bar and taking a glass of tea that JP poured him with a nod of thanks.

"Michelle just left. Jude's ex-wife." JP spoke up when the others didn't. Layla was looking down at her hands, and Jude was looking out the window. "Seems like she got a tip that Jude here had an overnight guest while the kids were visiting. She came in raging and took the kids, threatened not to let Jude see them again. You know, the usual," JP said in disgust.

"If it's the usual, then why …" Donovan began before Jude cut him off.

"She doesn't want Layla around, ever. Telling her what happened just made it worse because now I'm endangering the kids for …"

"Yeah, you don't have to repeat that part. We all heard what she called me," Layla said, crossing her arms over her chest and leaning over. Donovan could see how much whatever it was had hurt her, and he went over and sat by her at the table.

"Exes are a bitch, am I right?" he said easily, and she choked out a laugh that turned to a cry. He put an arm around her and looked at Jude reproachfully.

"They're my kids," he said beseechingly. "Layla can stay over with Lindy and Dean when the kids are here, and I'll be right here if she needs anything." Layla wouldn't look at him, and Donovan couldn't blame her. He knew Jude knew he was fucking this up entirely, but the guy was in a bad spot. He decided to give him a break.

"Come stay with me. When I'm not home, Presley is and vice versa," Donovan said easily. Jude frowned at him, not liking that answer any better.

"Wait—you're *living* together?" Layla asked in astonishment.

"Well, not exactly, but we tend to stay at whoever's house has the next day off. But you could both stay at my place until this blows over. My sister's there, too, so the house is never empty," Donovan told her reassuringly.

"Your sister with the baby," Layla said bleakly, closing her eyes. "Or Lindy with her baby. Or Jude with his kids. I can't!"

"Hey, what about Seth?" JP asked, speaking up. "He's your step-brother, and he's just down the road. His wife Libby is home a lot, and Seth works just up the street. No kids," he pointed out. Layla seemed to consider it. Jude looked temporarily relieved. It was a little closer than his place anyway, Donovan figured. "Or your dad's ..."

"No," Layla interrupted. "Not my dad's. He has heart problems, and the farm is too isolated."

"Um, I probably shouldn't mention then ..." JP began uncomfortably. They all looked at him, waiting. "Well, Dean said Lindy called him. Or called her mom. And anyway, they're coming over."

"Oh my God, Jude. Stop him. Don't let my dad see that," she said urgently, grabbing his hand and squeezing it. Jude nodded and headed out, and Layla slumped in her chair. "I didn't want him to know," she said softly, deflating.

"Everyone who loves you needs to be aware what's going on. There's something I don't like about this, besides the obvious," Donovan said thoughtfully. "You know him better than anyone. So, what's his end game? What would a guy like that want from all this?"

Layla sat up, thinking. "I hadn't considered ... but you're right. Noah always has a plan. Always. And it's rarely straightforward." Donovan could practically see the wheels turning. "I need to think about this."

"Look, you know him better than all of us. If you could tell us about him, the stuff you know that no one else does, we could figure this thing out. See what his next move is going to be," Donovan suggested. When Layla blanched, he put a hand over hers. "Look, I know it's going to be hard. I can't even imagine how hard this is for you, but this guy is straight out stalking you. If you're in danger, we need to know everything we can. Everything," he urged her. "No one is judging you, but we need to stop *him*."

"Okay," Layla said. "But once. And everyone together. And some parts I don't want my dad to hear," she said, looking into his eyes.

Donovan nodded and then met JP's eyes over her head. "Can you ask Lindy if we can come over? You're still renovating here, and they have the room. Tell them I'll call in pizza."

Chapter 29

Just over an hour later, Donovan walked with Layla over to Lindy's, watching her nervous glances around her. He didn't blame her for wondering if she was being watched even now. There was no guarantee she wasn't—even inside Jude's place. JP had gone ahead, and Donovan matched his pace to Layla's slower one, understanding her reticence.

"Hey, JP said Michelle got a tip about you and Jude," Donovan began.

"It's not what you think," Layla said, her face flushing pink.

"I wasn't thinking anything, and it's not my business anyway," Donovan said easily. "Sounds like Jude was being a good friend to me."

"Yes," Layla agreed, relieved that he hadn't read anything into it. "It's not like … I mean, the kids were there … we wouldn't …" She broke off, frustrated that she felt like she needed to explain herself.

"My question is where she got the tip," Donovan said, cutting into her excuses. "Who do you think gave her the tip, Layla?"

"Oh my God," Layla stopped dead in her tracks, her face growing pale. "Noah," she breathed. "But why?"

"That's the question. That's the big question. What does it serve? What's he doing?"

They walked into the house silently and headed to the living room where everyone was getting comfortable. Lindy was putting the baby in a bassinet in the corner, and JP was standing by, talking to her. Dean was quietly talking to Theodore and Jude, and Keely was looking out the window toward the street and sipping from a glass of wine. She was the first to turn when they came in but waited patiently for them to be ready.

Donovan could see Layla assessing everyone and gathering her courage. He squeezed her shoulder and then cleared his throat. All those eyes turned toward him, and then to Layla.

"My baby," Theodore said, moving to Layla and wrapping her in a bear hug. Donovan could see the emotion all over his face and could see that Layla was trying her best not to cry. "Good to see you, Donovan," he said over her shoulder.

"You, too, sir," Donovan answered, feeling the stab of discomfort that came from talking to his girlfriend's father. He felt like he could be asked his intentions at any given moment, and he hadn't even begun to think about his intentions for the long term. He'd only just realized he was in love with Presley. He shook off the thought and remembered to prioritize. Right now, he needed Layla's story. Something was gnawing at him, some realization he felt like he was overlooking, but so close to grasping. He'd already called Presley and updated her on the afternoon's summit, promising to call her on his way to work to fill her in.

"Want to tell us why we're all here?" he asked, as he sat back down beside Keely, his wife and Lindy's mom.

"Not until the rest get here," Donovan said, adding a "sir" as an afterthought that made Theodore grin. "I don't want her to have to go over it more than once."

"Seth's on his way," Keely spoke up, leaning into Theodore's side. Donovan looked from Keely to Lindy and noted the strong resemblance in all but the eye color. Keely was stunning and not in the condescending "for her age" way. She was just stunning. Lindy had that same quality but wore it more casually, with her own artful elegance. Of course, Presley and Layla had their own fierce beauty.

He had to admit this was a family of beautiful women, but it was the strength that impressed him. The door opened and a few minutes later another beautiful woman walked in. Donovan said hello to Libby and watched her find a place near Lindy and Layla, laying a comforting hand on Layla's trembling one. He figured Noah had picked the worst possible family to mess with. These women were the real steel magnolias, he thought with admiration.

"They're something else, aren't they?" Seth said softly, coming to stand beside him.

"You ever get used to it?" Donovan asked him, still looking at the women.

"Not really. Just like you never stop being thankful for it. That's my rock there," he said nodding at Libby. Libby looked up, not hearing him but sensing him nonetheless, and smiled.

"Wow," Donovan said. "I mean, really. That packed a punch," he murmured to Seth.

"Yeah, that's my girl. How are things going with yours?"

"Oh, we're working around a nightmare schedule right now, but she's good. She's on shift until later tonight, but I'll be at work by then."

"Hence the early dinner," Seth said with a nod.

"Yeah, I guess we should do this," Dean said, walking up and standing beside them. "They're something else, aren't they?" He looked over at the women with a smile. Theodore got up and joined them while the women talked softly to Layla.

"Is this a private meeting?"

"No, sir," Donovan answered quickly.

"You can quit that and call me Theodore. How's my other girl?" he asked Donovan easily.

"She's ..." Donovan's voice trailed off, and he stopped. Unassuming. Reserved. Nice guy. He felt a chill and actually shushed his girlfriend's dad who started to speak. "Wait," he ordered and then started pacing. Something about Presley. It was floating there in his mind.

"Tell me about Noah," Donovan snapped looking at Layla.

"Well, he ..." she started hesitantly, watching Donovan in

confusion. In fact, they'd all stopped what they were doing to watch him.

"No, just tell me about him physically. What's he look like, sound like?" Donovan asked.

"You think you've seen him," Dean said with certainty, going over to stand by Lindy. Seth moved to Libby's side, and Keely stood up to join Theodore, taking his hand in hers. Their fingers linked, and they turned toward Donovan, their eyes following him as he paced.

"He's tall. Just shy of six feet. Red hair, dark red. A little bit of a Southern drawl. Not much really," Layla shrugged helplessly, looking at the others. "I'm not doing a good job of this."

"He'd blend in," Theodore said quietly. "Except for the hair."

"Your average nice guy," Libby said softly, looking at Donovan with fear creeping into her eyes.

"We were talking on the way over," Donovan began, letting those pieces click into place.

"His end game," Layla said anxiously.

"What?" Jude asked, speaking up for the first time since Layla had come into the room. "What's the end game?"

"Someone called Michelle." Layla looked up and met his eyes. "She got a tip from someone about me."

"I didn't think of that," Jude said, taking a seat slowly. "You think ..." He trailed off and looked at Donovan.

"Why? Why would he do that? You said he would be the type with a plan, a game. Why call Michelle unless ..."

"You're thinking it was a distraction," Dean said matter-of-factly. Donovan nodded, thinking hard. He might be wrong. There was a slight chance he was wrong. He was really hoping he was wrong.

"Here," Layla said, scrolling through her phone. It took her a minute, and Donovan waited impatiently. "This is him."

Donovan took the phone and stopped moving. Stopped

breathing. He looked at Layla sharply. "This guy?" he asked, his voice soft. His face had drained of all color, and Layla looked up at him in confusion. Dean took a step toward him and Seth put his hands on Libby's shoulders. JP crossed the room to stand beside him.

"You've seen him," Dean said. Donovan closed his eyes briefly and then looked at Theodore with something like panic and pain.

"Shit. Shit," he said, reaching into his pocket for his phone and pulling it out. He dialed a number and called.

"What's going on, Donovan?" Lindy asked, getting up to pick Maya up from the bassinet in the corner of the room. She was still sleeping, but Lindy held her close. "Who are you calling?"

"Shit, she's not answering," Donovan muttered, and Theodore grew pale. Donovan looked up, and JP tensed beside him. "We were wrong. He's not after Layla. He's going for Presley. We're all here, and he's going for Presley."

***

Presley poured another cup of coffee and promised herself it would be her last for the night. After all, she wanted to go home, shower, and crash into bed. She didn't want to be up sleepless because she'd had far too much caffeine. If she was lucky, Donovan would join her before she woke up, and they'd have a whole day together for once. She wanted to enjoy it.

"Everything good?" Erin asked her from the desk.

"Looks good so far. It's been slow enough tonight. Of course, it's a full moon, so it won't stay that way. In fact, I think I'm going to take five and grab something downstairs. You want anything?" she asked Erin, glancing at the clock. Couple more hours, and she'd be off shift. She wanted something sweet, and she was pretty sure she'd spied some of that espresso cheesecake on her way up this morning.

"No, I'm good. Take your time. I'll give you a buzz if there's anything," Erin said absently.

"Alright. I'll take the stairs, though, and try to be quick anyway."

"Just don't get locked out again," Erin said with a grin.

"Ha. Ha," Presley said, rolling her eyes. "I've got my shiny new key card. Wes gave it to me on the way up."

"Good man," Erin said, reaching for the phone to answer a call.

Presley jogged down the stairs. She'd felt restless all day. She'd been trying to keep busy and not think about what Layla was dealing with. Donovan was there. She'd be fine. She'd be surrounded by family, and Donovan would call her later and fill her in. They'd go over together and see her tomorrow. Nothing to worry about, she told herself.

"Dammit," she thought, as she entered the cafeteria. Derrick was sitting by himself, nursing a slice of the same cheesecake she was after. "Damn," she said again quietly.

"That one," she said to Felicity at the counter, nodding to the slice of cheesecake she wanted and feeling thankful that he hadn't gotten the last piece. "I am not letting him ruin my dessert, too," she said with a grimace.

"Yeah, I almost spit on it, but he'd have seen," Felicity said with a grin. When Presley looked up in surprise, Felicity smiled. "Team Presley for the win," she said with a laugh, passing her the cheesecake. Presley thanked her, paid with her card, and took the cheesecake with her go-cup of coffee to a table across the cafeteria, facing away from Derrick.

She took her first bite with her eyes closed and then groaned in exasperation rather than ecstasy when she felt the shadow fall over her. Well, a figurative shadow at least. "Oh my God," Presley said. "Can't you take a hint?"

"You always did treat food like a religious experience," Derrick said with a smile she'd have once called charming but now termed "smarmy".

"And you're desecrating my temple," she told him sharply. "Go away. Go bother Amber," Presley said with annoyance, turning back to her cheesecake and praying he'd leave.

"Look," Derrick said, sitting down uninvited in front of her. Presley let out a long-suffering sigh and looked at him pointedly. "I'm sorry about the thing with Amber. We know you weren't behind the things that happened. I'm sorry she said what she did. I didn't know she was going to confront you."

"Have you *met* Amber?" Presley asked sarcastically.

"Anyway, I'm sorry. Well, we're sorry, but she's never going to say that to you. She's just a little jealous of what we had ..."

"You can just stop right there," Presley said, interrupting him. "What we had is over. Tell Amber she doesn't have to worry about me."

Derrick sat silently watching her eat. Presley could feel him and wondered why he was still there but figured she'd find out eventually. "So ... you still dating that guy from the elevator?"

Presley almost choked on a laugh. Elevator Guy. Derrick didn't even know that's what Donovan still called him. "Yeah," she said when she finally stopped chortling long enough to take a drink.

"I don't know why that's funny."

"Inside joke," she said with a cryptic smile.

"Good talking to you, too, Presley," Derrick said with a roll of his eyes. "Anyway, I apologized."

"Yeah, duty done," she told him, looking at her cheesecake pointedly and ignoring him. "We're good. You're free to go."

He walked away, but Presley could still feel him watching her across the room. She wasn't sure what his problem was today. She turned to shoot him a dirty look but didn't see anyone there. Weird. She was sure someone was watching her. He'd probably just walked away, she thought with a feeling of unease.

She looked at the last bite of cheesecake and decided she wasn't that hungry after all. She tossed it and took a final drink of coffee, hoping it would keep her energy up for these last couple of hours. She looked at the elevator and considered it before heading to the stairs instead. She reached for the door and opened it up, waiting for the overhead lights to engage before heading up.

Chapter 30

"What do you mean he's going for Presley?" Layla asked, growing pale.

"Look, we have to be quick. Theodore, keep trying Presley," he snapped, as he knelt in front of Layla. He could see Theodore calling and Keely standing beside him sending texts. "Don't stop until she answers."

"I'll try the hospital," Libby said, getting up to make the call in another room.

"I don't understand," Layla said.

"This is Noah?" Donovan asked again. "I've seen him twice before." He gathered his thoughts and tried to put them together quickly. "Is she answering?" he asked Theodore.

"She's not," he said, looking at him with growing fear. "I'll keep trying."

"We have to go," Donovan said. "I'll explain on the way."

"I'm with you," Layla said. "She's my sister."

Donovan nodded, as Jude spoke up. "I'm coming, too."

Dean groaned in frustration, tapping his leg in anger. "We'll stay," Lindy said, grabbing Dean's hand. "I'll keep trying Presley, and Dean will call the cops. Okay?"

"Yeah, do that. Any word from the hospital?" Donovan asked Libby as she came back in.

"She just went off shift," Libby said, tears running down her cheeks. "Erin said she left half an hour ago, but she's calling security to check now."

"Damn!" Donovan said, then suddenly a thought struck him. "Wes—I've got the security guard's number. Seth, can you call him? Libby, check with anyone she worked with. See what you can find out about where she went. Text me anything. Don't call. Keep the line open for Presley."

"I'm coming with you," Theodore said. "You've got the SUV. You have the room."

"Not with your heart condition, no sir," Donovan told him. "Presley would kill me. I'm going to get her home safe, but you have to stay here." He looked at the older man steadily.

"That's my little girl," Theodore told him fiercely.

"And I'm going to go get her," Donovan replied, just as fiercely.

"I'm going with him," Jude said firmly.

JP walked into the house. Donovan hadn't even noticed him leaving. He saw him pass Jude a gun.

"You know I carry, right?" he asked Jude in exasperation. "Cop," he said, pointing to himself.

"Won't hurt to have backup," Jude answered evenly.

"I don't have time to argue. Don't shoot anyone by accident," Donovan warned him. "We're going. Text only," he reminded them. "We'll bring her back," he said with a nod to Theodore.

"Hey, where did you see him?" Jude glanced over at Donovan. "You said you saw him twice. Where? How do you know he's after Presley and not Layla?"

"I saw him at the hospital. Twice," he said grimly. "The first time he was heading up to Labor and Delivery wearing a black shirt and a ball cap, talking about the doctors and nurses up there. We had a full conversation on the way up. The second time, I had car trouble in the parking lot, and he was going to give me a lift before the security guard came out to help."

"Oh, shit," Dean breathed.

"Yeah," Donovan said with a nod, turning to the door. "He was never after Layla."

Donovan ran down the stairs with Layla and Jude. "As if I'd take a shrink as backup," he muttered in irritation, running a hand through his hair. "And one with a man bun of all things."

"I assure you that the man bun doesn't stop me from shooting straight," Jude returned easily. "Want me to drive?"

"No, I've got this. We train for this."

"You got lights on this thing?" Jude asked.

"I won't use them unless I have to. I don't want to give him any warning we're coming."

Jude climbed in the back, letting Layla have the front seat. Donovan glanced over at her. "You okay?"

"Why isn't she answering the phone?" Layla asked hollowly.

"Her phone could have died," Donovan said with a shrug, starting the car and shooting out into the street. They saw Beth and Jamie heading into a house around the corner, the lights highlighting the two humans and two dogs paused on the porch watching them go. He saw them turn from the door and head toward Lindy's place, and nodded absently. It would be good for them to have more people there. He had to admit it would have been good to have Dean in a crisis, but he glanced in the mirror at Jude with his set jaw.

Jude met his eyes. "So, calling Michelle was just what? Him messing with us?"

"It worked, didn't it?" Donovan answered. "I might have put it together sooner, but it was a distraction. All those pictures," he muttered.

"You saw them?" Layla asked, coloring.

"I didn't go into the bathroom," he assured her. "Lindy had Dean bar the door," he told her with a quick glance. "But the pictures. The book on the floor was Presley's, not yours, right?" Layla nodded. "The pictures. Almost all of them had Presley in them, even the ones in the house. The ones of just you were a distraction. The one of the two of you together was meant to look like a threat to you. So, we all come here, and who's thinking about Presley?"

"Oh my God," Layla said. "Drive faster."

"I'm on it," Donovan said. "Tell me what you know about him and Presley."

"Oh, well …" she trailed off, looking at him uncomfortably. "He was kind of … he tried to build a bond with her," she said, shrugging when Donovan glanced at her sharply.

"She's your sister," he said, a question in the statement.

"She didn't do anything about it, but he wanted her to think there was something between them. And then there was an incident where they almost had a car accident, and he touched her in a way that made her uncomfortable. She thought it was an accident until later."

"He touched her?" Donovan asked softly, cursing under his breath. "Finish it. What else?"

"Beth told her about Naomi being hurt by him, and then she told me. That's when it all came out, and we broke up. Lindy and Dean were having Maya, and Presley and Beth walked me up to Dad. Anyway, I moved into Presley's. Then he came by once, after. She didn't tell me about it until months later, but they had some words. In front of practically the whole building. That's when he went silent and left me alone," Layla explained, trying to sum up everything they'd been through.

"Let me get this straight. He tried to build a connection with her, touched her in a way that made her feel uncomfortable, probably gaslighted her about it, and then she's the one who outed him as a psychopath? Shit, shit, shit," he said. "It's been about her the whole time." His phone buzzed, and he tossed it to Layla. "Check that for me."

"Stop," Layla said. "Pull over," she told him sharply. When he did, she shoved the phone into his hands. "She's not there."

Donovan read the text from Wes. "She's been gone over an hour," he said aloud. "But her car's still there?"

"Libby just texted and said they saw her head to the parking garage, but there was no log of her leaving. Wes found the car. Her purse is in it," Layla swallowed audibly, her breath coming fast.

"You've got to breathe," Jude told her, sliding forward in his seat. "You can't panic now. Panic later. Where would he take her?"

"I don't … I don't know," Layla said, slowing her breathing and trying to think. Where? Where could he go?

Her phone beeped, and she picked it up off the seat. "Oh my God," she said. "Head back to Madison," she said, pressing a link on her phone.

"What happened?" Jude asked.

"Presley's got this emergency thing on her phone. In an emergency, she can hold down two buttons, and it sends out her location to her top three contacts." She glanced at Donovan's phone lighting up. "It'll send a series of pictures that the camera takes, and it sends a GPS location. She had it installed on both of our phones after the breakup," Layla breathed. "She's pressed it."

"Hand me Donovan's phone. I'll forward it to Dean," Jude said, his hand out.

"No need. My dad's the other contact. Call him. See if they're closer," Layla said. Jude took out his phone and called and was only on the phone a minute.

"Can they get there first?" Donovan asked, speeding up and glancing only occasionally at the screen to see where they were heading. It looked like it was near the lake, closer to Greensboro than Madison.

"Maybe. They certainly know the way," Jude said, meeting Donovan's eyes in the mirror. "It's Dean's lake house. Dean says he's at the cabin."

"Wait—have you ever been, Layla?" Donovan asked.

"Dean and Lindy were married there," she answered. "It's really isolated." She swiveled in her seat to look at Jude. "Are they on their way?"

"All of them but Seth and Libby. They're staying with Maya," Jude answered. "Lindy insisted on going, and Keely wasn't going to let Theodore go alone."

"Plus, Seth and Libby are Maya's godparents, so that's good," Layla breathed, wondering if Presley was safe. Presley was smart, Layla assured herself. Smarter than her, smarter than Noah. She had to trust in that. She turned and looked at Donovan. "You're in love with my sister."

"Yes," he said shortly, not taking his eyes from the road.

"You promised my dad you'd bring her back," she reminded him.

"I know," he said quietly. "Give me the next turn."

They drove in silence punctuated only by Layla's updates on the miles and minutes until they got there.

***

Presley pressed the buttons and then cleared her head. He hadn't even thought to check the inner pockets on her scrubs. She kept her phone close. He'd tossed out the one she used at the hospital without even realizing her personal phone was in her pocket. He'd tied her hands in front of her, a rookie mistake. She couldn't call anyone or send a text, but she could just reach inside and press the button and pray they would figure it out and come. She put the phone on silent and then slid it from her pocket to push under the cushions of the couch where he'd dropped her when they came in.

She knew he'd drugged her. She could still feel that quick sting and remembered feeling it as she put the keys in the ignition. She hadn't even checked the backseat. She'd just gotten in with nothing on her mind except a shower, sleep, and Donovan. She woke up shortly after they pulled up, and her first peek was enough to tell her exactly where they were. She'd been here a few times in the last year, after all.

Presley tried to stay still and keep her breathing even. She wasn't sure what he was doing in the next room, but there was no point in making a sprint for the door until she was sure of what was going on. Besides, she wasn't sure her body was going to work. She could only just feel sensation returning to her limbs. She couldn't even worry about what he'd given her, beyond figuring its effects out. She was too busy trying to figure him out.

Noah. She knew on some level that it wasn't over for her. Something was off, had been off all along.

"Did you sleep well?" he asked her, coming into the living room and sitting across from her on the couch. Presley didn't even try to pretend she was asleep. She just looked at him. He was wearing dress pants and a button-up shirt and looked freshly shaven, as if he'd been cleaning himself up since they got there. His hair was still the dark red it had always been, but she could tell that he hadn't quite washed all the dark out of it and could see traces of dye on the collar of his shirt.

He waited, and she decided that she wasn't going to start this with a pissing match over patience. "I'd say it's good to see you, but it's not," she said softly, trying to remember all the possible exits in a house she'd only visited socially.

"No need to be rude. We have all the time in the world," he said magnanimously, leaning back in his chair and sipping something amber-colored from a glass. Scotch, maybe, she wondered. She wanted to laugh. He really should have majored in drama, she thought. After all, he certainly had the flare for it. Some of her amusement must have flashed across her face because his tightened in anger. "We should catch up," he suggested, leaning back and crossing his legs casually. "Still fucking the cop?" he asked with a smirk.

Presley looked at him steadily, refusing to be baited. She thought about Donovan and wondered if he would shoot Noah if she asked nicely. Of course, she'd rather shoot him herself but being drugged and tied up without a gun wasn't exactly ideal. Instead, she decided to turn the tables. "I see you still have your man crush on Dean. Nice digs," she said, referring to Dean's cabin.

"It's been convenient. It's been easy to keep an eye on you from here. And no one ever thought I'd be just down the road," he said with a smile.

"Clever," Presley said dryly. "So why bother Layla then?"

"If everyone's looking at poor Layla, no one thinks about you," he said with a smile that would have seemed warm if she didn't know him. "In fact, I gave Jude's lovely ex-wife a heads-up today about your little sister's sleepover with the kids, and that should keep them occupied for a while."

A car at a nearby cabin backfired, and she nearly jumped out of her skin. She hated to give him the satisfaction. Noah looked at her with a wide smile, getting more comfortable in his seat. She'd shown fear, the last thing she'd wanted to do.

"They'll figure it out eventually," she said with an attempt at a shrug, wondering if they would.

"Do you think so? How?" he asked her. When she didn't answer, he smiled. "They'll figure it out when you don't come home, but the cop won't even catch on to that for another … what? … nine hours? We'll be gone by then," he said with a shrug, throwing back the rest of the drink in one shot.

"Where are we going?" she asked, her throat dry.

"You'll see," he said with a smile, getting up to refill his glass. Presley had a feeling, and she knew that it was now or never. He headed toward the table where she could see the gleam of a bottle of liquor and the metallic flash of a gun. She didn't know a damn thing about guns, but she knew it was no prop. He turned, and she ran, straight out the door. She could hear glass breaking behind her and willed her legs to move. All those early morning runs for donuts weren't a joke now. She could run for miles if she had to, even with her hands tied.

Chapter 31

"Here it is," Layla said. "Right. *Right*," she shouted when Donovan almost missed the turn. Gravel spit from the tires, and she prayed they wouldn't lose control. She could hear Jude cursing behind her and then gasped at the sound of a shot. "Did you hear that?"

"People hunt out here," Jude said tersely.

"Not usually in the middle of the night," Layla said. "Hurry."

"Going as fast as I can. Where the fuck is this place?"

"Almost there. Just around these trees. Slow down."

"I see it," he said, stopping the car abruptly and putting it into park. "Stay in the car in case we've got to make a quick exit. Keep it running. If Presley comes out here before I get back, just go."

"I am *not* staying in the car," Layla shot back.

"Layla, we have guns. You don't," Jude told her gently.

"Yeah, which is why I want to stay with the people with guns rather than on my own without one," she shot back, taking off her seatbelt.

"Good point." Jude got out and came around the car. "Take this." He released the safety. "Point and shoot if you have to, okay? Be careful. And when this is done, we're going to have a talk about us," he told her, leaning forward and kissing her quickly but firmly.

"You take the back, I'll get the front, okay?" Layla could hear Donovan tell Jude as they left her in the car.

She slid over into the driver's seat, pressing the lock button and holding the gun in her hands. She didn't like it, but she'd been to the shooting range a few times, just to help her feel more confident after Noah. She was sort of hoping she'd get the chance to shoot him. She saw Jude go through the trees in one direction and Donovan go the other way. She couldn't quite see for the tree line.

Layla knew it would piss Donovan off, but she turned off the running lights and moved forward where she could see the cabin. It was dark, and the porch lights were off. She could see one window lit, likely the lamp in the living room. She was far enough back to have a good view and, hopefully, not be seen. She put the car in park and waited, rolling down the window to listen.

***

Jude headed for the back door of the cabin and wondered if Layla was safe in the car. He'd been an idiot earlier. Michelle had come in and taken the kids, and he couldn't lose them, not again. But he had to stop letting her call all the shots with his kids, too. If he got out of this whole fucked up situation alive, he was planning to tell her so. He had a right to see his kids, and he had the right to move on with his life.

Then maybe he'd ask Layla out on an actual date. It was ridiculous to keep pretending to be friends when they both knew there was so much more between them. He crept slowly, missing the gun already. Well, at least he could throw a pretty good punch. JP had taught him how to do that ages ago.

It was dark, and he tried not to think about snakes. After all, there was probably a madman with a gun inside. The last thing he should be worrying about was snakes. But he worried all the same and increased his pace, wondering how Donovan was doing. And missing Layla.

He wanted to get this whole thing behind them, make sure Presley was safe, and move on with their lives. Man, he thought, this guy had done a bang-up job picking a creepy lair. I mean, no offense to Dean, he thought, but this place was spooky at night. Probably cleaned up better in the daytime.

He kept to the edges of the trees and then darted over to the door. He turned the handle gently, but it was locked, as he expected. He wasn't sure if Donovan expected him to break it down or wait.

They hadn't exactly had time for a chat about it. He heard something inside and decided to wait and listen. He figured he needed to be ready to react to whatever happened next.

***

Donovan stepped out of the woods, trying to judge the distance to the door. He didn't like being this exposed, and he wondered how long it took the police around here to respond. They couldn't have had much of a head start. He started to move out of the shadows to the cabin when he saw the door open and Presley run through. He knew she ran. She'd said it enough. He thought it was a sort of joke that she would go for a run to the donut place a few miles away and then run home.

But he'd never seen her run.

She flew out of the house like a shot. He was about to call out, but Noah came out right behind her. She headed toward the road, toward Layla. Noah picked up speed, and Donovan yelled for Jude and followed. It was dark, and Presley was a blur on the road ahead, running in a zigzag pattern in a way that would have made him proud if it didn't tell him one thing.

Noah had a gun.

***

Layla could see it all unfold in front of her. Presley running out of the house, Noah behind, Donovan on the edge of the woods following behind. She could even make out Jude. She yelled out Presley's name but instead of calling her over, she made a split-second decision. She saw the moment her sister saw her and yelled "run" instead. The second Presley ran by the car, Layla flipped on the lights, shining them directly at Noah. She didn't have a chance to think. There was really only one way this could end.

***

Presley couldn't even think about why Layla was here. She heard *run*, and she ran.

She put everything in to it and went into a sprint. Layla was in the car, and Noah had a gun. She had to get to help, fast. She heard the scream behind her just as headlights turned in her direction, with blue lights not far behind. *Thank God*, she thought. *Thank God*.

***

Theodore stopped the car and opened the door. Presley shot into his arms. Safe. She was safe. "Your sister?" he asked. She looked back, toward the driveway behind her and Noah. She shook her head.

"I don't know. She told me to run," Presley said, feeling a surge of guilt. "We have to go back."

"Get in," he told her. Presley climbed into the back with Lindy and Keely. They didn't have time to ask anything. The car shot forward the second the door closed, and Lindy began pulling Presley free from her restraints.

***

He was really going to have to start running with Presley, Donovan told himself as he sprinted behind them. He was gaining on Noah, but he could see him raising the gun in Presley's direction. He thought about raising his own, but he couldn't afford to miss and hit either Presley or Layla. He heard Jude in the dark behind him and wished for some light.

Like an answered prayer, the light came on. He squinted in the brightness and realized what was going to happen next. He couldn't do anything to stop it, so he just braced himself.

***

Layla didn't even think. She saw Noah step into the light with his gun raised, and she reacted, throwing the car into drive and hit the gas. She felt the impact and saw the flash of surprise in Noah's blue eyes right before he went flying, the gun flying with him. Her own mouth formed a matching O of surprise. She put the car in park with shaking hands and opened the door.

She could hear the slide of gravel as a car came to a stop beside her. She heard voices, but she couldn't take them in. She just stood beside the door looking at the body in the driveway. She felt Presley come up beside her before she saw her.

Presley looped an arm through hers, and their dad came up to stand beside them, Keely just behind him. "Did you hit him with your car?" Presley asked, breathlessly.

"No, I hit him with Donovan's car," Layla answered carefully, letting out the breath she'd been holding.

"You know," Presley told her, as Donovan and Jude came stumbling up the driveway. "Hitting an ex with a car is supposed to be my signature move." Both sisters burst out laughing.

Donovan walked up and shook his head in total mystification, exchanging a look with Jude. "The shock," he murmured as he turned to take in the scene with a professional eye. "You'll have to tell us what's so funny later," he told them as he moved forward to mark the gun's position in the driveway, careful not to touch it, while Jude reached down to check for a pulse. Both sisters clutched each other, tears rolling down their cheeks.

"Is he dead?" Theodore asked quietly beside him.

"No, just knocked out. Probably needs a hospital," Jude said with a casual shrug, nodding to the uniforms coming up the driveway and stepping aside to let them work.

"Too bad," Theodore said quietly, reaching his arms out to hug both his daughters close. He looked at Donovan and Jude over their heads. "Thank you."

"We didn't do anything," Donovan said with a slight smile. "One daughter ran, the other ran him over. You raised some tough daughters."

"And when you're done with them, I think we're going to need a minute," Jude told him patiently.

"Wait your turn," Theodore said, a smile tugging the corners of his mouth.

The second he let go, Presley shot into Donovan's arms in a display of affection so strong that Theodore headed over to the officers with Keely to give them their privacy. He noticed that Layla moved a little slower toward Jude but ended up in his arms just the same. Jude rested his head against hers, kissing her hair. Theodore put his own arm around Keely and began to feel how late it was. "Let's sleep at Lindy's tonight," he told her softly.

"I'd love that, but I think we're going to be here a while." They walked over to join Dean and Lindy who were hanging back watching the action. Lindy had already sent Seth a quick text to let them know what happened.

***

Presley just let herself be held. Donovan was crushing her ribs, but she didn't really blame him. She was holding on pretty tight herself.

"Don't ever do that to me again," he told her severely.

"Believe me, I don't want to," she replied with a laugh, starting to shake. "It's just the shock," she managed before sliding down to sit on the ground. He sat beside her and called for a paramedic to check her. "I'm fine," she kept saying, allowing herself to be checked out but refusing to go to the hospital.

"How'd you figure it out anyway? Was it the text?" she asked him when the paramedics finally left her alone. She glanced over to where an officer was taking statements from her mom and Theodore. Another was with Dean and Lindy while other officers cordoned off the area. It was surreal.

"No, Layla was describing him, and I realized I'd seen him twice before," Donovan told her. "At the hospital," he explained. She paled. "Two conversations. I knew then that it was never about Layla. She was just the distraction he needed."

Presley nodded. "He took me at the hospital. Waited in my car and drugged me. I woke up here and sent the text before he realized I had my phone. Which is under the couch cushions by the way," she said, nodding toward the cabin.

"Let's get it and see if we can go home," Donovan said.

"Whose home? Yours or mine?".

"I think we should crash in Madison tonight. We can head back into Athens in the morning. We can't stay at Layla's. You don't even want to see that. But maybe with Lindy or over at Jude and JP's. One of them will take us in," he said, slinging an arm around her shoulder

"Not Lindy's," Presley said, coloring slightly.

"Don't tell me you have a secret crush on our resident firefighter," Donovan said with a laugh.

"No, my dad will stay at Lindy's tonight, and I want to sleep with you," Presley said firmly. An officer shot them an appraising look as they walked by.

"Can't keep her hands off me," Donovan said with a grin.

"You know what I mean. I don't want to be far from any of them, but I could use some time alone with you."

"Let's see if we can stay with Jude," Donovan said. "Or Seth, if that's better. Pretty sure your sister is staying with Jude."

"We lived together. That's not really an issue. The house is plenty big enough," Presley said, taking a deep breath and heading toward the cabin and the officers waiting for her there. Donovan spoke to the ones he knew while she slowly climbed the porch steps and entered the house along with the officer who'd gotten the basics but needed her to walk them through it.

She saw Donovan take in the couch cushion on the floor and spilled liquor pooling on the cabin floor where Noah had knocked it over as he ran out. On the other side of the couch was a sight that stopped her dead in her tracks. Rope. Weights. Masking tape. She looked at Donovan and then at the officers wandering the room.

"There's a boat docked here, right?" one of them asked quietly. She felt her throat go dry and nodded. Donovan wrapped his arms around her, and she leaned back for a minute.

"I don't even want to know right now," she told him quietly. She broke away from him long enough to grab the phone on the couch, waving it at the officers who nodded at her to take it. She turned back to Donovan and leaned into his arms. His chin rested on top of her head, and she murmured into his chest, "Later, after all this is over, can we please talk about this your place/my place problem?" She felt him smile into her hair.

"That was my plan all along."

***

Much later, after they'd given their statements and waited to be cleared, Jude held onto Layla and started apologizing. Again. "Seriously, quit. You were an ass. I get why. They're your kids."

"I'll take her to court if I have to, but she can't stop me from seeing you. Or seeing my own kids."

Layla paused. "When you say *seeing* me ..." She trailed off.

"I will be your friend if that's what you really want, but I'd like to take you out on an actual date."

"Like dinner and everything?"

"Wherever you want to go."

"Okay," she said with a nod.

"Okay?" he asked her, raising her chin and looking in her eyes.

"Okay," she agreed, closing the distance and kissing him. Someone whistled, but she didn't stop to see who.

Chapter 32

Lindy lit the candle and whispered fiercely to Dean, "You better have been joking about the trick candle." The others began to sing.

Happy birthday to you. Happy birthday to you. Happy birthday, dear Maya. Happy birthday to you.

The baby clapped her chunky hands together, and Dean and Lindy leaned forward to help her blow out the candle, which wasn't a trick one at all. They smiled, and cameras flashed.

"I am not eating from the cake the baby spit on," Donovan muttered.

Presley nudged him "That's why they have a tiny cake for her and a big cake for everyone else," she said with a laugh. "She really is the prettiest baby."

"I know," Libby agreed, standing beside them with a cup of lemonade. "I can't wait to see what ours looks like," she said with a smile, leaning against Seth who wrapped his arms around her. They had just announced that their adoption request had been approved. In another couple of months, they would be parents, too.

"Do you get to make requests?" Layla asked curiously, as she watched Jude play in the garden with Gryffindor, Kelsey, and Connor. They had been surprised that Michelle had allowed them to get the kids for the Fourth of July holiday, but it turned out she wanted to go to the beach for a week with her new boyfriend, so it worked out.

"I guess some people do. We don't care about that. We just want a healthy baby," Seth said, and Libby nodded. "Our baby."

"Our grandbaby," Keely said with a smile, coming over with Theodore. "I'm going to throw you the biggest baby shower."

"It'll be nice for Maya to have someone to play with," Theodore said. He turned to look at Presley and Layla pointedly.

"Okay, we're going to get cake before he starts asking us about future babies," Presley said with a laugh, wrapping an arm around her sister and heading over to the table. "What about it though?" she asked her sister quietly. "Do you think …" She nodded toward Jude and the kids.

"I don't know. One day maybe. It's too soon to say. But I'd like to think so," Layla admitted. "What about you and Donovan?"

"No plans. We're just enjoying living together for now," Presley said. "And I think Vashti is happy to have her space back, to be honest."

"If I'm placing bets on anyone, it's those two," Layla said, nodding to Beth and Jamie who had come in and released Lizzie and Darcy on Gryffindor and the kids.

"You think so?"

"Well, Naomi suspects. But it's their business," she said with a shrug. "Are you still doing the marathon with Libby?"

"We're training," Presley said with a nod. "You should come with us."

"I'll be there cheering you on, but no," Layla said with a laugh. She'd be there with bells on and signs held aloft, ready to shout her through to the finish line. Because sisters should show up for sisters.

Presley looked at her sister and wondered how a year could change so much. A whole year had passed since Maya's birth. They'd lived together, survived a stalking, and watched Noah sentenced. It had been a busy year, she mused over a bite of cake. She closed her eyes in bliss as she bit into it. She did love cream cheese icing.

"I forgot about you and your religious experience with food," Donovan said as he walked up.

"You know, Derrick said the same thing to me," Presley said with a quirk of her eyebrows.

"When did you talk to Elevator Guy?" Donovan asked, sitting

down and taking a bite of his own cake.

"The day of Noah."

"How come we're just now hearing about this?" Layla asked.

"You know, getting drugged and kidnapped was a little bit of a distraction," Presley said with a roll of her eyes.

"You were kidnapped for all of three hours," Layla reminded her with a laugh.

"It still counts," Presley pointed out. "Anyway," she continued, "he came up and apologized for his crazy girlfriend and ... Huh."

"What?" Donovan asked curiously.

"It just occurred to me that it was probably Noah who was doing all that stuff to Derrick and Amber. Anyway," she said with a shrug, "he apologized and then asked me about the guy from the elevator." She cast a smug look at Donovan.

"What'd you say?"

"I told him I was definitely still dating you," she answered with a grin.

"Are you a little sorry you didn't run over him?" Donovan asked sympathetically.

"No, that's Layla's signature move, now," Presley said, laughing when Layla puffed out a sigh and left. "She won't say it straight out, but you know that had to have felt good."

"I only wish I'd thought of it myself," Donovan agreed. "You want some of those?" he asked, nodding to the yard.

"What, dogs? Not with my schedule," she answered with a shake of her head, taking a bite of cake and closing her eyes.

"No," Donovan corrected, "kids." Presley's eyes popped open and she started choking on cake. He patted her on the back, passed her his soda and waited. "I was thinking four."

"Four. Kids?"

"I mean, I could deal with more if you wanted, but who has the time?" he asked philosophically.

"When did we agree to one?"

"We didn't. Which is why I'm asking."

"Have you been drinking?" she asked him seriously.

"One beer, earlier," Donovan admitted. "But I mean it. You, me, kids, maybe even a dog. Though I like cats okay, too."

"I think you should get out of the sun. Maybe cool off in the baby pool," Presley told him with a small smile.

"That's not a no," Donovan pointed out.

"No, it's not," she said with a smile, taking another bite of cake and feeling the sun on her face. It was hot, but it felt really good. And the cake really was a religious experience.

***

Layla helped the kids change into their bathing suits and then watched Jude put sunscreen on them before setting a timer on his phone to reapply. "I'm not going to lie," she whispered as she wrapped her arms around him. "This whole dad thing looks pretty sexy on you."

"Are you sure you're not looking for Dean?" Jude asked with a grin. When she only laughed, he reminded her. "I'm glad you like it because I think we can talk Michelle into letting us have them all summer." He looked at her to gauge her reaction. It might be a long summer.

"Really?" she asked, absolutely delighted. "Because I had some ideas on things we could do." She started telling Jude about the kid-friendly activities in town she'd been wanting to check out, and he reached out and pushed a dark curl back behind her ears. All the dark shadows that had followed her since Noah had faded. She'd even stopped having all but the occasional nightmare. She just looked happy. Midway through her list of activities, which she probably had saved on a spreadsheet somewhere, he leaned forward and kissed her.

"Hey, that's rude," she told him, pushing him back and laughing.

"But I take it you approve."

"We'll do all the things," he assured her with a smile. Then the smile slid off his face. "Except for the thing you mentioned with the snakes. Let's skip that one," he told her seriously.

Layla laughed, and outside Kelsey and Connor laughed in the baby pool with Maya while the dogs chased each other around the adults, and Seth went to the gate to help Vashti in with her baby. They heard a car pull up and knew that it would probably be Libby's sister Rachel with her kids. The yard was full, and somewhere Theodore and Dean were squaring off at the grill while Dean and Donovan traded pot shots at each other's choice of career. She loved this place, these people.

Layla pulled Jude's face closer to hers, as JP quietly took over the grill while the others were arguing, and Keely walked with Beth and Libby around the yard talking babies. She rubbed her nose against his and then kissed it before taking his hand and heading out into the sun with the others.